ⁿᵉNeon Church
Journal

CHARLES LEMAR BROWN

Broken L Press

To my kids,
Brandy, Kara, Sarah, Brenton, Makela, Beth, and Seth

WEEK 0—PROLOGUE

Sometimes people screw up their lives a little. Sometimes they screw it up a whole lot. And for some people, their whole life seems to be one big screw up, a never-ending road of bad choices which leads to a dead end in the middle of nowhere. If you think the road a person takes to get to such a place is a hard one, you should hear about the journey it takes to get back.

I was thirty-two when I found myself at the end of the road. I stood in the living room of my Granny's little white country house and stared out across the pasture at the cattle grazing. Years of running from one rodeo to another, riding bulls, hard drinking, and wild women had finally left me bankrupt. When I say bankrupt, I'm not talking financially; I'm talking mentally, emotionally, and spiritually. I was dragging rock bottom, and as hard as I tried, I couldn't see any light above. I had dug the hole so deep and so fast that darkness was all I could find or feel.

I had gone where I always go when I need wisdom—to Granny's house. The peace that I always find at Granny's is like no other peace on this Earth. I suspect that it has something to do with her direct line to God, but whatever the reason, it's where I go.

"Runt," that's the handle Granny tacked on me at birth, "maybe this is a good thing. Maybe this is where you turn your life around."

"Ain't so sure, Granny," I returned, "Fifty-two weeks of court ordered batterer's intervention classes, at least a year of probation, and I was just trying to stop her from bashing my head in with a lamp."

"That may be, Runt, but you had plenty of opportunities

before that to make choices that would have led to a different outcome." There was an edge to Granny's voice that I'd heard before but not in a long while. "You could have walked away. Maybe had you not been drinkin', you'd have had the sense the good Lord gave you and gotten out of that relationship before it went so far."

"Maybe," I agreed aloud, but inside, I knew it wasn't just the alcohol. Something deep down inside of me was broken.

"Runt, I've been patient, Lord knows I have," Granny's voice softened, "but I'm not getting any younger. This ranch is going to be yours one day, and I think it's time you take a bigger hand in it."

"What are you saying, Granny?" I turn from the window to face her, "I do my share of the work around here."

"When you're here," Granny's steel blue eyes met mine and held, "but you're not always here. Between the rodeos and carousing, you're more like a hired hand than the rancher you're gonna have to be to keep this place running when I'm gone."

"Granny," I smiled and winked, "you're gonna live forever."

"Dang it, Runt, I'm being serious," her eyes flashed. "Don't try to charm your way out of this with a cute little smile. It's time for you to grow up."

"Okay, okay," I couldn't remember the last time I'd seen her this riled. "You're right, I'm sorry."

"You know, Runt, I keep a journal," she said, her voice softening once again.

"Didn't know," I replied half-heartedly, turned back to the window, then asked, "What for?"

"Each and every day after I read my Bible, I write down what I've learned from it," she answered.

"Okay." I wasn't sure where this was going.

"Maybe it would help if you kept a journal and wrote down what you learned after each one of the classes the judge said you have to go to," she suggested. "I think that might help. I surely do. You'll do that for me won't you now, Runt?"

"Yeah, sure, Granny," I sighed, but I had my doubts that what she suggested would do me any good.

WEEK 1—BUILDING PARTNERSHIPS

I'd rather have the head of my pecker slammed in a truck door than be here. Call me crazy, but that was the kind of thoughts that were running around in my head as I sat at the table in the back room of the Tri-County Family Services offices. Family services, now that's a hoot. Half the fellas sitting around this table don't look like they have families, and the half that do look like normal, everyday hardworking guys. Who am I to talk? I've got a kid, a boy, nine years old. His name is Luke, and Granny says he's the spitting image of me at his age. Great kid. Wish I could see more of him. But then there's the ex. If she wasn't such a bitch, maybe I'd be a better father, and wouldn't be in this mess.

Tri-County Family Services offices this place is called. Offices may be stretching it a little. It is housed in a renovated and partially remodeled Family Dollar Store stuck between Suzie Q's on one side and the Wine to Water All Faith Christian Church on the other. Suzie Q's has a big neon sign in its front window that reads: Adult Toy Store. Suzie Q's is done in a sexy, flowing pink, cursive script with ADULT TOY STORE in bold white block letters just below. The church has its own neon sign: two green palm trees that frame the word Oasis with blue ocean waves shining below them. I'm pretty sure I've seen the exact same sign hanging on a wall behind the pool tables in a bar somewhere on the rodeo circuit, but I can't remember exactly where that might have been.

The sign on the front door of this place where I've been sentenced to attend meetings simply reads: Family Services, the words embossed in tiny gold letters. Nothing fancy on the outside or inside. The building is old. The furniture is old. Even the air feels stale and moldy.

Just inside the front door is a chipped, black, formica countertop. To the left of it in what I suppose could be called a lobby, are a couple of square folding tables with metal chairs around them, and to the right is a round, white, plastic table accompanied by two matching chairs. Beyond the table, a long hallway leads past a couple of offices to the room where we all meet.

The only table provided for our use is long, rectangular, wooden, and scarred from years of use and misuse. It takes up most of the room and seats ten comfortably. There are fourteen mismatched chairs around it, some metal fold out, some wooden kitchen table chairs, and a couple of black square-back office chairs. By the wall at either end of the table are another three mismatched chairs.

Miz Nancy followed the last fellow in and stood just inside the door while he took his seat. She is the counselor who will be leading our classes. One class a week for fifty-two weeks, and I will have completed the court-ordered, state-mandated Batterer's Intervention Program. It's gonna be a long year.

Eleven guys are seated around the table. Four of the chairs against the walls are occupied. No one looks excited to be here.

"We have a new member tonight," Miz Nancy said pointing at me. "Introduce yourself and tell us why you're here."

I wasn't sure if I should stand or stay seated. I decided to stay in my seat. Most of the other members just stared at their paperwork or the chipped tabletop, but one young guy who was wearing a faded red t-shirt with a surfboard centered on its front looked me right in the eye and waited.

"I'm Hank," I told her, and she motioned for me to address the guys at the table, so I turned my attention to them. Surfboard was still staring at me with a perfectly expressionless poker face, and I was trying to decide if I liked him or not.

"I'm here because me and my girlfriend got into an argument. We were in a hotel room and we'd been drinking a lot.

She picked up one of the tall metal lamps from the desk, swung it like a bat, and laid my head open. Took thirteen stitches to close it up." I stopped and looked up at Miz Nancy.

"But why are you here?" she asked.

"Well, when she drew back to swing the lamp again, I tried to stop her. I grabbed at the lamp, but I missed it and hit her in the mouth. It was an accident but when the cops got there her lip was split and still bleeding. The room was a mess and there was blood all over the place from my head and her mouth, so they hauled us both to jail. Court ordered me to pay fines, make retributions for the damage to the motel room, and told me I had to complete this program or go back to jail. I choose the program." I shrugged and sat quietly not knowing what else to say.

"Okay," Miz Nancy said after several seconds of silence.

"Welcome to the class," Surfboard nodded. "I'm Dan."

Several of the others murmured greetings, and few even looked up. I felt a little embarrassed, tried to hide it with a smile, and nodded in response.

"Dan, you want to tell our new member why you're here?" Miz Nancy asked.

"Sure," Dan said, "I'm here because I backhanded my wife and split her lip. We'd been arguing, and she told me to get my things and get out. I told her to go to hell, I paid for the house. She shoved me and said I was an asshole. I backhanded her into the wall. I tried to apologize, but she wouldn't listen. I left to cool off, and when I got back, her mother was there with a cop. They arrested me and took me to jail. This is week thirty-two for me. I've got twenty weeks to go."

"Anyone else?" Miz Nancy looked around the room, and no one volunteered. "How 'bout you Manuel?" She suggested, staring hard at the short, skinny Mexican kid that sat across the table from me.

"Again Miz Nancy?" Manuel shifted nervously in his metal chair. "I ain't so good at this," he complained.

"You're getting close to the end," she countered. "You got,

what, sixteen or seventeen more weeks and you're gone? You should be getting used to this by now."

"Ain't never gonna get used to this," he shook his head and then began. "I'm Manuel. Me and my ole lady, sorry, my wife, we was fighting over her getting a job. I was drunk and didn't want her getting a job. She said she was tired of not having enough money for food. I took my belt off, and she ran out the front door. I caught her before she could get in the car and was whooping her with the belt. The neighbor lady called the cops, and when they got there, I tried to run, but they caught me. They put me in jail for a while, and when I got out, they said I have to come to this class with Miz Nancy. I am here because I drank too much, and I hit my wife with my belt. Is that enough Miz Nancy?"

"Yes, Manuel, that's just fine. And I hope some of you recognized that Manuel held himself accountable by admitting what he had done." She stared sternly at several of us as she picked up a copy of the week's lesson from the table and turned her attention to the first page.

I stared down at my packet of papers. I had scanned through its three pages while I was waiting for the other members to sign in and pay the weekly charge for being in the class. I was still not sure what it was about partnerships we were going to discuss, and my role in the class was still unclear.

"Someone read page one," Miz Nancy ordered.

The big burly Grizzly Adams looking man sitting at the far end of the table started to read, and I followed along. At the end of the page he stopped, and Miz Nancy made a few comments about different partnerships and asked if anyone had questions or anything to add. No one did. Page two and three followed the same pattern, and then we were instructed to turn the packet over and use the backside to write down our thoughts on the class and the program.

"Since this is your first class, Hank, you can just comment on what your first impression was," Miz Nancy said to me and then to the rest of the class, "I want some thoughts from the rest of you on the program, also."

She stepped back out into the hall, and everyone went to work. After a minute of thought, I scribbled a couple of sentences about the incoming process being a lot less painful than I had expected, and I hoped future lessons would be a little easier for me to understand. After that, I sat staring at my paper, waiting for the others to finish.

Miz Nancy came back into the room, and slowly, the sound of pens scratching against papers subsided until finally the last guy, a tall, square-shouldered hippie with a soul patch on his chin, laid his pen down. A glance around the room at the boredom on the faces of the men who were trapped here with me made me wish I'd brought a bottle of good ole Jim Beam and fifteen shot glasses. Oh, hell make it sixteen, Miz Nancy looked like she could use a shot too. On second thought, alcohol is against the rules for all of us guys until we finish our fifty-two weeks of classes, so I guess the whole bottle would have to go to Miz Nancy. Then again, that just might make the class a helluva lot more interesting.

"Austin, tell me something you like about this program," Miz Nancy ordered the guy who I figured was the youngest of our group. He was maybe five-six and couldn't have weighed more than a buck twenty-five, and had shaggy blonde hair and steel blue eyes. It was hard for me to imagine him being abusive to anyone. The dark brown company shirt he wore had the name of a local heat and air company above the left pocket.

"I like the counselor." He looked sheepishly up at her and smiled.

"Nice try." Miz Nancy shook her head. "No brownie points for you. You got three weeks to go, and you're gonna do every one of them. And you better get your account caught up by then or you aren't going anywhere."

"But I really do think you're a good leader," Austin said defensively. "You're hard but you're fair, and you work with us if we're in a bind."

"Okay," Miz Nancy smiled, "but I was serious about the

payments and the time. Now, what are some things you don't like about the program?"

"Paying thirty dollars every week and fifty-two weeks is too long," he answered without hesitation.

The reactions of the others made it evident that they agreed whole-heartedly with Austin. Miz Nancy quickly explained that both of those were state mandated and could not be changed. After questioning several others and getting similar responses, she asked if anyone had anything else written on their papers about what they didn't like about the program.

"I don't much care for the coffee," I spoke up.

"What coffee?" Miz Nancy asked, then looked at me confused and added, "We don't have coffee.

"I know," I returned. "That's what I don't like about it."

Several of the others chimed in, and the hippie suggested that we should have donuts or some kind of pastries. Grizzly Adams made the observation that at AA meetings, they make coffee available. Miz Nancy made it clear that this wasn't an AA program, and if we wanted coffee and donuts, we could damn sure bring them ourselves. After that, she dismissed the class with a reminder that she had better get all her pens back.

As each of us filed out past her, we handed her the last sheet of our package, which was an attendance sheet. At the bottom of the sheet were five blank lines. A brief description of what we had learned from the night's lesson was to be written in this space. On mine I had written: Better partnerships make better relationships.

WEEK 2—DEFINING NEGOTIATION AND FAIRNESS

If there is a hell on this Earth, I've found it, and here I am for the second week. Yippee-fuckin'-A! Someone should tell the new guy, and by someone, I mean someone besides me. He's an old guy, maybe in his sixties with a big white beard. Oh shit, I know where I've seen him before. It's Santa Claus! Holy shit! Santa kicked Mrs. Claus's ass!

I was still staring at him when Miz Nancy called everyone to the front to sign in and pay up. I got up and fell in behind Santa. I noticed that the other guys seemed just as curious about this new arrival as me. Everyone lined up along the wall in the narrow hall. On the opposite wall are "How To Identify Abuse" posters and pictures drawn by children of various stages of family life. My eyes are drawn to one particular drawing of a dad pushing his young son in a swing with the mother looking on. It's done in Crayola and reminds me of my son.

"Hank," Miz Nancy called my name.

I made my way to the front of the line and took a seat at the little round white table where we sign in. I paid my thirty dollars, scribbled my John Hancock on the log, and received a receipt for the thirty, rose and headed back to the conference room. As I passed him Santa smiled and nodded at me. I thought what in the hell is wrong with this guy. Is he always this happy?

Back in the room, I gathered up a packet from the corner of the table and began to read over it. I realized there would be a new packet of papers for each week's lessons and felt a little bit like I was back in high school. I hated high school. Lord, this is going to be one hellavu a long year.

I found that after the initial reading material there was a questionnaire I was supposed to fill out about my wife/girlfriend/ live-in/latest-one-night stand/significant other/insignificant other/ or someone of that nature. The questions ranged from Who makes the money? to Who pays the bills? to Do you want kids and if so how many? On the back page were more questions. Do you approve of drinking, smoking, or using other drugs? Okay that's interesting. Other drugs. So is drinking considered a drug? Is smoking considered a drug? I answered yes, yes, and no.

Halfway down the page, number ten stopped me dead. It simply said: Define "love." I just sat there and stared at those two words. I thought of Granny and my son and felt like crying. *Cowboy up, you pussy*, I scolded myself. Miz Nancy saved me. She looked tired tonight. She's maybe forty or a little older, real pretty with strawberry-blonde hair and big brown eyes. She wears glasses but I don't think she's had them very long because she still messes with them a lot like she's not comfortable with them. Tonight, she had her hair pulled up in a ponytail.

"We have a new member tonight," Miz Nancy said as all eyes turned to Santa who was sitting in one of the chairs along the wall just inside the door. "Jacob, introduce yourself and tell us why you're here."

"I'm Jake," the new guy stared, around the room as he spoke, "I'm here because I blacked my wife's eye. We had been arguing for two days. I was in the kitchen pouring a glass of milk when she came in and gave me a smug little look."

I looked down at my papers. Everyone was staring at Jake like they were waiting for the punch line of a joke. I thought, man, if he says anything about cookies, I'm going to lose it.

"I'd had enough, so I threw the milk in her face. I was closer than I realized, and the edge of the glass hit her in the eye and blacked it. I know I shouldn't have done it."

Wow! I wondered what the Clauses could possibly fight

about for two days. Did he catch her blowing an elf, or was she bitching about the reindeer shitting on the front lawn? The images kind of screwed up the whole idea of a sweet jolly life at the North Pole that television had left in my head as a child.

"Anyone else?" Miz Nancy pushed her glasses up on her nose and looked around the room. After a few seconds of silence, "Maybe you could share, Freddy."

I'd noticed Freddy at the meeting last week. He looked like an over-sized Shaggy from the Scooby-Doo cartoon. Only he had jet black hair and more facial whiskers than Norville Rogers sported in the movie. He was sitting in the same black molded plastic chair that he'd been in the week before. It was in the far back corner. He shifted nervously and stared at his paper.

"I'm Freddy," he said. "I'm here because of this situation I got myself into. I've been sober for a long time now. Haven't had anything to drink and no drugs. I used to get messed up, but I don't anymore. Anyway, this situation, it was not a good situation. I think this is week twenty-two for me, if I've figured this right."

"Okay, Freddy," Miz Nancy said as Freddy shifted back and forth in his seat, "but you need to work on telling us what you actually did."

"Yeah," Freddy shook his head, "I'll work on that situation. I just don't like to talk about the past."

"Yes, but that's why we're here, Freddy." She said somehow stern and compassionate at the same time, and then she turned to the rest of the class, "Someone start reading on the first page of the packet."

Dan started reading. He read really well. When Miz Nancy stopped him and asked for someone else to read, Jake chimed right in. I can read. I don't even mind reading, but I felt a little unsure about reading in class. Dan and Jake didn't seem to have any inhibitions about it, though. When Jake reached the end of the material, Miz Nancy instructed us to finish the questionnaire that followed and stepped out of the room.

Five minutes later, she returned, and we went over the questions. After much discussion, it was generally decided that who makes the money, who decides how to spend the money, and who does the housework depended on the particular situation and could be different for different couples. We also discovered that a "clean house" can mean something different to different people. On the What does a "clean house" mean to you question, I put 'not cluttered'.

Do I want children? Well, I already have a son, so I guess that answers that question. Then Miz Nancy asked if we had kids, did we want anymore? I realized that I hadn't really thought about it. Do I? I don't know. Would I, could I be a good father? I really didn't get much of an example from my own dad. I thought about my boy. I haven't been much of an example to him. No, having more kids probably wasn't such a good idea for me, I decided. Kind of made me sad. Made me wish I was a better dad… a better man… a better person.

"Okay," Miz Nancy said, "number ten says define love. Someone tell me what you wrote there."

"Sex," Grizzly Adams mumbled beside me. Everyone chuckled and Miz Nancy shook her head.

"Typical, Mason," She scolded. "I should have known it would be you."

Mason, so that was Grizzly Adams name. Mason shrugged and smiled. Miz Nancy explained the misconception that sex was love and how detrimental it was to a good relationship. She said sex was an important part of any relationship, but love was necessary for a lasting partnership. Several of the guys put forth feeble attempts at defining love. Everyone seemed to be struggling with the concept.

"When you love someone more than you love yourself and put them first," Jake said.

We turned our attention to him. He was looking at the tabletop, and his smile had disappeared. It was like he was looking into some hole in time, and the picture made him sad.

After a second, he shook his head like he was trying to clear his vision and said, "I don't know, maybe, just maybe, that's what love is or what I thought it was. I don't know."

Someone had really messed Jake up, I decided, and I felt a little sorry for him. Did I love anyone that much, I wondered? I couldn't think of anyone. Would there ever be anyone like that for me? Looking at Jake, I wasn't sure I wanted to chance that kind of pain.

We moved on to the question of religion and what part it should play in a marriage. I thought of Granny. If anyone could pray someone into heaven, she could do it. I tried to remember what I'd been taught about such things when I was young, and found nothing—nothing at all. How could that be? I wondered. I believed in God and Jesus and the Holy Ghost. I tried to remember the last time I'd opened a Bible; the last time I'd owned a Bible. Maybe I should go to church with Granny on Sunday.

When we finished the lesson, I'd written something in all of the spaces provided, except number ten. It was still blank.

On the bottom of the sheet I had to turn in I wrote: In a good relationship you have to negotiate. It's give and take. Both parties have to be willing to compromise.

WEEK 3—USE OF NEGOTIATION AND FAIRNESS

I arrived fifteen minutes early tonight. I told myself it was just a fluke, but I know that's not true. Last week's session got under my skin somehow, and I want to learn more about being a better person. I figured I'd be the first one in the door, but when I got to the classroom, there was Jake, already seated and reading through this week's lesson. His black-rimmed glasses were perched on his nose. He looked up when I walked in, smiled at me, and asked, "How was your week?"

"Good," I answered with a grin, "and yours?"

"Can't complain," he responded looking over the top of his glasses.

"Howdy," Freddy spoke from the corner and shocked me. I didn't realize he was there.

I nodded at him with an, "Evening."

I wondered which of them had arrived first as I picked up my packet of papers. I thought about taking the seat beside Jake but decided against it since that was the seat Mason usually took. There was something that seemed to draw me to Jake. Maybe it was some repressed childhood memory of how nice Santa Claus was supposed to be, or maybe it was that, even seated in this stuffy, cramped room, he looked at peace.

I sat down, flipped through my packet, and found that I couldn't concentrate. My thoughts kept going back to Sunday morning. I'd driven Granny to church like usual. I helped her out of my pickup, and she had disappeared into the church. Usually at that point, I would have driven off and found something to do for an hour and a half. Sunday, I couldn't seem to make myself leave. I just sat there in the pickup, scared.

Scared of what?… of failure?… of the past?… of the future? Scared of what my life had become and scared that it would never change. I was afraid if I stepped through the front doors of the church, everyone in the sanctuary would turn and stare at me. I was afraid they would see right through me. Afraid a big red *B* would magically appear on my forehead, a *B* for batterer, and they would run me out, maybe even with stones.

I took a chance, slipped in, and found my way to Granny's pew. I kept my head down and didn't make eye contact with anyone. As soon as I was seated, the preacher stepped to the pulpit, welcomed everyone, and asked the congregation to bow their heads as he asked God into their service. God? It was hard enough for me to face the congregation. The thought of facing God was too much. I wanted to jump up and head for the door, then Granny reached over and patted my knee, and I bowed my head.

The preacher's message was from the book of Mark. I remember that and the story, but not the chapter and verse. It was the story of the crazy man who came out of the caves when Jesus got to shore. He had a bunch of demons in him and Jesus sent them into a herd of swine. The swine ran into the sea and drowned. The preacher said in today's world there were a lot of demons, like depression, PTSD, alcoholism, drug use, and several others. He said Jesus could help people today, just like he helped the man in the Bible. All I had to do was ask Jesus to help me.

After the service was over, Granny proudly introduced me to everyone as if I was the most perfect gentleman in the world. They all shook my hand and were very polite. It was very nice. When I helped Granny into the truck and shut the door, I checked my reflection in the glass and was relieved there was no *B* on my forehead.

Miz Nancy came in and brought my attention back to the present. She was smiling and looked rested. She reminds me of someone, but I can't put a finger on who. I think it's someone in the movies. "Tips on how to build a healthy love life with your spouse," she began to read the front page of the week's lesson. She stopped after the first bullet and talked about it. Her voice was a little raspy. Not too deep, but not too high. I decided it was a very nice voice. I liked to hear her read and a lot of what she had to say made sense.

After reading all fifteen bulleted points and expounding on each, she instructed us to answer the questions on the next two pages. As usual, she disappeared up the hall and left us to it. First, I sat wandering where she went and what she did for the five minutes she left us alone. Then, I stared around the room, watching the other members hard at work. Not really into it, I finally forced myself to concentrate and work on the questions.

After five minutes, Miz Nancy returned. I had six of the seven questions answered. The last one was giving me some problems. The question wanted to know how my partner and I had resolved our last argument. I no longer had a partner. I'm not sure you would have called what I had with Shelby a partnership or just another fling in a long history of flings.

"How responsible are you for your own happiness?" Miz Nancy read the first question and asked for volunteers to read their answers.

"Completely," Jake spoke up.

"That's right, Jake." Miz Nancy smiled. "You can't blame your unhappiness on your partner. You make the choice to stay or leave, so you make the choice to be happy or unhappy."

"What if you feel like you don't have a choice? Like you've got to stay for the kids?" Dan asked.

"You always have a choice," Miz Nancy told him. "You have to also think about the kids. What does the constant cussing and fighting do to them?"

"I guess so," Dan said. "Never thought of it that way."

"Okay, next question, what does equality look like in a relationship?" Miz Nancy moved to number two.

"What's good for the goose is good for the gander and vice versa." Jake said.

"Give me an example," Miz Nancy ordered.

"Well, for instance, if it's okay for her to go out with her friends," Jake explained, "then it should be okay for me to go out with the guys."

"Good," Miz Nancy agreed. "Anyone else?"

The class continued to answer the questions, but I tuned out. I watched Jake. He seemed lost again, like he wasn't really there. I wondered where he went when he disappeared like that. For the next few minutes, I simply watched Jake. How could this old man be violent? The final question arrived. It asked us to explain the last conflict we had been in and how it had been resolved. Miz Nancy said we all had to read what we had written.

When my turn came, I told the class that my last conflict had been resolved by the police and the courts. I explained how I hadn't been in any conflicts since I got out of jail. One after another, the members spoke, and then it was Jake's turn.

"The last conflict I had was with my now ex-wife. I can no longer have any contact with her. There's a protective order," Jake explained. "I told her I was sorry before she got the protective order, but I guess it was never really resolved. I guess it never will be, unless divorce is a resolution."

Jake was the last one to speak, and when he finished, the room was silent. For a long moment, nobody spoke. I could physically feel his pain from across the table. It was a new experience. I had never felt bad for someone before, especially not for someone who was essentially a stranger.

"That's everyone," Miz Nancy said breaking the tension in the room. "Make sure I get your sheets before you leave."

At the bottom of my sheet I wrote: Tonight, I learned I have a choice in everything I do in life. I learned that for every choice I make, there is a consequence. I learned that I should think about the consequence before I make a choice, not after I make it.

WEEK 4—CONCLUSION OF NEGOTIATION AND FAIRNESS

Miz Nancy was out in front of the Water to Wine All Faith Christian Church finishing a Marlboro Light when I pulled up twenty minutes early tonight. Kind of explains why her voice is a little raspy and where she goes for the five minutes after introducing the lesson. I can't really blame her. Dealing with a dozen or more pissy men who act like they don't really want to be there must be trying.

I figured I'd be the first one in the door. I told myself it was because I wanted to see who got to the meeting first, Jake or Freddy, but I think maybe the idea that these classes could be helping me become a better person has something to do with it. I still have doubts, plenty of them, and Granny says it's normal to have qualms about the process, but she thinks I should try to keep a positive outlook.

When I got to the room, Jake was just sitting down with his packet. Freddy was nowhere around. One question answered. Jake looked up and greeted me with a half-smile.

"How was your week?" he asked before I could say anything.

"Good," I answered, then asked, "how was yours?"

"Okay, can't complain," he replied, pulled his glasses out, put them on, and started to read the packet.

It occurred to me that he wasn't quite himself tonight. He seemed a little frayed at the edges, like an old lasso that's been overused and is starting to come unbraided. I wandered what was bothering him and realized I was a little worried for him. I wasn't sure when the last time I worried about anyone was, and there I was fretting over a complete stranger. I wasn't sure if these classes were helping me or just making me crazy.

After the usual sign in and pay up, Miz Nancy asked for a volunteer to read the first page of our packet. Dan began to read after a few seconds, and I tried to follow along. One part of the lesson asked us to try to think using our partner's brain. In other words, we were supposed to imagine how our most recent (or current) partner would answer the questions. The further along in the lesson Dan got, the lower Jake's head drooped until finally he pushed his glasses up on his forehead and pinched the bridge of his nose. It was a quick action and only lasted a few seconds. Nobody else seemed to notice, but I did. Someone had really done a number on this old fellow.

"Okay then," Miz Nancy's voice brought my attention back to the group, "take a few minutes to answer the questions, and we'll go over them. I expect everyone to participate, so for those of you who haven't had much to say lately, be ready to speak up." Then as usual, she headed up the hall.

Everyone got busy writing.

"Question number one," Miz Nancy said as she reentered the room with her packet some five minutes later, "How are you unique? Someone tell me what you wrote down."

"I work hard," Dan answered.

"That is a good quality," she agreed, "as long as you make time for the family. Someone else."

"I'm quiet," A young black guy whose name I don't remember spoke up.

"That can be a good quality as well, unless you want someone to talk to you." Miz Nancy smiled at him. "Someone else?" she waited a couple of seconds and then, "Hank, what did you write down?"

I looked at the blank space on my page and said, "Ma'am there isn't much unique about me. And on the next question, I don't have a partner."

"There is something unique and special about everyone including you, Hank. You don't get off that easy. Think of something, and we'll come back to you. And, Hank, if you don't have a partner, then write down a unique quality you'd like to see in a future partner. Now, who's next, and just so we're all clear, everyone is going to answer every question tonight."

"I fix things," Jake spoke up while I mentally wrestled with ideas to fill in the blank spaces.

"Good," Miz Nancy nodded, "and what do you mean by you fix things? Things like a broken washer?"

"Yes," he answered, "and any problems which might come up?"

"You have to be careful there," she advised. "We'll get into this in another lesson, but sometimes a woman doesn't need a problem fixed, she just wants you to listen."

"That's where I come in," Freddy announced from his usual corner. "I'm a good listener."

Miz Nancy smiled, "Good, Freddy, good."

After everyone had answered and I thought I was off the hook, she looked right at me and asked, "Hank what have you got for us now?"

"I'm pretty good with animals," I said. It was the only thing that came to mind.

"Okay." Miz Nancy didn't seem to know where to go with my answer.

Mason, on the other hand, had no trouble with it at all, "Maybe I should introduce you to my ex," he said. "She's a real cow."

"Mason!" Miz Nancy scolded as the room filled with laughter.

"Well, she is." Mason laughed, held his hands three feet apart and added, "got an ass this wide."

"That's the same thing you said a couple of weeks ago about your current girlfriend," Miz Nancy cocked her head to the side and gave him the look. "See a pattern here."

"Yeah," Mason shook his head. "My first wife was

beautiful, so beautiful. When she left, I guess my standards just went to hell."

"Okay, enough," Miz Nancy warned. "Someone answer question two. How is your partner unique?"

"On a good day, she made me feel like I was on top of the world," Jake spoke up, "and on those days, she was truly beautiful."

"Remember last week you said, and we all agreed, that we are each completely responsible for our own happiness?" Miz Nancy reminded him.

In my mind, I flipped Miz Nancy the bird. I stared across the table at that bearded old man. He nodded, shook his head, and sat silent while the rest of us answered one by one. I didn't hear a single word the other members said, and when I was called on, I still hadn't written anything down.

"Hank," Miz Nancy said my name again, "have you thought of a quality you'd like to have in a partner."

"Yeah," I said, "I want someone who makes me feel like I'm on top of the world every day of my life."

She shook her head. "Good luck with that."

When I looked over at Jake, he was smiling. Chalk one up for the good guys. Not that I'm a good guy, not by a long shot, and maybe Jake's not either, but he gives me hope.

The rest of the questions had to do with respecting each other's privacy, how we would accomplish it, how we would give our partner some 'me time', and how we would use ours. Answers varied drastically as the members were in so many different kinds of relationships. Some were still married to the spouse they had abused, some had new partners, and some had no partner at all. Generally, it was agreed on that everyone needs some time away from a relationship.

I tried to remember what had gone wrong with my marriage. My ex-wife Liz and I were only married for four years, and it had ended seven years ago or there about. Had it really been that long? My son turned nine last month, and he was almost two when we split, so yeah, I guess it had been that long. I remember lots of fighting, followed by a lot of make-up sex, followed by lots of fighting. But for the life of me, I couldn't remember what we fought about.

Come to think of it, I couldn't remember what the fight that landed me in these classes had been about either. I tried picking through the haze of what little memory I had of that night and came up with nothing. I can remember a lot of booze. I recall the motel room and her denim mini skirt. I can recall the red lacey thong panties and matching push-up bra, but I don't remember what started the fight.

The last seven years of my life seemed to be a non-stop loop of the same old same old. Every six months or so, there would be a new girl in my life, but it would end with the same old story. I looked at my life and hated what I saw. Behind me, a path of destruction; in front of me, uncertainty, and inside of me, fear.

"Tonight is Austin's last meeting," Miz Nancy announced when the last of the questions had been answered. "Austin, it's time for you to tell us what you've learned from the program."

Austin stood. He placed his hands on the tabletop and stared at them as he spoke. "Well, when I first started, I kinda thought the program was just a bunch of B.S. Then some of it started to really help me in my relationship. Me and my ole lady, sorry Miz Nancy, my wife haven't had any really bad fights in a long time, and the kids are doing better. A lot of what I learned here will help me have a better marriage and a better life. I think that's it. I think that's all I've got. That okay, Miz Nancy?"

"Yes, Austin, that's good." Miz Nancy smiled.

She dismissed the class and stood by the door, waiting for our papers. Jake took a long time finishing his, and I piddled with mine, not wanting him to be the last one out of the room. He finally rose, stepped around the table, handed her his paper, and disappeared up the hall. Before I handed it in, on mine I wrote: Tonight, I learned that everyone is unique, and everyone is special in some way. I learned that everyone needs some space in a relationship. I learned that when I am in a relationship in the future, I need to try to concentrate more on what makes my partner special.

What I didn't write was: I learned that I seriously need to get my shit together.

23

WEEK 5—CONSEQUENCES OF NEGATIVE FAMILY BEHAVIOR & ACCOUNTABILITY

They say shit rolls downhill. Well, that may be true, but I think sometimes shit doesn't roll at all. Sometimes it jumps on you like a three-hundred-pound sumo wrestler who just caught you banging his little sister. Well, tonight everyone in our wonderful little group must have pissed off their respective sumo wrestlers because walking into the building was like trying to ride your favorite Harley through a hundred mile an hour shit storm with no helmet and no goggles. I'm pretty sure that everyone will be picking fecal matter out of their teeth for the next week.

It all started before I even arrived. A middle-aged white guy who hadn't been coming to the meetings showed up early, which would have been fine except he showed up wasted. By the time I arrived, he was on his way to the pokey, and Miz Nancy was in a conference with her boss. I would say it was a 'behind-closed-doors' meeting, but the door was most definitely not soundproof, and neither Miz Nancy nor her boss was exactly happy.

"I know you have a soft spot for these guys because of your brother and his problems," Miz Nancy's boss said loudly as I eased down the hall.

"I think we should leave my brother out of this," I heard Miz Nancy's voice, "I have never missed work or even been here late."

"No, but there have been a lot of times that you were so tired, I was afraid you would fall asleep trying to lead the classes," her boss's voice raised enough that I was still able to hear it halfway down the hall, "I'm just saying, you have a soft spot and you can't let your feelings…" Her voice faded out and I didn't hear the last part as I slipped into the meeting room.

The only person in the room when I got there was Jake. He had shaved off his beard and cut his hair short. At first glance, I almost didn't recognize him. He looked twenty years younger. As usual, he gave me a half-smile when I walked in and asked how my week had been.

"Okay," I said. "What's that all about?" I asked, pointing back up the hall towards the office.

"The police were here when I got here," he explained, "and took some guy that was drunk or wasted or both out. As soon as they were gone, Miz Nancy and her boss started arguing. I didn't feel like it was my business so I came back here. About the time I sat down, I heard a door slam. In this room you can't hear what they're saying, but as you can tell from the tone of their voices both of them are pretty riled up." He shrugged and went back to reading his packet.

Forty minutes later, twenty minutes after our scheduled start time, Miz Nancy called us to sign in. Two of the three men who were called before me got none too nice lectures about the need to get their accounts current. I paid my fee, signed in, thanked Miz Nancy, and was happy to slink back down the hall and out of harm's way.

"I had a visit with my boss," Miz Nancy said as she walked in and stared around the room. "If your account is not current, you have two weeks to get it current. For those of you who have been missing classes, be warned. If you miss three in a row, you're out. If you miss more than seven times, you're out. If you come in here drunk or using or if I suspect either, you're out. I will call the police. You will go to jail. Do we understand each other?"

"Yes ma'am," Jake answered. Several of the others echoed his response. I just sat and stared at her. It was Julia Roberts, that's who she reminded me of, Julia Roberts from the movie Erin Brockovich, and the similarity was uncanny. I tried to remember when I'd seen the movie or even why but couldn't.

"Effects on children who live with domestic violence," She began to read the first paragraph of the packet. When she reached the end, she asked someone to read the section entitled: How are children affected by violence?

Jake read the twenty-six bulleted statements that followed. As he read through them, I thought of my own son. I had called his mother earlier in the week to arrange to see him on Saturday. Of course, she had plans with him and wanted to know if I wanted him after church on Sunday. After a twenty-minute argument, I agreed to pick him up after church.

Dan read the next section, and a new guy with a faded yellow Tweety Bird tattoo on his right bicep finished the back of the first page. By the time we got through page two, I was scared shitless. The physical effects my son could possibly suffer from witnessing domestic violence made me ill. Somehow, it had never occurred to me what his mother and me fighting could be doing to him. The possible emotional, behavioral, and social effects made me want to walk out, drive to the ex's house, apologize for ever being a douchebag, and promise to never fight with her again. It also made me want to protect him in a way I'd never wanted to before.

I had never been physically violent with my ex-wife, but our arguments had often escalated into foul screaming matches during which all rules went out the window. As far as I was aware, none of the guys she had dated had ever been physically abusive either, but now I was worried about how badly and in how many ways I had screwed up my son. It was a gut-wrenching realization.

"Now," Miz Nancy said, "I would like each of you to tell me how your family life was when you were growing up. Who would like to start?"

"I had a good family life," Jake shared. "My mom and dad raised me and my two sisters. They were good, kind parents. We were poor, but I don't think we ever really even realized it. Life was just good. I can't complain about anything from my childhood."

"That's good," Miz Nancy smiled. "Who's next, and just so we're clear, everyone is going to share."

"I'll go," Manuel spoke up. "My mother raised me and my brothers. There are three of us. My dad left when I was three and a half. I'm the oldest. I don't remember him. After he left, I never saw him again. Mom worked all the time, and my grandma helped watch us. We got by, but I never really had a man to look to, so it's been hard trying to figure out how I'm supposed to act as a husband and a father."

"You have a son and a daughter, right?" Miz Nancy asked.

"Yes." Manuel smiled.

She called on Freddy next. As usual, he was not keen on sharing. It took quite a few attempts and several questions to get his story out. One after another, all shared until there was only me left. I sat quietly hoping she had forgotten about me, but she hadn't.

"Hank?" She pushed her glassed up with the tip of her right index finger.

"My Granny raised me." I looked at her and shrugged.

"And?"

"We got by okay." I shrugged again.

"Hank," her tone was flat and hard, "you can either share, or I can ask questions until I'm satisfied."

"I don't remember my mother," I told her, my tone matched hers. "Granny said she left before I was two. My dad was a bronc rider and a rodeo clown. I kinda remember him. He wrecked his truck and died when I was six. He was a drunk. Granny had… has a pretty good size spread and raises cattle. Her husband, my grandpa, died of a heart attack when I was six months old, so I don't remember him either. Mainly, it was just me and Granny and sometimes some guys she hired to help her work cattle. She took me to church every Sunday."

I didn't know what else to say, so I just sat there. After a moment, Miz Nancy instructed us to fill out our sheets and hand them in before we left. I had so many thoughts and emotions running around in my head that it took me a good minute to gather them into words I could write on my paper. In the end I wrote: Tonight, I learned that abuse can have terrible effects on kids who have to live through it. I learned that I need to be more aware of what I say and do around my son.

I handed her my paper and walked out, feeling like the world's shittiest dad. It wasn't until I was outside in the cold that I remembered I'd left my black Stetson hat on one of the chairs. Returning to the room, I met Jake coming up the hallway. He had my hat in one hand and his own in the other. He smiled, handed mine to me, and told me to have a good week.

Outside again, I realized that there were far more cars in the parking lot than usual. It was then it dawned on me that there was a light coming from the church next door. As I watched, Jake opened the door to his truck, dropped his folder in the driver's seat, closed the door back, and started for the church door.

What made me do it, I couldn't tell you, but I followed him. At the door, he removed his hat, and I did likewise. Inside, rows of white, plastic folding chairs were lined up facing the back wall. A small, raised stage with a very plain wooden podium served as a pulpit. A short, stout-looking, older gentleman was addressing the few members present as I took a seat beside Jake.

"Tonight's study comes from the first chapter of James," he said. "Would someone like to read the first eight verses?"

Someone near the front of the church read loudly in a deep baritone, and then the man behind the pulpit prayed. What followed was a discussion of what the verses meant. It was not your usual service but a discussion. Several of the members participated while others, like myself, sat quietly. After about an hour, the leader announced to the newcomers that next week's reading would come from the second chapter of James, another prayer was said, and everyone got up to leave.

"You come here often?" Jake asked as he stood up.

"First time," I answered, "and you?"

"Second," he returned. "I wandered in last week after the B.I.P. class. I don't have time to get back home to my regular Wednesday night service, so I thought I'd come here for now."

We walked out together. Without a word he nodded, got into

his truck, and drove away. I stood shivering in the cold until he was out of sight. I tried to remember the last time I'd opened a Bible. I couldn't. Ten minutes later, I pulled into a space in front of the Dollar General, went in, purchased a new King James Bible, and headed home.

WEEK 6—PLANNING FOR NON-VIOLENT RELATIONSHIPS & SELF ACCOUNTABILITY

Even a blind squirrel finds a nut every once in a while. Somewhere in my distant past some very wise, or very wiseass, kin of mine had bestowed upon me these magnificent words of wisdom. As I sat at the table waiting for Miz Nancy to call us to sign in, it occurred to me that this past week had been like finding a little nut—a tiny kernel of hope in an otherwise shitty existence.

Thursday, I had called the ex and asked when it would be possible for me to see my son again. She told me Sunday after church, and I did not argue, just said okay and thanks. I couldn't remember the last time we had talked without yelling and cussing. It was kind of nice. Friday and Saturday, I worked mending fences at the ranch during the day and read my new Bible in the evening. I read the second chapter of James, and on Saturday evening, I sat and discussed it with Granny.

I spent Sunday afternoon with Luke, riding the four-wheeler around the ranch. We took Granny out to her favorite hamburger joint before dropping her off at the church for the evening service. On the way back to the ex's house, Luke told me he'd really had a good time. It felt like another tiny kernel of hope.

On the flip side, I have to admit that I'm still scared shitless. Most of my life, hope has just been a prelude to a massive heartbreak, a fucking train wreck waiting to happen. So, now I'm looking over my shoulder and listening for a long, loud, screaming whistle.

* * * * *

For tonight's lesson, there is a short paragraph explaining the reasoning behind the exercise. Following that, there are two pages of material that is formatted in two columns. The right column is filled with ideas that batterers hold, and the left column has positive self-talk. It took a little while, but eventually most of the class began to grasp the idea.

For instance, right column, batterers blame ex-partners or ex-spouses for causing anger to escalate to rage. Left column, batterers should use self-talk, reprograming the thought process to realize everyone is responsible for their own anger and any other feelings they may be allowing themselves to have. I gotta tell you, this was not an easy concept for me. I struggled with the idea.

On the second page, right column, batterers think of themselves as bad, evil people because they have been abusive. Left column, batterers should self-talk, acknowledge the abusive behavior as mistakes they have made and learn from them so they do not repeat them. This one was a little easier.

When the class had finished both pages, Miz Nancy instructed us to turn the second page over and do five of our own. She warned that she did not want to see any of the examples reworded. She wanted new material, and everyone would share all five of theirs, after which she retreated up the hallway.

I drew a line down the middle of the paper and sat staring at it. The front door opened and then closed. Five minutes and Miz Nancy would be back, but I could not think of one single idea about abuse that I held, and I sure as hell didn't know what I was supposed to do to self-talk myself into a new thought process. I looked around the room and felt relieved when I realized that nearly everyone was in the same boat as me. Except for Jake, everyone was staring at blank pages.

"A little help here, Jake," Dan broke the silence.

"What?" Jake asked as he looked up from his scribblings.

"I think you're the only one who got this," Dan shrugged. "You think you could help us out?"

Jake looked around the table and then back down at his paper. He pushed his glasses up and pinched the bridge of his nose. I thought he was going to ignore Dan.

"On the right side of my paper I'm writing beliefs I have, and on the left side, a more positive way to look at the situation. I guess you could call it self-talk if you want to, I prefer positive-talk," Jake explained shifting his glasses back into place.

"How 'bout an example?" Manuel chimed in from the far end of the table.

"Sure," Jake said. "Belief: If I can't make this work, then I'm a bad husband, so I need to fight for this relationship no matter what it takes. Positive-Talk: It's okay to step back from a relationship that is going badly. Something like that anyway."

"Thanks," Dan said and started jotting something on his paper.

After a minute or two, everyone was writing. Like clockwork, Miz Nancy wandered back into the room and found us all hard at work. She stood in the doorway for a few minutes, allowing us to finish, and then she asked if someone would read one of their items.

"Belief: The kids will be better off with a mom and a dad even if abuse is happening," a stocking looking guy with prison tattoos on both arms and his neck spoke up, "Positive-Talk: (he nodded at Jake) Kids need a peaceful place to live."

This was the first class he had attended since I began, and nothing had been said about him introducing himself. I was beginning to understand that some of these guys missed from time to time and some of them were here to make up classes they had missed elsewhere during the week. Just because I hadn't seen them before didn't mean they were new members.

Without waiting to be called on, Jake read aloud, "Belief: I'm too old to start over again. Positive-Talk: I ain't dead yet, so I can start over if I want."

Dan chuckled and everyone smiled. Jake half-smiled himself, but his heart wasn't in it, I could tell. He's eyes were far off again. He was picturing his ex-wife, and I was beginning to wander if Jake would ever *want* to try again.

Tweety Bird tattoo guy from last week went next. "When she loses control, she makes me lose control. Positive-Talk: I can choose to let her throw a fit and remain calm. I don't have to lose control."

"Very good, James," Miz Nancy spoke up from the doorway.

After everyone had read one belief and positive-talk, we went around the room again. I began to wish I had time to write everybody's comments down for future reference. Except for Jake and maybe Dan, I was pretty sure this wasn't the kind of crowd for such an exercise. Crazy, though, here we all were doing it, and it felt right somehow, even felt good.

Jake was the last one to read, "Belief: God doesn't like divorce." His voice waivered. "Positive-Talk: God doesn't like abusive people."

A long minute passed before anyone made a sound. I don't know what the other members where feeling, but somewhere deep inside myself, I was excited. Excited, yeah, I guess that's the right word. I was excited to try life with a more positive attitude. I was excited to leave the old me behind and start forward. I was excited because I felt like life could be different, better, nice. I thought to myself: Belief: No matter what, life is eventually going to kick you square in your nads. Positive-Talk: Start wearing a metal cup."

Miz Nancy broke the silence by asking for our papers, and everyone got busy writing their closing remarks. I wrote: Tonight, I learned that turning negative beliefs into positive thoughts is a very powerful way to combat abuse.

We turned in our papers and I followed Jake out the front door and headed to my truck for my new Bible. I had parked at the back of the short parking lot, and as I shut my truck door, Miz Nancy turned out the lights in the counseling center. When she did, it seemed to make the neon signs on the other store fronts stand out. On the left was Suzy Q's, and on the right The Wine to Water All Faith Church.

I'm not sure what a revelation is or if I'd recognize one if it bit me on the ass, but as I stood beside my truck looking at the building in front of me, I thought I might just have had one. With the counseling office darkened, the neon signs on each of the other buildings shone more brightly. On my left was Suzy Q's 'Adult Toys' sign and on the right the churches 'Oasis' sign. It was like two neon lite pathways led from my feet to the doors of each establishment.

On the left, my old life and one hell of a party. On my right, the chance for a new beginning, a new life, a more peaceful life. I wanted to move forward, but I froze. My feet refused to move. It was like someone or something had super-glued my boots to the asphalt.

"Headed to the Neon Church?" Tweety Bird tattoo asked as he open the door of his truck parked next to mine.

"Yeah," I answered, adding. "Me and Jake have been going."

He smiled, got into his truck, and pulled away. I found my feet and followed the path to my right.

WEEK 7—NON-ABUSIVE COMMUNICATION TECHNIQUES I

Some call it routine; some call it a rut. Call it what it you want, it sucks. Deep down inside, I know I'm on the right path. I know I'm becoming a better person, but this week has been a constant battle not to do something stupid. Thursday night, I called the ex and asked when I could see Luke. Sunday afternoon was the answer as usual. I bit my tongue.

I was mad. Mad clear through. A voice in my head said, *what the hell let's do it*. So, I got in my truck and drove. When I stopped, I was setting in the parking lot of a bar arguing with myself. The biggest part of me wanted to waltz through the door and not come back out until I was completely shitfaced. A very small part kept trying to get me to drive back home and go to bed.

I shut off the ignition, opened the door, and stepped out. As I closed the door behind me, the door to the bar opened and Miz Nancy stepped out into the night air with a man. I could tell the man was having trouble standing and Miz Nancy was supporting him. My first instinct was to go over and help her, but then I remembered, that because of the charges against me, I wasn't even supposed to be here. As I watched, she managed to get him into her car. She closed the door and for just a second her face was illuminated by the light from the other side of the bar's door. She looked tired and frustrated.

She moved from the passenger's side of her car to the driver's side. I stood perfectly still and prayed she did not see me. The palms of my hands started to sweat, and I wanted to wipe them on the front of my jeans. I did not need any more trouble.

I recalled the comment I had overheard as I passed the office the night Miz Nancy and her boss were arguing. "Because of your brother and his problem," she had said.

Sometimes when a person can't help those closest to them, they try to compensate by helping as many other people as they can. I had to wonder if that is what drove Miz Nancy. Her brother had a drinking problem. Not that I'm one to judge.

Standing there, I took a hard look at myself. Did I have a drinking problem? I didn't know for sure, but I knew I didn't want to have one. I got in my truck, drove home, and read the third chapter of James.

On Saturday, I had a long talk with Granny about what I'd read and the troubles I was having.

"Satan is out to kill, steal, and destroy," Granny said after listening to my woes.

"But I'm reading the Bible and trying to pray," I shrugged. "So, shouldn't it be getting easier?"

"Doesn't work that way," she answered.

"Then how does it work?" I asked.

After a minute's thought, she cocked her head to the side, squinted, and smiled, "You've been in a few relationships. You know when someone is losing interest, and you try harder."

She stopped there. I just looked at her. I knew she was trying to tell me something, but it just wasn't getting through. She let it sink in for a few seconds longer and then continued. "You been running wild for a long time. You been killing your own spirit, stealing your own peace of mind, and destroying your own salvation. Satan didn't really need to do anything; you were doing it all for him. Now, you're starting down the right road, and he doesn't like it. He's going to work, and, Runt… it won't get easier anytime soon.

So, there it was. For all of you morons like me out there that think the road back from hell is a short walk across a neon lit parking lot into a Neon Church, or any other church for that matter, it's NOT.

Sunday, after attending church, I picked up Luke. We spent some time at the lake canoeing. I took a couple of fishing poles, and we wet a line. It was still too cold to expect anything to bite, but on the way back to his mom's, he told me he sure would like to go again. I figure that meant he enjoyed himself.

Monday, Tuesday, and Wednesday rolled along like every other Monday, Tuesday, and Wednesday had for the last seven months, the weeks of monotony broken up only by the Wednesday night meetings of the Court-Ordered Society of Batterers. I found myself sitting across from Dan and wondered if any of the other class members were getting something out of these classes.

Jake greeted me with his usual question about my week and a smile when I walked in. Freddy grinned from his corner seat, and some clean-cut new guy, looking nervous as hell, nodded from his seat at the far end of the table. Inside, I chuckled. In a few weeks, the nerves would be gone, and the confusion would set in. I wanted to tell him that Granny says change is never an easy thing, but I didn't. I just picked up my packet and began to read through it.

After the customary sign in and pay, Miz Nancy read over the first couple of pages. She seemed to be in a bad mood and looked tired. After the close call on Thursday, I knew why but what the hell was I going to do, I couldn't even figure out my own life.

Before heading off for her evening cigarette, she instructed us to fill out the two exercise pages. Page one was titled: Rules of Communication and page two: Reflective Listening. Page one had eight rules on it, the first was: Keep it simple. Our task was to explain each rule in our own words. I wrote: One Issue = One Incident. The second page was much harder. In this exercise, we read a statement from a female and had to supply the reflection of her feelings. In other words, she says something, and we are supposed to finish the sentence that begins with "You feel…"

Unsure of how to answer the questions, I stared around the

table. A few of the guys were attempting answers, but most of them seemed as lost as me. Miz Nancy appeared and asked someone to read what they had written on number one of exercise one.

"If the argument is about money, don't let it become about everything that's wrong with the relationship," Jake offered. Like Miz Nancy, he looked haggard, as if he hadn't been sleeping well.

"Good, Jake," she nodded, "but remember, this doesn't have to be an argument. It can be a discussion. And if it is about money, it should be about one instance of money."

Jake smiled weakly and nodded his agreement.

Through the next couple of questions, I watched Jake over the top of my packet. There were noticeable dark half-circles under his eyes, and he looked pale. I found myself worrying about him.

"Number five: Avoid bringing up the past. Someone?" Miz Nancy had stepped up behind me, and her voice just above my head jarred my thoughts back to the present discussion.

"Don't bring up old shit," the tattooed fellow at the end of the table spoke up.

"That's one way to put it, Frank." Miz Nancy cocked an eyebrow his way. "In other words, stick to the topic at hand and don't bring the past into the current discussion. Number six: Talk for yourself, not for you partner."

"Don't put your thoughts in your partner's brain," Jake spoke without looking up, "or head, maybe," he added as if speaking to the packet in front of him.

"Good, very good," Miz Nancy agreed. "When you have a discussion with someone, it is never good to assume that you know what they are thinking."

Jake removed his glasses, laid them on his packet on the table in front of him, and pinched the bridge of his nose. Miz Nancy directed the group to the next question. After a moment, he retrieved his glassed, sighed deeply, placed them back on, and glanced over at me. I nodded. I didn't know what else to do.

"The goal is not to win but to cooperate on a goal." Miz Nancy read the last of the questions in the first exercise. After several of the members responded with similar answers about working together, Miz Nancy moved us to the next exercise. As she did so, I suddenly realized it had never occurred to me that you shouldn't try to win an argument. It dawned on me then that if someone wins, then someone must lose, and if it is your partner/girlfriend/wife, then in a way, you also lose, so no one really wins.

The first example on the second exercise said: "When you scream at me I want to crawl in a hole and hide. I never know what to expect." Following were the words, "You feel…", and we were required to explain what emotion she was feeling as briefly as possible.

"Someone, please, share," Miz Nancy requested.

"You feel scared. You're not sure where it's going," the new guy offered.

"Not bad, Garrett. Now she knows you understand," Miz Nancy said.

"But why?" Frank raised his hand. "Why is it necessary?"

"It is a tool. A tool used to slow the conflict down and make you think about what she is feeling. And maybe give yourself some time to find some compassion which will overshadow your anger," Miz Nancy explained.

"But this really works?" Dan wondered, adding, "I think if I did this, my girl would think I was being sarcastic and get pissed."

"Yes, that can happen," Miz Nancy agreed, "but if she is made aware of this technique, if the two of you are willing to practice it, it can come in handy."

The remainder of the exercise went without a hitch and then Miz Nancy introduced Garrett and asked him to explain why he was attending the classes. He's tall and stocky. Put a black and white striped shirt on him and give him a whistle and he'd look like he just walked off the field after a Sunday afternoon football game. He looked down at the table as if to get his bearings.

"I was seeing three different girls," he started. "I had an open relationship with two of them, but the third thought we were exclusive. When she found out she wasn't, she came to my apartment and took an aluminum baseball bat to my car. The alarm went off, and by the time I made it downstairs, she had already smashed both headlights, cracked the windshield, knocked a side mirror off, and was starting on the driver's window. She didn't see me coming. I grabbed her from behind and threw her across the pavement. She lost the bat and I picked it up. I smashed her front windshield, and when she came at me, I threatened her with the bat. That's when the cops showed up."

"Most of the time, we have some other members share," Miz Nancy informed him, "but tonight, we're out of time, and I've got a terrible headache, so another time." And then to everyone, "Fill out your papers and make sure I get them before you leave."

* * * * *

The church next door was closed and the parking lot almost empty when we exited the center. Jake stood beside his truck, staring at the neon sign. I walked out and asked him why he thought there was no service and what we should read for next week.

"Don't know," he said. "Maybe just the next chapter of James."

We stood there quietly together, him looking at the front door of the church, me looking at my scuffed boots. It was a weird couple of minutes.

"Something on your mind?" he asked.

"Well, um," I began, hesitated, and began again. "I was wondering, well, um…"

"I find it best to just spit it out." He grinned, and there was a funny twinkle at the edge of his eyes. I felt like I could ask him anything.

"In the meeting, you got really quiet after the question you

40

answered, 'don't put words into your partners brain'," I said and paused.

"Yes?" he urged.

"Well, I wondered if there was more, if you could explain." I asked.

"In my marriage, often my wife, or I guess my ex-wife, would decide she knew what I was thinking, especially about some woman, and when we would argue, she would tell me what it was I thought."

"And was she, ever right?" What made me asked that, I don't know.

"Never," he said without hesitation. "She was the love of my life, actually, she probably still is, and I never wanted or even thought I wanted another woman. Still don't for that matter."

"Never felt for a woman like that," I admitted aloud, more to myself than to him.

"I hope someday you do." He smiled. "It's a very special feeling."

All the way home, I wondered if there would ever be someone who would make me feel the way he felt about his wife, and part of me wondered, after seeing him hurt the way he did, if I ever wanted to find that someone.

Before I had handed my paper in, I had written: I need to learn to shut up and listen more. I need to make sure in future relationships that I give my girlfriend a chance to communicate her feelings and try to understand those feelings.

It seemed like I was learning a lot, but in order to put it into practice, I needed a girlfriend. After talking with Jake, I felt more confused than ever. I guess that's just how some weeks go.

WEEK 8—NON-ABUSIVE COMMUNICATION TECHNIQUES II

The opposite of love is not hate, it is indifference. That's what Granny told me when I told her about my conversation with Jake and wondered aloud how Jake didn't hate his ex-wife. Granny's statement started me thinking, and indifference has been on my mind all week. I look back over my many relationships and how they ended, and I guess, for the most part, I'm indifferent. Except for maybe, my son's mother, I don't feel much of anything for any of the other women in my past. These classes and Jake are really messing with my head.

On Friday, I was mending fence at the back edge of the range. There's a stretch of land that gets no radio reception at all. I like to listen to music while I work, so I selected a CD from the center console and slide it into the player in my truck. It was Blake Shelton's *Pure BS*. I grinned, it just seemed right for the time.

After several songs, he started singing about an old boy that had screwed up his life bad. One line caught my attention, something about taking enough wrong turns to get to the town of Sorryville. I stopped stretching fence and just listened to the words. In the song, he wonders if he was born the way he was or if he was a self-made man. I've never met Blake, so I was sure surprised he knew my life story.

On the way back to the house, I thought to myself that after working all day a beer sure sounded nice. Somewhere in the recess of my brain, a little voice that sound a lot like Granny was questioning if I could stop at one. A much louder voice that could only be Miz Nancy was dead set against it, and then Jake's voice overshadowed both women and asked if I'd called about visiting my son this weekend. I hadn't.

When I rolled into the front yard, I was so frustrated I just felt like screaming. I got out of the truck and headed in to take a shower. As I stepped up on the porch, I heard the house phone ringing. I tossed my work gloves, sunglasses, and keys on the counter and grabbed the phone. It was Liz.

Turns out she was to be a bridesmaid in one of her girlfriend's weddings, and her mother, who was supposed to watch Luke, had decided to go off with her friends to Las Vegas for the weekend. Did I want the boy for the weekend? She could drop him off around noon on Saturday. After a quick yes, I hung up the phone, sat down on the couch, and cried like a big baby.

That night, I sat on the front porch and read the third chapter of James in my new Bible. The chapter explained how the tongue is the hardest thing in the world to tame. I read it twice and mulled it over as I watched the sun sink from the sky in a magnificent splash of orange and red. I'm not sure, but I think the chapter's meaning is if you want peace and happiness, you better have God leading your life. Before I got up from the porch, I closed my eyes, bowed my head, and prayed, "God, please help me. Thanks. Amen." It was the first time I could remember speaking to God since my son was born.

The weekend was the best I can remember. Luke and I spent all of Saturday and Sunday after church fishing and running around the ranch on the four-wheeler. By the time, Liz picked him up late Sunday evening, both he and I were sunburned, windblown, and worn out. Monday and Tuesday flew by, and even though I got to the center twenty-five minutes early, Jake still beat me. He was seated in his usual spot, looking over his packet. He seemed rested, looked better than he had in several weeks.

"How was your week?" I asked with a grin, beating him to the punch.

"Good, really good." He grinned back. "I got to talk to all my kids this week."

"How many kids do you have?" I asked.

"Seven," he said with a smile and went back to his packet.

I slid into my seat, grabbed my packet, and sat staring at the page. I couldn't concentrate on the lesson in front of me. I was still trying to wrap my mind around seven kids. Jake was most definitely full of surprises.

The night's lesson was another exercise in listening, reflective listening to be exact. Since we'd already done one about listening, I figured it would be easy. It wasn't. This time we weren't allowed to use the words 'You feel'. Instead, after a dialogue from a female, we were supposed to simplify what she had said and repeat it back to her.

For instance, she says: "This is a big joke to you. You think I'm a big joke. Every time I try to talk to you about something I think is a serious matter, you tune me out. You've got something else on your mind, like your job, or the football game on the television. Anything but me."

To which, according to the example on our paper, the man should respond: I don't listen to you and I tune you out.

"So, I just repeat what she said in less words?" Freddy asked from his corner.

"Yes," Miz Nancy said.

"Don't make much sense to me," James interjected. "If I repeat back to Tweety what she said in the first place, she'll think I'm makin' fun of her, then there'll be hell to pay."

"Not if she understands the process," Miz Nancy stated, "kind of like last week's lesson. You will have to explain the process to your partner before using it. Did any of you talk to your partners after last week's exercise or maybe even use the technique?"

Dan was the only one to raise a hand. He looked sheepishly around the room and shrugged, "I'm tryin'."

"That's good." Miz Nancy smiled at him and then

proceeded to let the rest of us have it. She explained in some very colorful terms how we would only get as much out of the program as we were willing to put into it. When she got finished, we went over the rest of the exercise. At the end of the lesson, she gathered our exit papers and wished us all a good week, encouraging us to use what we were learning in class in our relationships.

The Neon Church was still open, so I followed Jake into the room and had a seat. We had missed the first part of the service and got in on the middle of the discussion. One of the fellows was saying the tongue was the hardest thing to control. By the end of the discussion, I was pretty sure I'd been almost right in my thoughts on the chapter but still wanted to ask Granny about it.

On the way home, I thought about what I'd written on my exit sheet: I learned I have not been very good at listening in my past relationships, and if I am ever going to have a meaningful, lasting relationship, I have to learn to be a better listener.

WEEK 9—NON-ABUSIVE COMMUNICATION TECHNIQUES III

The first thing a fella better know is that a temptation is like a woman. The second is she will not always give you a warning shot. Oh yeah, now and then she does, like a sexy little blonde in a mini skirt that throws a wink your way at the dance hall. More often than not, though, she's the red head who walks up, grabs your cock and says, "Buy me a drink?"

This week, temptation has played it both ways with me. Thursday, I called the ex, hoping I'd get to spend the weekend with my son again. No can do, she had plans with him on Saturday; I could have him Sunday as usual. I was tempted to drive into town for a bottle of Jim Beam, drive back, and drink it dry. After careful consideration, along with the knowledge that I had to move cows on Friday, I decided to reread the first chapter of James instead. For some reason, it helped.

Friday went smoothly. Tom Jack, an older gentleman Granny hires to help around the place, came over to lend a hand. We finished the jobs we had to do late in the afternoon, and Granny had fried chicken and the works ready when we made it back to her house. We visited while we ate, and Granny asked what I'd been reading. I told her the first few chapters of James, and we discussed them. I was really surprised at how much Tom Jack knew about the Bible. I thought he was just an old cowhand.

Saturday morning, a Sheriff's deputy showed up at my door before the sun was up. I was sitting at the kitchen table, having my morning coffee, when I saw his truck turn in at the end of the drive. The light from the barn illuminated his light bar, and I went into a scrabble. Old habits die hard. By the time he'd knocked on the door, I remembered there was no alcohol in the house, and all my guns were at Granny's since by law I was not allowed to have them while I was on probation.

"Got some cows out over on the west side of the property," he said in explanation when I opened the door.

"Sure they're ours?" I asked through the old wood framed screen door.

"Got your Granny's brand on'em." He nodded. "Want me to go on up to her place?"

"Nah," I told him, "I'll get'em back in."

Ten minutes later, I was on my four-wheeler and headed across the pasture. It took me all morning to get the cows back in and fix the fence. A big old hackberry had split, and half of it had taken down three T-posts and thirty feet of wire. I finished up, made a sweep of the west pasture, and got back to the house about noon.

Granny's old red and white pasture truck was in the front drive, and Granny was sitting in the rocker on the porch. She smiled when I climbed up the steps. She handed me a stack of mail, stood up, pulled my head down and kissed me on the forehead.

"By the time I heard the cows were out, I also heard you had everything done," she said. "Just wanted to check on you and say thanks. Now, I better get back. I've got dough rising for bread. We're having a dinner after the morning service tomorrow."

I stretched out in the rocking chair she had vacated and flipped through the mail, mostly junk except a notice it was time for my annual cleaning from my dentist, and a letter with no return address written in a very female handwriting. I dropped everything on the bench beside the rocker and stared at the envelope. I turned it over, then back. I placed it under my nose and sniffed. Why I don't know.

"Yeah, that was stupid," I said aloud and opened it. Inside, I found a letter from Shelby. She is the reason I am in the program. Okay, I'm the reason I'm in the program. Shelby was the girlfriend who helped get me there. She was writing to let me know that she had forgiven me for splitting her lip open and thought we should give it another chance. She apologized for the way she was contacting me, but explained that after I changed my phone number, the only way she knew to get to me was through Granny.

I stared at the letter, put it down, picked it up, read it again. Now, to say that Shelby was good in bed would be a massive understatement. Temptation smiled; I smiled. At the end of the letter she had written, "P.S. Call me" and had included her phone number.

The crazy thing about temptation is that once she gets in your head, she's all you can think about. Liz called Sunday morning to tell me Luke was sick, and I couldn't pick him up. I said okay and went right back to thinking about Shelby. At church on Sunday, I could not even begin to tell you what the sermon was about. Monday and Tuesday went by in a cloud, nothing on my mind but Shelby. I picked up the phone a dozen times to call her, and every time, I couldn't.

I thought about talking to Granny. I decided against it. If I'm honest, it was because I knew she would have said it was a bad idea, and I wanted to hold on to the possibility for a little longer. I knew I was not in love with Shelby. I didn't hate her for what had happened. I guess it all came back to the indifference Granny had mentioned last week. Truth be told, I hadn't been laid in months, and I just really wanted to tap that one more time.

* * * * *

Wednesday found me arriving early to the meeting. I needed to see Jake. Why? I needed advice. Why, Jake? I don't know. Because he was a man? Because he had been through something similar? Because he was close to the age my dad would be if he was alive? Maybe all of the above.

Jake must have heard me coming down the hall, because he caught my eye as soon as I cleared the door, and asked, "How was your week?" and grinned.

"Man, you wouldn't believe it," I said as I sat down.

"Really?" He removed his glasses and laid them on the table.

"Yeah, my old girlfriend sent me a letter," I told him.

"The one from the motel that split your head open with a lamp?" He leaned back and cocked his head to one side.

"Yeah, that one," I answered.

"And what did you do?" he asked.

"Nothing yet," I shrugged. "What would you suggest?"

"Are you in love with her?" He looked me dead in the eye.

"Not really." I shook my head. "Just thought it might be fun to hit it one more time."

"You're about the same age as my oldest son." Jake leaned forward and rested his elbows on the table, "so, I'm gonna give you the same advice I would give him. You're not getting any younger. If you ever want to have a wife and a family, it's time to grow up. If you don't love her, if you don't see her as part of your future, and if you really want to have a better life, then don't answer the letter, just let it go. That's what I would tell my son. That's my advice, take it or leave it, it's free."

He sat back, put on his glasses, picked up his packet, and began to read. For a second, I felt like cussing, but the feeling passed and with it the weight of the world lifted. The temptation was gone. Like smoke in the wind, it disappeared, and in that instant, I could have hugged that gray-haired old man.

One by one the other members showed up, and we followed the usual routine. The meeting itself went well. The best part of the packet was a list of rules for fighting fair. The first rule was: Only fight by mutual consent. The concept of it ever being acceptable to fight was something brand new for me. I always figured couples should never fight. Miz Nancy explained how unrealistic the idea of couples never fighting was and said, in healthy relationships, couples learn to fight fair.

Some of the week's rules were very similar to last week's exercise, but one of them was: Never quit. In other words, the fight only ends when a lasting resolution to the problems has been reached. Another rule was: Never try to win. Miz Nancy said if one partner wins, then the other one loses. If this happens, the loser will begin to resent the relationship. The list really opened my eyes. I almost wanted to find a woman, build a relationship, and have a fight—almost.

The last rule of course was: NO VIOLENCE.

Miz Nancy dismissed the class in her usual manner, and before I followed Jake to the Neon Church, I wrote on my exit paper: I learned that in a healthy relationship, fighting is okay if everyone fights fair and there is NO VIOLENCE.

What I felt like writing, but didn't, was: Temptation Zero; Old Jake One.

WEEK 10—DEVELOPING HEALTHY RELATIONSHIPS I

They say God works in mysterious ways. I ain't sure if it was God or some other force, but this week was interesting, to say the least. I'm still trying to wrap my head around it. Granny says it might just be the miracle we've been waiting for, but I should take it slow. Myself, I'm not sure whether I ought to run forward, run backwards, or just spin in circles.

Friday evening, Granny sent me to Walmart for a bill of groceries. Now, the nearest Walmart is thirty miles away and just across the state line. I make the trip down, gather up the groceries, and push my cart in line at the first register. The conveyer belt was piled high with groceries, and the shopper's basket in front of me was overflowing, so I settled in for a bit of a wait.

"How old are you, young man?" a voice behind me asked.

I turned to find a lady I figured to be about Granny's age smiling up at me. She had one of those jolly faces little ladies have that just melt your heart, and then she gave me a mischievous grin.

"I'm thirty-two, ma'am." I smiled.

"Well, I would have never guessed it, you look younger," the grin grew bigger, "and you sure fill out those Wranglers well."

I'm pretty sure the tomatoes in my basket were a lighter shade of red than my face. I stammered a thank you and smiled like a shit-eating possum.

"Oh, don't worry," she waved a hand. "I'm seventy-three years old, and I've got grandkids as old as you. It's just that I'm too old to worry about what I say, so I say what I want. It's one of the privileges that comes with age, and I take full advantage of it."

"Yes, ma'am," I said, not knowing what else to say, and started to turn away.

"You're in pretty good shape," she said looking up at my straw Stetson and then down at my scuffed work boots. "You work on a ranch?"

"Yes, ma'am," I said. I was starting to feel like those were the only words I knew.

"Which ranch?" she asked.

"My grandmother's," I said, then added, "The Broken L." I noticed she only had a few items, so I asked her if she'd like to go ahead of me. She smiled and thanked me and eased her cart up in front of mine. The belt moved, leaving space for her to unload her purchases, a few groceries and a couple of pastel blouses.

"These are on sale. A really good price." She held up one of the tops to show me as she spoke. "You should tell your wife about them."

I held up my left hand to show her I wasn't wearing a ring and said, "I don't have one of those."

"Oh, so you're not married?" The mischievous grin flashed back. "Well, I've got a granddaughter who needs a husband."

Once again, I put the tomatoes to shame. Her cell phone rang, and I let out a slow breath as she reached in her purse and took it out. Saved by the cell.

"Better take this," she said after looking at the number. "It's my sister."

She answered the phone, and I began to examine the beef jerky and candy bars that are always strategically placed near the check out. I was raised to understand phone calls are private, so I tried not to listen.

"Yes, I'm checking out right now," she spoke into the phone. "Yes, at Walmart, and I think I may have found Dottie a husband."

My head snapped back around so fast I may have sprained a neck muscle, and I'm pretty sure I blushed all the way to my pinky toes. I couldn't even begin to form a sentence, and the cashier was trying so hard not to laugh that I was pretty sure she was going to wet herself.

"Yes," the lady continued, "he's a rancher, and he does fill out a pair of Wranglers. Yes. No. Okay, I will. See you in a bit."

As soon as she hung up, she started flipping through her phone. I was at a loss. I wanted to turn away. I thought about running, but I couldn't move, I couldn't speak. And then she flipped the phone around and show me a picture of a very beautiful young lady with big brown eyes.

"That's my granddaughter," she stated.

"She is beautiful," I stammered, and she truly was.

"She's divorced. I think you should meet her. If I give you her phone number will you call her?" she asked.

In all my life I had never been in a situation quite like this one, and I honestly did not have a clue what to do. The only thought in my head was, Granny will kill you. I don't know why that thought was there or even if it was true, but it was there and so I said, "Ma'am, she is beautiful, but I just wouldn't feel comfortable calling her. She doesn't even know what I look like."

"Okay, then," she said and looked me right in the eye, "let me take a picture of you and I'll give her your number. If she wants, she can call you."

The next thing I know, I'm posing for a picture in the checkout aisle in Walmart and giving the sweet little lady my phone number. It later occurred to me that in the picture there would be a big blue lighted number one indicating the counter number just above my head. At the time I wondered if it would make a difference.

"My names Joani Walters." She stuck her hand out.

"I'm Hank Wilcox," I said as I shook her hand.

The cashier had finished scanning her items. She paid the lady, put the last bag in the cart, turned, and said, "It was nice to meet you, Hank. We live east of town in the big red brick house on the hill just past the Cowboy Church. Come visit anytime."

I smiled and nodded, "It was very nice to meet you too, Mrs. Walters." I blushed.

"Not Mrs. Walters," her eyes twinkled, and she smiled, "just Jo. That's what everyone calls me. See ya."

And she was gone, leaving me staring at the cashier. Someone behind me in line let out a chuckle, and I blushed again, but I did not look back.

I checked out, drove to Granny's, and dropped off the groceries. No phone call came that night. I spent most of Saturday piddling around the ranch.

I dropped Luke off after our Sunday visit and was sitting on the front porch when the phone rang. I had all but forgotten about Mrs. Walters when I answered it.

"Hank, you don't know me," the sweetest voice I'd ever heard said, "but I'm Dottie. My grandmother said I should give you a call."

After an hour-long conversation, during which I poured my heart out and confessed to nearly every bad deed I'd ever done, including why I was taking the batterers' classes, for reasons I may never understand, she asked me if I would call her the next evening.

Monday morning at breakfast, I told Granny about the call, hoping she might have some opinion about what I should do, and she just grinned. As if my life was not confusing enough.

That night I called Dottie. We talked so late into the night that I found it hard to get up and around Tuesday morning. The day blurred by and that night I resisted the temptation to call her for a third night in a row. I wasn't sure what kind of message that would send.

Walking into the meeting Wednesday night, my head was so messed up that I almost didn't acknowledge Jake when he asked how my week had been. I recovered in time to tell him it was good but not before the old fox sensed something was up. He cocked his head to the side and raised his eyebrows. I shrugged.

I sat down and picked up the packet from the table in front of my seat. The exercise for the evening was for us to create a plan for non-violent behavior in our relationships. Before Dottie had called, there had been a spark of desire growing somewhere deep inside me to be a better man, but now there was a full on five-alarm fire blazing out of control. I desperately wanted to be a better man.

After we had read the lesson, our worksheet asked us to identify our trigger—the thoughts, behaviors, and situations that would bring out the violence in us. I had some trouble with thoughts and situations, but on the behavior, I wrote screaming and cussing. I hate for someone to scream and cuss at me.

When Miz Nancy asked for someone to share, most everyone was quiet. Then Jake spoke up, "On thoughts, I wrote I'm tired of this shit. Twenty years and nothing's changed. On behavior, I wrote the silent treatment and running me down. And on situation, I wrote talking in circles."

"Okay," Miz Nancy looked across the table at him, "why did you stay for twenty years?"

"I thought it would get better. I thought she would change or that I could change enough to please her. Maybe for the kids. Anymore, I don't know." He took his glasses off and laid them on the table.

"Sometimes, it helps to answer the tough questions." Miz Nancy smiled at him. "Sometimes, not so much, but maybe." She shrugged.

He smiled back and nodded. I thought how crazy it was that sometimes the right question just opens a whole new world.

"Someone else, question two." Miz Nancy said.

Question two asked us to explain how an abusive behavior built within us from beginning to end. No one seemed to want to volunteer.

"Everyone will share on this one, boys." Miz Nancy's eyes narrowed as she looked around the room. I'm pretty sure Freddy was considering crawling under his chair.

"I'll go," I said. "First, I get quiet, then if I'm pushed, I'll raise my voice. There's a good chance the F-word will start flying, and after that, most of the time I just leave, but the last time, things went too far and my girlfriend ended up with a busted lip. For me, that's how it goes with girls; with guys it's different."

After I opened the ball, everyone took their turn, and for the most part, with some slight variations, their stories were very similar. Freddy, of course, had a little trouble. At one point, I was pretty sure Miz Nancy came very close to the end of her 'pattern of escalating abusive behavior'. Freddy must have sensed it, too, because he quickly admitted that he had used the F-word himself and that he had laid his hands on a partner in a relationship. However, it was a long time ago, he said, and he had changed since then.

The last question for the night required us to have a plan for calling or going to see someone when we needed help because we were feeling angry. The only one I had ever gone to in time of trouble was Granny, so I put her name down.

The meeting ended as usual. I wanted to leave so I could call Dottie on the way home, but somehow, it seemed wrong not to go to the Neon Church with Jake. After the service, we walked across the parking lot together.

"You call her?" he asked.

"Huh?" My head was on the phone call I was about to make.

"The old girlfriend you punched. She sent you a letter. Did you call her?" he repeated his question.

"Oh, no." I said, "No, I didn't, but something strange happened this week."

And I told him the whole story. He listened patiently, smiling and nodding from time to time. By the time I had finished, I felt like a complete and total moron.

"This could be the one," he said with a smile. "Just take it slow, son."

As I climbed into my truck and dialed Dottie's number, I was thinking about what I'd written on my exit paper: I learned that it is very important to know how violence within myself is triggered and the pattern that it follows. I also learned that it is important to have a plan and a support system in place.

WEEK 11—DEVELOPING HEALTHY RELATIONSHIPS II

Doubt is like an early morning autumn fog. It creeps in when you're not paying attention, and it makes it hard to see. I spent the week running circles in my mind. Every evening, I visited with Dottie on the phone, then I curled up and slept the most peaceful sleep I'd slept in a long time. But during the day, while I was working, I'd wonder if I was being duped. I had never actually met Dottie. Her grandmother could have shown me a picture of anyone and said it was her. I knew it didn't make sense, but then nothing had been making any real sense to me lately.

On another front, I still hadn't gotten rid of the letter from Shelby. I had decided I would not call her. She was the past, and I could see no future with her in it. Still, I couldn't bring myself to throw the letter away. In my mind, I justified it. You wouldn't throw away a coupon for a free steak at the Texas Roadhouse, would you? No, you would not, unless, of course, it had expired. And this letter had not expired and was kind of like a coupon, only it was for something much better than a steak.

"If it's too good to be true, then it's probably not true," I said to Granny one evening at dinner. "Isn't that what you always say?"

"What's your problem, Runt?" she looked up at me from her plate. "You're talking to a nice girl for a change, and you look like you're ready to bolt."

"That's just it, Granny. How do I know she's a nice girl?" I laid my fork and knife down and shook my head.

"You've been talking to her nearly a week, and you haven't figured out whether she's a nice girl or not?" She laid her fork and knife down and stared across the table at me. "Runt, you are slow."

Just like Granny, straight to the point, no punches pulled. Flustered, I shrugged and said, "She sounds nice. She's real sweet, but what if she's hiding something? What if she has four kids, she's not telling me about? What if the picture Mrs. Walters showed me really wasn't her at all, and she's fifty years old and looks like Aunt Gertie?"

"Then I reckon when you meet her you ought to shake her hand, tell her it was nice to meet her, and turn around and run like hell." Granny snorted a chuckle and picked up her fork.

"Granny, I'm serious!" I pleaded.

"'Have I not commanded you? Be strong and courageous. Do not be frightened, and do not be dismayed, for the Lord your God is with you wherever you go.' That's Joshua one, verse nine." She pointed the fork at me.

"Okay, Granny," I said, "but what does it mean?"

"It means that if she seems to be a nice girl, then you give her the benefit of the doubt until she proves otherwise." She lowered the fork. "You aren't married to her, you're just talking, taking it slow, very slow." She raised the fork again and aimed it at me. "And it means you trust in your God."

Talking with Dottie broke up the monotony of the week, and it seemed like I barely turned around and it was Wednesday. I got held up by a train on the way into the meeting and was nearly late. Miz Nancy was signing everyone in and taking money when I slipped through the door. Jake raised an eyebrow and grinned at me as I found a place down the hall at the end of the line.

"Hank," Miz Nancy called out.

I stepped to the front of the line, handed her my thirty dollars, and started to sign.

"Everything, okay?" she asked as she slid the money into a worn bank bag.

The question caught me off guard. I finished signing my name, shrugged, and answered, "Yeah."

"You were almost late," she stated flatly, as she filled out a receipt.

"Train," I said in explanation.

"Leave earlier," she suggested sternly, tore the receipt from its book, and handed it to me.

"Yes ma'am." I took my receipt and skedaddled down the hall.

A few minutes later, Jake stepped into the room, took his seat, smiled, and said, "How was your week?"

"Good," I nodded. "It was good. How was yours?"

"Not too bad. My oldest son was down, and we had lunch Saturday," he said.

Miz Nancy stepped in and said, "Someone read the story." Her tone was flat and hard.

Dan started reading immediately, and everyone followed along as if their life depended on it. The situation reminded me of my second-grade teacher, Mrs. Stanton. She was a short, plump lady with a loud shrill voice. When it was your turn to read and you had lost your place, well, let's just say it's been over twenty-five years since I was in her class, and I still remember clearly the last time I lost my place. Tonight, as Dan read, the same fearful tension filled the room. It's just crazy how a little bitty ole thing like Miz Nancy can affect grown men in such a manner, but then again, every one of us knows that just seating in these classes every week only goes so far. At the end, we still need her to sign off on our exit papers for the court.

The story Dan was reading was about a fellow who had nearly completed his batterers' classes. In it, he wrote a paragraph about how the classes were helping him, but several things he included showed he had a long way to go. When Dan finished reading, Miz Nancy instructed us to answer the questions on the next two pages, and she disappeared up the hall. The minute the front door closed behind her, a collective sigh filled the room.

"Wow!" Freddy said from his corner, and everyone laughed.

The questions about the story mainly wanted us to identify the problems we saw with the fellow's paragraph. His two biggest errors, as far as I could see, were that he worked so much he didn't have time for his family, and he held money over his wife's head. What I got out of answering the question was that I should make time for my family.

The final series of questions got more personal. The last three asked what my role as a parent was, how was my relationship with my wife/ with my kids, and what steps could I take to make these relationships better? I was just finishing up when Miz Nancy returned. She seemed less stressed after the cigarette and even managed a smile as she asked someone to share their response to the first question.

When we finally got to the personal questions, Miz Nancy announced everyone would be sharing their answers for this one and asked for a volunteer to begin. Dan and Jake both started to speak and then paused like polite people do.

"Go ahead, sir," Dan said.

Jake nodded, smiled, and started again. "My kids are all older. Except for my youngest son, they're all out on their own. He's in his first year of college, so really my role is just to be the best example possible and help them through life and with the choices they must make. On how my relationship with my wife is, well as most of you know, I no longer have a wife, so I'll let y'all decide whether that's a really good thing or…"

"A really good thing," Dan cut him off. Several of the guys that attended regularly nodded in agreement.

Jake's smile grew bigger as he continued, "As for my kids, my relationship with them has never been better. And as far as what steps can I take to improve these relationships, I guess I just need to keep good lines of communications open with them all."

"No wife, better relationship with kids," Miz Nancy spoke up. "A correlation there, perhaps?"

Jake looked up at her, and you could almost see the wheels turning. He nodded and smiled. I could have hugged Miz Nancy.

When they made it around to me, I said, "My son is nine. I haven't been much of a father to him, but lately, since I started these classes, I've been trying harder. I haven't been very nice to his mother, my ex-wife, and so it's kind of a work in progress. Let's see, question one and two, I think I've answered. Steps to make relationships better, I guess it's just going to take time and effort on my part. I reckon I need to spend as much time as she'll let me with my son and try as hard as possible not to argue with her."

"It's good that you are admitting you played a part in the problem, Hank," Miz Nancy said, "and you're right. It will take time, and it will take consistency. You can't try for a little while, give up, and then come back and try again. Remember that."

"Yes, ma'am," I said, and I felt just like I had back in second grade when Mrs. Stanton called on me to read and I knew exactly where to start.

I don't know if Miz Nancy had something pressing she had to do or if she just felt sorry for us because she had been so short, but she let us go a few minutes early. She followed the last member out the door, locked it, got in her car, and drove out of the parking lot. I stood on the sidewalk with Jake and watched her leave, then the two of us walked down to the Neon Church, and once inside, we found our seats.

The week before, we had finished the book of James and Brother Jim, the fellow who led the services, asked if anyone had something they would like to read next. One fellow asked if we could study Proverbs, and so we started Proverbs.

Every night for the past week, I had read the first chapter of Proverbs. I discussed what I had read with Granny, and we talked a lot about it. This new routine felt good, but somewhere deep down I was scared. I always seemed to screw my life up just about the time things were going good, and now, I had so much more to screw up. Suddenly, the thought of messing up other people's lives bothered me.

The service ended with a prayer, and I walked with Jake out to the parking lot. It was beginning to rain a little when I climbed inside my truck. I wanted to call Dottie, wanted to visit with her, but something held me back. I took Shelby's letter from above the visor, opened it, and read it again. When I finished it, I had a deep desire to call and talk to her. It was just a matter of time before I screwed up. Why not just get it over with? Then I remembered what I had written on my exit paper: I learned that if I want to become a better person and build better relationships, I have to be consistent and never give up.

I put the letter back above the visor and called Dottie.

WEEK 12—PARENTING SKILLS FOR FATHERS

They say time heals all wounds. Well, it's been my experience that a fifth of Jim Beam will do the job just as effectively and in less time. It's weird how thoughts like this come to you at the strangest times. The ex-wife agreed to let my son stay over Saturday night if I took him to church on Sunday. I'd asked for him all day Saturday because I heard the fish were biting. As I hung up the phone with her, I considered taking her a bottle of Jim Beam when I picked him up. I figured what the hell could it hurt? If seven years hadn't healed the wounds I'd caused, maybe the whiskey would.

Of course, I didn't take it. Luke and I had a wonderful Saturday evening and a better Sunday. After attending church with Granny, we found a couple of hours to fish one of our ponds. Seven good size bass and a five-pound catfish filled out stinger by the time we had to head back to the house. I taught him how to clean the fish and promised him we'd have them for dinner the next time he was over.

When I took him home, I barely got the truck stopped before he bailed out shouting, "Mom! Mom! I caught a fish!"

His excitement was infectious. The three of us stood in her front yard as he enacted how he had reeled his first catch in. She scrunched her nose up when he walked her through the cleaning process, but she was still smiling. In the end, he scrambled into the house and left us standing alone, grinning at each other. For a brief moment, it was nice, then the silence crept in and it felt weird.

"Thanks for letting him stay over," I said as our smiles faded.

"No problem," she returned. "Maybe next weekend, you can pick him up on Friday night. I mean, if you want to?"

"Yeah, yeah. That'd be great," I stammered and was very glad I hadn't purchased the whiskey.

Monday and Tuesday, I stuck close to home, checking the stock and the fences. When I passed the liquor store on my way to the Wednesday meeting, I shook my head and laughed. *Maybe it takes about seven years for the wounds to scab over*, I thought. *Now the healing will start. Yeah, if you don't screw it up, huh.*

Jake and Freddy greeted me as soon as I cleared the door. The atmosphere in the building was much less tense than it had been a week ago. I spoke to each of the men and grabbed a packet from the center of the table. The week's lesson was designed to help us differentiate between punishment and discipline. I thought they were one and the same until I started reading through the pages.

Once the preliminary sign in and pay were through, Miz Nancy started the class. It was instantly apparent that this was a subject she was passionate about. I could not think of a class, up to this point, that she had been this into. She mentioned a son and a daughter as she explained the difference between discipline and punishment. It was clear early on that punishment was not good and discipline was preferred. It took her a little while to wind down, at which point she instructed us to answer the questions and headed out for a smoke break.

As soon as she exited, the sound of pens scratching across paper filled the room. No one seemed to have a problem with the night's lesson. By the time Miz Nancy returned, everyone had finished writing.

"Freddy, were you disciplined or punished as a child?" Miz Nancy asked the minute she stepped back into the room.

Flustered, Freddy stammered, started to speak, stopped, and then just stared at her. "Disciplined or punished?" she repeated.

"Well, you know, Miz Nancy, it's like this. I guess it

depended on the situation. Different situations called for different things. I guess you'd have to be more specific. Like what is the situation? Can you tell me that, give me a situation?" he spoke rapidly.

"Freddy, you don't need a situation," she said. "I'm not asking if you discipline or punish. I'm asking when you were a kid, did your mom and dad punish or discipline you?"

"Oh!" the light bulb flashed on. "A little bit of both I guess. Dad was mostly in prison, and mom was a church going Christian lady. Mostly, dad didn't discipline us much cause he didn't see us much, prison and all. He'd be out for a while, and then he'd go back in. I guess he kind of hated to whoop on us 'cause of that. Now mom, on the other hand, she could really light into you. Not that it wasn't needed. It's just that sometimes she could get really wound up."

"Hank, same question," Miz Nancy said as Freddy finished.

"Oh, well," I said, "as I've told y'all before, I don't remember my mom, and I only have a few memories of my dad. I remember him whipping me once or twice when he was drinking, but Granny put an end to that pretty quick. So mainly, Granny took care of me, and I'd have to say discipline. She was always trying to teach me to be accountable and such."

Each member was required to answer the question. Their stories varied from no discipline, no punishment, not even much attention to getting slapped, beaten, and punched. One member even told how he was burned with lit cigarettes as punishment. When the last member had shared, there was a solemn silence in the room. I felt for those who had been raised with abusive parents and was extremely glad Granny had raised me. I made a mental note to give her a big hug and thank her.

"Often, the way you were raised has a major effect on the way you raise your children." Miz Nancy broke the silence. "Now, I want each of you to tell us if you feel like you discipline or punish."

No body spoke as a minute dragged by. "Discipline with a dash of punishment," Jake finally spoke up.

Dan who went next and each member in turn gave short answers one way or the other. Once everyone at the table had answered, the room grew silent again. I looked around at the men present. To say the lesson was thought provoking would be an understatement. I could see it in the eyes of every single member, and I had never wanted to be a better dad than I did right there in that moment.

"Okay, now you have something to think about as fathers," Miz Nancy pushed her glasses up as she spoke. "The last item asked you to list three questions you have about the difference between punishment and discipline. Someone read me one of your questions."

"Is taking away a cellphone punishment or discipline?" James asked.

"Neither, it's murder," Frank answered. "Don't you know your kid will die if you take their phone away?"

Miz Nancy laughed with the rest of us and then said, "It kind of depends on the situation." Before she could continue, all heads turned to Freddy in the corner. He had tuned out so he didn't catch the joke and looked completely shocked when he realized everyone was looking at him. That brought on the chuckles.

"Now listen," Miz Nancy continued, "if there is a lesson learned and it changes the behavior, it's discipline. If you take it away just to be mean, that is more like punishment."

After everyone else had gone, she called on me. "Is this class punishment or discipline, or both?" I read the only one of my three questions that had not already been asked by someone else.

"Punishment," several members answered in unison.

Miz Nancy just smiled and shook her head. "Make sure I get your exit papers before you leave," she ordered.

"Hey, wait," I said. "You didn't answer my question."

She just kept smiling. "And make sure I get my pens back," she added and turned and left.

I looked around the room at the other guys. A couple of them laughed out loud, all of them were smiling, and Jake just shrugged and grinned. I shrugged back and wrote: Tonight, I learned the difference between punishment and discipline. I learned that I was lucky in my raising and that I want to be a good dad. I also learned that I have a lot to learn.

67

WEEK 13—CO-PARENTING SKILLS

What doesn't kill you makes you stronger. I've heard it from Granny since I was young, and I'm sure in a sense it's true. But sometimes before you get stronger, you get really messed up, like so messed up you don't even know the man-in-the-mirror messed up. Friday evening, after I showered and before I drove over to pick up my son, I stood looking at my reflection in the mirror.

Now, it's not like I'm horribly disfigured physically or anything, it's just that, standing there looking at myself, I honestly did not recognize the man looking back. I could not remember the last time I really felt like I knew who he was or even if I ever had. It was a very sobering experience. I began to wonder who I was and who I wanted to be. Granny likes to quote a verse out of the Bible. It says, "I can do all things through Christ which strengthens me." I don't know where it is in the Bible, but the thought gives me courage. I'm starting to think maybe I can become a good man.

Dottie and I visit on the phone every night now. We've discussed the possibility of meeting in person, but neither of us is quite ready for that yet. Dottie says when it is time, it will feel right. Granny says she ain't gonna live forever, and I better stop dilly dallying around. How does life get so confusing?

The weekend with my son seemed to pass in the blink of an eye. We spent most of it on the four-wheeler but did find time for a little fishing. Sunday evening, I dropped him back at his mom's and stopped by Granny's for a spell. As we visited, I realized just how close she and my son were becoming. It had been just me and Granny for so long, I wasn't sure how I felt about sharing her.

Monday, a trip to the feed store took up half the day. Cleaning out the barn and unloading the truck into it took up the rest of it. Tuesday, I spent searching the pasture for a cow that didn't come up when I fed. I found her late in the afternoon. She had torn up one of her back legs and was limping badly. It was well after dark before I got her up into the corral and finished doctoring the leg.

* * * * *

The first part of Wednesday's lesson was on parenting skills. According to the packet there are four parenting styles. Authoritarian, Authoritative, Indulgent, and Neglectful/Laissez-Faire. The explanations kind of reminded me of the old fairy tale about the three bears. Authoritarian was too harsh. Neglectful/Laissez-Faire was too lenient. Indulgent was too much like a friend and not enough like a parent. And of course, Authoritative was just right, so they all lived happily ever after.

Our first page of questions concentrated on what our childhood was like. How was your father as a parent? Your mother? How did your father treat your mother? The first question, I answered briefly from what I could remember. I figured my father was Neglectful/Laisse Faire, unless he was drunk and mad, then he was Authoritarian. On mother, I had no answer, and I don't think Granny had ever mentioned anything about my mother's and father's relationship. I was surprised to realize how little I really knew of my parents. I made a mental note to talk to Granny about them.

The next several questions were about my mother/father's parenting styles. Since Granny had raised me, I used her to answer the questions. Granny had been the perfect parent. I can't recall her ever whipping me. She just never had to. I had always hated it if she was mad at me and tried very hard not to upset her. I flipped the page over and was about halfway down the backside still answering questions when Miz Nancy returned.

"How's it going?" she asked.

I looked around and noticed that everyone was still working. "Got a few more," Jake told her as he continued writing. Miz Nancy nodded and headed back up the hall.

Five minutes later, she waltzed back in. I'd just finished the last question.

"Okay, what was your father like?" she asked. "Let's start with James and make our way around the table. Freddy, there is an empty seat at the table, why don't you scoot up here and join us?"

Freddy in his usual seat against the far wall, looked shocked, but started scooting, as James said, "He was brutal. A real asshole. My first memory of him is when I was maybe five. I was in my toybox, digging a toy out of the bottom, and he came in, got mad about the mess in the floor and kicked me in the head. Knocked me out and scared mom pretty bad."

Albert, the quiet young black man, had been there from the first night I'd attended. His attendance had been kind of hit and miss. He went next, "My dad was pretty hard on me and my brother. He always said he wanted us to be better than him. He didn't know his father. He gave us whooping sometimes, but he wasn't bad."

"I never knew my father," Joel said when Albert finished. Joel was a thick Mexican man about my age, I think. He had 'Sanchez' tattooed down his left forearm. He'd move in from another class, and so I don't know his story. "I was three when he left. My mom had me and then two more kids, my brothers, before I was three. He left the day after my baby brother was born, and mom never married again. She never even dated as far as I know."

Each member took their turn and the stories varied. Jake had a great father, and, of course, I couldn't say much about my own father. By the time we had gone around the table and started on what our mothers were like, I was beginning to realize how hard it would be to define the word normal. For me, growing up with Granny was my normal. For Joel, having only a mother was normal. For James, having an abusive father was normal. So what one person thought of as normal might be completely different from what someone else considered normal.

The next series of questions dealt with our own parenting style. It was still hard for me to consider myself as a true parent. I figured I parented my son roughly the same way Granny had me, but it was strange to have to think about it. The whole exercise was making me more aware of how little thought I'd put into being a parent. I realized this was something I could not approach with my usual 'fly by the seat of my pants' attitude.

"Next question, how did your parents let you know they loved you and how do you let your kids know?" Miz Nancy moved us along.

"They said it, and now I say it to my kids," Jake spoke up.

"Okay, someone else," Miz Nancy said.

"Dad never showed love, my mother would always say 'love ya' and kiss us on the forehead when she tucked us in at night," James said. "I'm not much on saying it, but I do tuck my kids in and kiss them on the forehead."

"Good," Miz Nancy said looking around the room. Her eyes stopped on me.

"Granny has always been good at telling me she loves me," I said, "I guess the way I show it is I take my son fishing. I'm trying to spend more time with him."

As the other fellows answered, I tried to remember if I had ever told my son I loved him. I couldn't remember and it bothered me. I decided it was something I needed to fix if I wanted to be a better father.

The lesson ended, we handed in our exit sheets, and Jake and I headed for the Neon Church. Outside, solid sheets of cold rain met us, and the church was closed. A woman in a bright yellow raincoat and blue jeans hugged the wall under the canopy in front of the church.

"It's closed," she said as we stepped under the overhang ourselves.

"Oh, okay," Jake said, twirling his straw Stetson in his hands, then asked, "you okay, you need a ride ma'am?"

"Sally, my name's Sally," she answered, "and yes, I could use a ride."

"I'm Jake," he introduced himself, "and this is Hank." He indicated me as he stuck out his hand.

Sally shook his hand. As she did, the raincoat fell open, and underneath, she wore a tightly stretched white t-shirt, and it was very evident that she wasn't wearing an undergarment. She offered her hand to me next. I shook it and looked at Jake. I couldn't tell if he hadn't noticed or if he was just really good at hiding it.

"Where are you headed?" Jake asked.

"Just across town. About five minutes." She gave him an address.

"I can take you," he said as placed his hat on his head.

"Okay."

"See you next week, Hank," he said as he pointed his truck out to her. "Have a good one." And then they were both running for his pickup.

I stood in front of the church and watched until his vehicle pulled out of the parking lot and then started for my own. *Damn, Jake.* I thought to myself. On my way out of the lot, I called Dottie and spent the ride home visiting with her.

Standing in front of the mirror before getting into bed later I thought of what I'd written on my exit paper: Tonight, I learned that there are good parents and bad parents. I learned that there is more to being a parent than just having kids, and I learned that I want badly to be a good parent.

WEEK 14—PERSONAL GOALS AND SAFETY PLANNING

My dad sat on the front porch of our little ranch house. I was so glad to have him home, glad that Granny had agreed to let me come up to his house to spend the night. He'd been away for what seemed like a long time to a four-year-old. Granny's house was just over the hill, and as I ran my plastic horse along the top of the porch railing, I could see smoke rising from her chimney.

Dad had his chair leaned back against the side of the house, feet crossed at the ankles, with the heel of his boot resting on the top rail. My plastic horse began to buck just like the one's dad rode at the rodeos. I imagined myself on the horse and dreamed of winning a new buckle just like the one Dad had showed Granny when he came home. The horse bucked harder, head down and hooves up, he bucked right down the rail and into the side of dad's boot.

Off balance, Dad spilled from his chair and onto the porch, and the horse fell from my hand. The drink he wouldn't let me have a sip of spilled all over his shirt and down the front of his jeans. It made his new belt buckle look funny. One second, he was sprawled on the floor, the next he was on his feet taking off his belt. I reached down to pick up the horse, and as I stood up, he swung the belt. The buckle caught me midback and sent me sailing. I landed, rolled over and looked up into my own face. Confused and sickened I fought for clarification. The last thing I remember before I woke in a sweat was me standing over my son with a belt in my hand, ready to swing.

I laid in bed and cried. How long, I couldn't tell you, but I slept badly the rest of the night, and when I rolled out in the morning, my eyes were swollen and sore. I have never whipped Luke, never had reason to. Even when he was little, all I had to do was say no in a rough voice and he'd tear up. So, where the dream came from, I had no idea.

At breakfast, I told Granny about the dream. She quit washing dishes and sat down at the table with me. I watched her as she neatly folded the dishtowel, placed it on the tabletop, and patted it thoughtfully. When she looked up at me, there were tears in her eyes.

"You are a good man, Runt." Her voice was soft, "Don't ever believe any other way." She paused, wiped a tear away and continued. "That wasn't just a dream, it was a memory. Just after you turned four, it happened. Your daddy had a mean streak in him, and when he was drinking… well."

"But the house, Granny," I asked, "where was it?"

"Just over the hill yonder," she answered, pointing south and a little east. "The summer your dad died, there was a pasture fire and the old house caught. I suppose we could have saved it, but something in me just wanted it gone. I let it burn."

"Granny, at the end of the dream it was me, not dad. It was me and Luke."

"You are not your dad. I would know. I raised both of you. You've been down some rough roads and maybe done some things you're not proud of, but you are not your dad. Runt, I hate to say it about my only child, but your dad was just no good. The best thing that ever happened to him was your momma. And the best thing he ever did was sire you. After she died, he was…" Granny hung her head.

I got up from my seat, went around the table, squatted beside her, and looped my arm over her shoulder. She looked up and with a weak smile said, "Everything's gonna be alright, Runt. You'll see, everything's gonna be just fine."

And I believed her.

* * * * *

All the way to the counseling center, I wondered how Jake had made out after last week's class. I found myself kind of hoping Sally had tied him to her bed and rode him so hard he had trouble walking upright all week. I still had no idea what had caused Jake and Mrs. Claus to split, but somehow, I just couldn't see Jake as a bad guy.

He was seated in his usual spot, reading his packet like any other week, and when I walked in, he greeted me like nothing had ever happened. Freddy was the only other person in the room, and he was doodling on the front page of his packet.

"How'd it go last week?" I asked Jake across the table.

He lowered his packet, looked at me over the top of his black-rimmed glasses and said, "How'd what go?"

I grinned. So, this was the game he was gonna play. "How'd it go with Sally?" I asked.

"Oh, fine," he seemed confused. "Just fine, why?"

"I don't know," I answered, adding, "I've just been wondering if you got her home okay."

He lowered his head, pursed his lips, cocked his head to the side, and said, "I dropped her off at her apartment, watched from the truck to make sure she got inside okay, and then drove home."

Damn, Jake. I thought to myself, but said, "Okay," and shrugged.

A half hour later, we had all read through the packet, answered two full sheets of questions, and were discussing what we'd written on our personal goal's sheets. That was the first page of questions in the packet. Along the left side of the page we were to list our long, short, and immediate goals. Along the right side, we were to list things that could get in the way of those goals.

Dan shared first. His immediate goals were to finish the class, get his boat ready for the coming season (he's a fishing guide on a nearby lake), and impregnate his wife. Miz Nancy found the last goal to be very interesting, as did most of us. She told us that, in all her time leading these classes, that was a first. His short-term goal was to buy four more boats, hire some decent guides, and expand his guide company. His long-term goal was to have his house paid off in ten years and his guide company fully established.

Jake shared next. His immediate goals were to finish out the year at his job, at which time he was planning on retiring, and then help his youngest son with college. His short-term goals were to photograph all fifty states and finish the novel he was working on. He was hopeful that he could have it done in the next couple of years. His long-term goal was to have a thriving photography company and establish himself as a mystery author. When he finished sharing, I found myself looking at him and hoping someday to see his books on the selves everywhere I went. *I'm pullin' for ya, Jake,* I thought to myself.

Unlike Jake, my goals were simple. Immediately, I wanted to get these classes over with. Short-term, I wanted to find a building site for a little cabin somewhere on Granny's place and improve the quality of the cattle we were running. Long-term, I wanted to finish building the cabin, increase the size of the herd, and (even though I didn't share this one) maybe find a good woman, settle down, get married, and have a few kids. It felt strange to even admit that to myself let alone say it out loud.

The first page of questions for the night ended with a fifteen-minute bout between Miz Nancy and Freddy. Freddy had no idea what his goals were, and the harder she tried to guide him, the more confusing and funnier it became, until everyone but Miz Nancy and Freddy were wiping tears. Finally, in frustration, she gave up and moved us to the second part of our lesson: the safety plan.

On this page we had to identify the triggers and signs leading up to our own violent behavior, specify our behavior, outline steps to prevent the violent behavior, and list negative versus positive coping behaviors. Signs and triggers identified by the group included, flushed face, ache in the stomach, rapid heartbeat, and raised voice. Jake said that when he was angry, it was like being in a small dome, and everything outside the dome was foggy. Miz Nancy called it short-sightedness and said it was a common sign. James said that just before he lost it, he usually started screaming the 'F' word. Several other members admitted to the same behavior.

After each of us confessed to the violent behaviors for which we were responsible, Miz Nancy had us discuss, as a group, ways to keep a situation from escalating into violence. The first thing we decided was that walking away and getting some space was a good idea. Miz Nancy said it never hurt to take a drive to clear your head.

"Unless, you've been threatened with divorce if you leave the property," Jake spoke up.

"You or her?" Miz Nancy asked.

"Her first. She was afraid I was going to meet someone and have an affair," Jake said, "Then at the end, me. I just didn't think it was fair for her to jump in her car and leave if I couldn't."

"So, now neither of you can leave," Miz Nancy said, "and how'd that work out?"

Jake just nodded, shook his head in agreement, and said, "Yeah."

By the end of the class, I felt like I had a pretty good plan for myself to avoid violent behavior. I was also beginning to think that maybe it wasn't such a good idea for me to have alcohol. Not that alcohol was the source of all my problems, but as I looked back, I could see where it had played a big role in them. Maybe, just maybe, it was time to quit drinking.

Our class ended, and Jake and I headed for the Neon Church. Brother Jim was explaining how Proverbs four encouraged us to stay on the straight and narrow path when we settled into our seats. He said God had a plan for each of us, and if we followed God's plan, we would find peace and happiness even in this life. He explained how, in his life, alcohol had led him from the path God had planned for him and how it had taken him years to get back to it. This church he said was his way of giving back. He'd been sober for a little more than twelve years now and had opened the church three years ago. It was his hope that, through the church, he could help others find God and the path He had planned for them.

Several of the members told of their bouts with alcohol and drug use, and they all discussed the chapter. I sat quietly listening. Jake commented on a couple of verses he had enjoyed toward the end of the evening, and Brother Jim asked him if he would like to pray to close the meeting. Jake prayed and we were dismissed.

"So, about Sally," I said as we walked to our trucks, "I kind of got the idea she was interested in you."

"She was," Jake said.

"So," I returned.

"So, when I explained to her that my ex-wife was the love of my life and always would be, she decided she wasn't quite as interested anymore."

"I'm sorry, I didn't realize," I said, then asked, "so there's still hope there, huh?"

He looked at me with a sad smile and answered, "No, she's already seeing someone else."

"That was fast." I shook my head.

"Yeah," he agreed.

"So, you're just not ready, then," I mused. "Maybe somewhere down the line?"

"Doubt it," he said.

"Really?" I asked, confused.

"I guess when you love somebody the way I loved her, it changes you," he said. "It's complicated."

"Yeah." I agreed not knowing what else to say, but I thought to myself, *Damn, Jake, she really fucked you up, man.*

When I climbed into my truck, I found myself wondering what Jake had written on his exit paper. On mine I'd written: Tonight, I learned that there are signs and triggers before violent behavior occurs. I learned that I need to be aware of these signs and triggers in my own self. By learning to identify them, I can take preventive steps and keep violence from occurring.

As I pulled out of the parking lot, I called Dottie.

WEEK 15—DYNAMICS OF POWER AND CONTROL, DEFINING NON-VIOLENCE

Some fellow named Nietzsche once said the trouble with getting cross ways with a woman was that, when it was all said and done, the man was afraid he might have hurt her too badly, and the woman was afraid she hadn't hurt him badly enough. Dottie and I had our first disagreement during our Friday evening call. I wanted to meet her for a date on Saturday night, and she said she wasn't ready. I clammed up and got quiet; she said I needed to be patient, and shortly thereafter we hung up.

All day Saturday, I felt awful. A dozen times, I started to stop working and call and apologize to her. At three o'clock I called it quits. I'd worked all day and didn't seemed to have gotten anything done. I was physically tired, mentally exhausted, and spiritually frustrated. I parked the four-wheeler in the barn, jumped in my truck, and left Granny's house headed for my trailer.

A mile east and half mile south, I turned into the gravel drive that leads up to the old home. Up ahead, I saw a red Jeep Wrangler parked out front but didn't recognize it. I parked and crawled out of my truck, ready to give someone a piece of my mind for trespassing, and there on my front steps sat Dottie.

I stopped at the front of my pickup and just stood there staring at her. She stood up and smiled. I'd only ever seen portraits of her, so I hadn't known what she looked like from the shoulders down. She was wearing a light blue sundress with dark blue flowers on it. Her hair was pulled back in a ponytail, and she had on dark brown cowboy boots. And she was perfect.

"What are you doing here?" I almost choked getting it out.

"I felt bad about our argument last night," she said as she stepped down into the yard. "I wanted to apologize, and I was taught to always apologize in person. I'm sorry."

"Oh," I mumbled, frozen in place. "I should be the one apologizing. I shouldn't have been so pushy. I'm sorry."

I stepped forward finally and extended my hand. "It's so nice to finally meet you in person," I said.

Dottie stepped right past my hand, wrapped her arms around me, and the next thing I knew I was hugging her and saying, "Lordy, Dottie, I must smell awful."

"Been waiting a long while for this, don't really care how you smell." And then she let go and stepped back. "Well, how long is it gonna take you to be ready to go to dinner?"

As I showered and got ready to go out, I thought to myself, I guess Nietzsche never dated anyone like Dottie—but then it was still early. I guess I can only be partially optimistic.

Dinner with Dottie was great, Sunday with my son was wonderful, and the week slipped by right up to the Wednesday night class. Freddy was in his usual corner when I walked in, but Jake was nowhere around. I sat down in my chair and looked over at Freddy.

"Ain't seen him." He nodded towards Jake's chair as if he'd read my mind.

I grabbed a packet and idly flipped through it. I told myself that Jake was a big boy. Hell, he was probably just running late, but he'd never been late before. Several members arrived, and as each one took his seat, I noticed they looked at Jake's empty chair.

Miz Nancy called everyone up to sign in and pay. We lined up in the hall, and still no Jake. I and two members were left when the door flew open and in stepped Jake. I didn't know whether I wanted to punch him or hug him, so I said, "Howdy, how was your week?" as he stepped into line behind me.

"It was something." He smiled as he answered, and then Miz Nancy called my name.

The cycle of violence was the study for the night. One of the first pages in the packet had a picture of what resembled an old wagon wheel. At the top of the wheel was the word VIOLENCE and inside each spoke was an example of a violent behavior. On the back of the page was the word NONVIOLENCE and another wheel, and between the spokes were examples of nonviolent behaviors. We discussed the examples on each of the wheels. Next, we read a story about a violent incident and answered questions about it, but the most enlightening page was the one that explained the cycle of violence.

It showed a circle. At the top was the word Abuse, then running clockwise, Guilt, Excuses, Normal Behavior, Fantasy, Set-up, and back to Abuse. Miz Nancy explained that in a truly abusive situation, the abuser moves through this cycle. First, they abuse, then they feel guilty. Sometimes, they even apologize for their actions, but often, even in the apology they make excuses. Eventually, they resume what seems to be normal behavior, but often, during this time of seeming normality, they begin to fantasize. They start spending more and more time thinking about all the things that the person they have abused has done wrong and how the abused should pay for those wrongs. Then, the abuser will set the abused up so that they feel justified in abusing them.

I thought of my own experiences and found that, while the cycle made sense, it did not really apply to me. My relationships did not last past the first go around. If the problem escalated to screaming and cussing, I was usually gone. The only time it had ever made it further, I ended up in these classes.

As Miz Nancy was explaining the cycle, I noticed Jake was writing something out beside each step as she went along. When the circle was completed, he looked up and saw me staring at him. He smiled and nodded as if it was all coming clear. I wanted badly to read what he had written and hoped Miz Nancy would ask someone to share, but she didn't. Instead, she switched gears and began to explain how important it was not to rush into any relationships. She asked us how long we thought it took to get comfortable with someone. Several members took guesses and finally James said, "Six months to a year."

"That's about right," Miz Nancy said and began to break it down for us.

Jake flipped his packet over to the back and started jotting something down on the blank page. I noticed Miz Nancy was watching him as she talked, and when he finished and put his pen down, she said, "Jake you've been scribbling on your paper all night long. Now, I'm curious. I gotta ask, what did you just write?"

Jake gave a sheepish grin and began, "Well, I've been married and divorced three times, and at my age, you start to look for answers. Tonight has really helped me to see the cycle that has been the demise of my relationships. In all of them, I was either married, engaged to be married, or already living with them before I'd known them six months. My tendency to rush into relationships was a real revelation, and so I just jotted down a reminder to myself for the future."

"What does your reminder say?" Miz Nancy wanted to know.

"Think Dumbass," he said as he flipped his paper around and showed her. It was written in all caps and followed by three exclamation marks. "I think I'll tack it above the computer in my office, so I see it every day."

I, along with several other members, nodded, and Miz Nancy grinned and shook her head. Jake laid his paper back down, and Miz Nancy said, "Not a bad idea and not a bad way to end the class, make sure I get your exit paper and put my pens back before you leave."

Because of the time change, it was still light outside. I noticed the Bradford pear trees planted along the edge of the parking lot had started to bloom as I walked with Jake to the Neon Church. A soft breeze brought all the smells of early spring.

Our class had run so long, Jake and I had barely sat down when Brother Jim asked for someone to close the meeting with a prayer. I felt a little let down. I'd read the chapter for the night and wanted to know if my thoughts matched up with everyone else's. Jake must have sensed my disappointment because, instead of standing up when the prayer was over, he asked, "What did you think of the chapter, Hank?"

Before I realized what I was doing, I was telling him how I thought it was a warning not to be fooling around with the wrong woman. If you were in a relationship, you should not be messing with someone else. If you were married, you should be satisfied with your wife and not look elsewhere.

As I was finishing, Sally walked up. Jake stood up and stuck his hand out. She took it, and as they shook hands, I stood. When she released his hand, she stuck her hand out to me and I took it. Tonight, she had on a floor-length, red summer dress and plain brown sandals. The dress was padded, so her nipples weren't as noticeable as with the raincoat and t-shirt, but I could still tell she wasn't wearing a bra.

"Good to see y'all again," she said to both of us, and then turning to Jake, "I hate to be a pest, but could I bother you for another ride home?"

"No problem at all," he said with a smile. "We were just headed out."

I stopped at my pickup and watched the two of them walk on out to his truck. He opened the passenger door and helped her in, then shut it behind her. I hadn't seen that done in a long time and I thought to myself, *I should do that for Dottie.*

As I climbed into my truck, I realized I was getting a lot from my classes, but I was also learning quite a bit from reading my Bible and a little from ole Jake. I grinned and remembered what I'd written on my exit paper: Tonight, I learned that the cycle of violence repeats itself. If you are in the cycle, you must break the cycle for it to stop. I also learned that a lot of times your life can become one big cycle that is negative, even if it is not violent or abusive.

WEEK 16—COERCIVE BEHAVIORS

If you have ever seen two bulls fighting, you'll never forget it. It's amazing and scary at the same time. Two tons or more of muscle and hide on one side, snorting, pawing the ground, screaming and slinging slobber: on the other side, the same. They come at each other, heads down, shoving, snorting, screaming, sweating, in a cloud of dust and rage. Neither willing to yield, they hurl everything they've got at their opponent until one of them gives up. And that's just the first round. There are no bells, no referees, no rules. When the loser catches his breath, he has two choices, walk away or continue the fight. Each battle can last for several minutes, but the war can last all day.

On Saturday, the neighbors bull found a hole in the fence and came a visiting. Our bull didn't take to kindly to him showing up unannounced, and the war was on. By the time I got there, they'd tore up a good size patch of pasture, and both still seemed to have plenty of fight left in them. There was nothing to do but sit back, watch, and wait. Two hours later, the neighbor bull decided he had enough cows over to his place and our cows didn't look so good anyhow, so he conceded the war and headed home.

As I set about fixing the fence, it occurred to me that the battle between good and evil, right and wrong, was a lot like two bulls going at each other. Television shows, movies, and stories would have you think it was like a little devil and a little angel sitting on your shoulder, whispering suggestions in your ear. Nah, it's like two bulls. What human nature wants weighs about four thousand pound and is meaner than sin. The Holy Spirit? ... well now, I reckon it depends on what a person's been feeding on as to what He'd weigh in at. But when the war begins, there's gonna be some seriously ugly battles waged.

I finished fixing the fence and started for home. I had to pick up Luke at six. Liz was going to let him stay until noon on Tuesday. I'd driven over to Dottie's Friday night. She'd cooked supper, and we had a good visit before I left her place. It was the first time in my life I'd known a girl this long and hadn't slept with her. For some reason, I was alright with that; it felt good, felt right.

It seemed like the whole week just disappeared, and before I knew it, I was walking back through the counseling center doors. I don't know if it was the weather or the fact that there hadn't been any new members lately, but Miz Nancy seemed to be in great spirits. Jake was all smiles and greetings as usual. Even Freddy seemed livelier.

The lesson for the week dealt with how an abusive person uses coercive behavior to manipulate another person. The first page was a circle showing the stages of the cycle. The second page was a list of tactics a coercive abuser might use. On the list was jealousy, controlling behavior, isolation, dual personality, just to name a few. Miz Nancy explained that not all behaviors on the sheet would be used in all relationships. She said some batterers might only be jealous and controlling while others might try to isolate their partners.

While she talked, I tried to work through my own relationships and identify the problems. As I worked backwards, I realized that I had never made it very far into the cycle with any woman. For me, as soon as they started acting jealous or trying to control me, I was gone. Except for my ex-wife, my longest relationship had been a little over six months. It made me sad to think on it. But then I remembered what Jake had said last week, *Think Dumbass*, and I knew I had to think on it if I hoped to become a better man.

I noticed throughout the lesson that once again Jake was making little notes to himself in the margin of his papers.

Towards the end of the session, I looked over and saw that he had drawn two circles, one inside the other, on the back of his packet. I don't think I've ever seen anyone try as hard as he has been to figure out what went wrong.

Miz Nancy concluded by telling us the reason the cycle continues to repeat itself is because it just becomes the norm. Once established, it works almost like clockwork. Sometimes, it speeds up a little; sometimes, it slows down a little, but the same pattern happens repeatedly. The hardest and most dangerous thing to do is to break the cycle because the abuser doesn't want to lose control over the abused, and when they feel the control slipping away, they often become violent or try to find other ways to manipulate them.

Before Jake turned his packet back over, he wrote in capital letters big enough for me to read across the table, FIND A NEW NORMAL, and underlined the word new twice. When he looked up and caught me watching him, he just grinned. There was a twinkle in his eyes I hadn't seen before.

On my exit paper I wrote: Tonight, I learned that sometimes the desire to control someone can lead to violent behavior and abuse. I learned to identify those behaviors so I would know if someone was using these kinds of methods against me and that it is wrong for me to use them on another person.

As we walked out to our trucks before heading to the church meeting, I asked Jake about the circles and the normal thing. He stopped at an older model flatbed and opened the door. When he looked up and caught my questioning look, he said, "It's my farm truck. I use it on the farm, or I did when I had a farm. My around town truck is in the shop."

"Okay," I said, repeating my question, "what about the circles and the normal thing?"

"Well, the circles were me figuring out the cycle my relationship has been in for the last twenty years, or was in. My ex-wife was a very jealous woman and very controlling. Trying to make peace with her, I let things go too far. By the time it all came to a head, I had been isolated from my family, I wasn't supposed to be on my computer even to work on photographs without her in the room, and she didn't want me to have a smartphone, even though she had one." He paused and shook his head.

"Wow," I said.

"Yeah, wow," he repeated, "From this side looking back, I must have been crazy. Mind you, I'm not making excuses. What I did was wrong, I know that, but to have let it go so far…? Anyway, the other circle was me correlating when I started being abusive, starting with me throwing things and ending with me blacking her eye."

"I've really never been in a cycle like that," I told him. "I'm more the up and gone at the first sign of trouble kind."

"Thinking about it and writing it down, I realized our cycle, my ex-wife's and mine, repeated itself about every four to six months." He shook his head, and we headed for the church doors.

"What about the normal?" I asked just before we got to them.

"Oh, that," he stopped and looked me in the eye, "that was a goal. For twenty years, I was spinning around in an insane cycle that I didn't understand and couldn't fix. For twenty years, that was the norm, the normal. I'm beginning to figure things out bit by bit. Ever since my wife divorced me, I've been lost. I've had no normal. I don't know what my new normal is going to be, but my goal is to figure it out."

There were several new people in the congregation, and they were well into the chapter discussion when we walked through the doors. Brother Jim looked up and nodded as we slipped down the aisle. Jake slid into a seat beside Sally, and I sat down next to him. As I half-listened to the discussion, I wondered what part she was going to play in Jake's new normal. I told myself it would be best not to ask; I didn't want to jinx whatever it might be.

On the way home, I called Dottie. While we talked, I thought about Jake's goal of finding a new normal. I decided I wanted Dottie to be a big part of my mine.

WEEK 17—CHRONIC VERBAL ABUSE

Funny thing about a person changing, it can't change their past. There's a line in an old Eagle's song that says, "things in this life change very slowly, if they ever change at all." On Friday, I ran into an old rodeo buddy at the feed store. It had been three or four years since I'd seen him, and he'd put on a bit of weight.

"Well, I'll be damned if it ain't Hank Wilcox," he said as he stuck out his hand and grinned. "You still tryin' to make eight on them bulls?"

"Nah," I said. "Retired. I'm helping Granny run the ranch. How 'bout you, Rafe? You still trying to pay bills from the back of a bronc?"

"Oh, hell no," he patted his stomach and laughed. "I found me a wife and got two little ones. We got a little place just west of town. We run a few longhorns."

"Know the place." I said, "I didn't know it was your spread. How did that happen?"

"Well, let's see," he thought a second, laughed again, and said, "I guess you could say I chased her until she caught me."

"Five years ago, if you'd have told me you'd be married and settled down, I'd have called you a liar." I shook my head.

"Yep," he agreed, "and I'd have knocked your teeth out." 'bout

"Yeah," I laughed. "We did tangle a few times, didn't we?"

He nodded, "I gotta go. Man, it was good to see you. Come around sometime."

As he drove away, I recalled a motel room in Wyoming.

He'd taken a couple of women there after a dance and their husbands found out. They'd driven to the motel together, paid the clerk to tell them which room their wives were in, and called him out. When Rafe stepped outside, one of them grabbed him, and the other one hit him. One husband ended up with a broken jaw, and the other one's nose will never be straight again. I heard the commotion and stepped out to see what was going on. My room was two doors down from his, and by the time I got to them, both of his assailants were out cold.

"Didn't know they were married," he shrugged his shoulders and said in explanation.

"What are you gonna do?" I asked him.

"Send'em home," he muttered as he opened the door, "but the damage is already done." Inside, the women were scrambling into their clothes.

He held the door open until they made it outside. We helped them get their husbands into the back of the truck they'd come in and watched as they drove off.

"Think I'll head on down to Vegas," he said as the taillights disappeared. "Don't reckon it'd be smart to be here in the morning."

I knew how hard it was to make those long drives on no sleep, so I asked, "Want I should tag along? I'm riding with Jeb; he can pick me up when he gets there."

"That'd be nice." He nodded, then muttered again, "Man, I didn't know they were married."

"Would it have mattered?" I asked.

He thought a minute, then said, "Probably not, but a fellow ought to know what he's up against."

After Vegas, I had lost track of him. Standing there on the loading dock of the feed store, I thought, man, if he can change, so can I. And I knew for the first time that I would find a way to change, even if it came slowly, even if it didn't change the past, even if it killed me.

Luke was off with my ex-wife's dad for the weekend, and

Dottie had gone south to visit with Mrs. Walters. I still couldn't bring myself to call her Jo. She was Granny's age and my raising just didn't allow for me to call her by her first name. So, I spent the weekend checking cows. About half of them had calved and the other half were all due any day. Sunday night, a late cold front came through, reminding everyone that the weatherman was not in control of the climate.

Monday morning, I woke up to an overcast sky, and by midmorning, the drizzle had started. The skies finally cleared up and the sun showed itself late in the afternoon on Tuesday. The grass sure needed the rain, but trapped inside, or cold and wet, for two days did nothing for my attitude.

* * * * *

"We have two new members, tonight," Miz Nancy said as she picked up a packet and handed it to a young man with dark hair and a neatly trimmed mustache. "This is Oscar."

"Hello, Oscar," the members said, and he nodded, reddening a little.

"And this is Keith," she said as she handed another packet to an older man with a bit of gray streaking his black hair.

"Hello, Keith," we repeated the greeting, and he nodded.

"Every member starts their classes by telling what they did to get here." Miz Nancy looked from one to the other and asked, "Which of you would like to go first?"

Oscar looked like he was going to be sick. Keith leaned forward, rested his elbows on the table, and said, "I'll go first." He looked down at the packet on the table, and I noticed his jaw clench and unclench. "I have a landscaping business—or did. I left one morning to pick up a load of materials up north. I was supposed to be gone for a couple of days, so I made a couple of stops around town, making sure my crews were all lined out." He paused. Clench, unclench, deep breath. "One of my new foremen needed a phone number, and when I reached for my phone, I realized I'd left it at the house, so I ran by the house to get it and caught my wife and my best friend in bed together."

Every eye in the room was fixed on Keith. I could hear my own heart beating in my chest.

"I grabbed this heavy, metal figurine shaped like a cat and proceeded to beat him to death. When my wife jumped on my back, I threw her off and into a dresser. She hit her head, and it knocked her out. When I got finished with him, he was unconscious. I thought he was dead. I called the police and…" he stopped and looked up at Miz Nancy and shrugged.

"Was he dead?" Dan asked from across the table.

"No," Keith answered flatly, "just in a coma for ten days."

"Okay," Miz Nancy said, everyone took a breath, and then, "Oscar?"

"My son's stepfather whooped him. He used a wire hanger and left him bloody. When I found out, I went after him." he said.

I looked at him and knew there had to be more to the story. Oscar would have to stretch to make five foot four inches and would have to be soaking wet to weigh a hundred and ten pounds. His voice had a prepubescent high pitch to it and an unusual squeak.

"So, what happened?" Miz Nancy asked what we were all thinking.

"Well, he was a big guy, and I knew he'd beat the hell out of me in a fair fight." Oscar squeaked, "so I took the tire iron out of the car. He answered the door, I said 'We need to talk'. I had the iron down by my side, and when he stepped out and before he could react, I laid it upside his head. He hit the ground, and I broke three of his ribs, his right arm, and his right leg."

I wondered what I would do if someone ever did something like that to my son. I hoped I never had to find out, but I could picture a very similar scenario.

When he finished, Miz Nancy asked, "Would anyone else like to share?"

"I backhanded my wife," Dan said.

After a pause, Manuel said, "I hit my wife with a belt."

"I busted my girlfriends lip trying to keep her from splitting my head open with a metal lamp," I spoke up.

Jake leaned forward and added, "I blacked my wife's eye with the edge of a glass."

No one else offered anything, and finally Miz Nancy said, "As you can see, the degree of violence that got you all sent to these classes are very large in range, like the behaviors of abuse can be, but no matter how abuse occurs, it is still abuse. Tonight, we are going to discuss verbal abuse, and for some, this doesn't seem like a big deal, but it is still abuse."

After reading through the materials and discussing our answers to the questions that followed, I realized how lucky I was to have grown up in a house where voices were never raised, and Granny was so encouraging. From the stories the other guys told, it became real to me that a lot of verbal abuse goes on in lots of homes. I thought of all the yelling and cussing that I'd been a part of in the last seven years, and I decided that I never wanted to have any part of it again.

At the end of the lesson, Miz Nancy asked us to turn our packet over to the back and write down three ways we felt we were getting better. I wrote (1) I'm more at peace, less angry. (2) I have been cussing less, hardly ever use the 'F' word anymore. And (3) I'm not in a hurry anymore. I wasn't sure if the last one was what she wanted, but it was true.

In less than three minutes, everyone at the table except for the two new guys, had finished. I figured we'd all have to share, but when the last guy laid his pen down, Miz Nancy said, "Okay, I hope you noticed how quickly most everyone was able to come up with their three ways. That tells me something is making a difference in your lives. I hope this class has a lot to do with it, but it should give you a good feeling when you see yourselves improving."

Man, she's good. I thought to myself. If she had asked us outright if the class was helping us, we would have hum-hawed around and never given a straight answer. This way, we could see it without having to admit it. Pretty cool stuff.

"Okay, Manuel, you're up," Miz Nancy said.

"This is my last night," he stood up as he began in broken English, "so what did I learn from this class. Well, I learn it is not okay to hit my wife. I learn it is not okay to get drunk and run from police. I learn I must treat my wife with respect and be kind to her. I learn I never want to have to be here again. No disrespect, Miz Nancy, I like you, the class no so much. Is that good?"

"Yes, Manuel, that's good," she answered, then said, "exit papers and pens."

Jake and I each shook Manuel's hand at the door and then headed for the church. My new Wednesday routine, B.I.P. class, Neon Church with Jake, and now, I guess seeing Sally, and then calling Dottie on the way home. Come to think of it, my whole week had turned into a routine. It wasn't too long ago that I was moaning and bitching about being in a rut. Now, it felt kind of nice. Crazy how time changes things.

As I listened to the phone ring and waited for Dottie to pick up, I thought about what I'd written on my exit paper: I learned tonight that verbal abuse can have terrible and lasting emotional and mental effects on a person. I learned that I do not ever again want to be verbally abusive to another person.

WEEK 18—ECONOMIC ABUSE

I do not recall ever putting a flame to an item from a relationship. It seemed cliché. Realistically, I couldn't wrap my mind around the action being helpful. Man was I wrong. On Friday, I used our old John Deere tractor to push brush into a burn pile. After returning the tractor to the barn, I drove a four-wheeler out, made sure the fire department knew it was a controlled burn, and lit it. By supper time, it had burned down to a few smoldering coals.

After a quick shower and change of clothes, I slid into the truck and headed for Dottie's. How and why some things happen the way they do I'll never know, but when I got the truck turned around and accelerated down the drive, the letter from Shelby fell from above the visor into my lap. At the end of the drive, I stopped and picked it up, wondering what I should do with it.

After a moment's thought, I turned around, drove out across the pasture to where the remains of the brush pile were smoking. At the edge of the coals, I found several partially burnt branches. Using them, I made a small fire and burned the letter. I did not read it. I did not even take it out of the envelope. I just burned it. As the last of the tiny white envelope disappeared in flames, I felt a weight lift off me like I would never have imagined. I'm pretty sure I floated back to the truck with a smile on my face.

After supper, I asked Dottie if she had any plans for the weekend. She didn't, so I invited her for a tour of the ranch on Saturday. She accepted and we spent Saturday bouncing around on my old red four-wheeler as I showed her the place, ending with a visit to Granny's.

Sunday after church, I picked up Luke, and we spent most of the day fishing. A day with Dottie, followed by a day with Luke; things sure seemed to be looking up in my life. Maybe, just maybe, everything was going to work out after all.

The last of the cows gave birth sometime Sunday night, and so it was time to start thinking about when to work them. Monday, I stopped by and visited with Granny, and we decided to wait a few more weeks. She said she would get a hold of Tom Jack and see if he could help. Tuesday slipped away, and just like that, another week had snuck past.

As I pulled into my usual space in the counseling center parking lot, I spotted Jake stepping out of his truck. I was surprised to see Sally exit the passenger side, speak to him, and head for the church. He met me at the door. As we entered the counseling center, I wondered what was going on with them, but decided it would be better to keep my thoughts to myself for the time being.

"I make the money, so I call the shots," Miz Nancy said to start our Wednesday class. I was preoccupied with questions about Jake and Sally as she continued. "In some relationships, this is the kind of thinking which causes what is known as economic abuse. Sometimes, a man will use money to control and keep his wife in line. This is a form of abuse. Hank, please begin reading page one."

It occurred to me that she knew she did not have my full attention, and I had been called out as a result. I wanted to say, "But Sally rode to class with Jake." Instead, I picked up my packet and began to read.

The first page, which I read in its entirety, explained the purpose and procedure for the evening's class. When I finished, Miz Nancy instructed us to fill out the next three pages of questions and exited up the hall. Five minutes later, she stuck her head back into the room. Like almost everyone else, I was still hard at work answering questions. She retreated from the room and I heard her office door open. Ten minutes later, she returned.

"Question one, I think money is…?" she read from her packet, "Dan, how did you finish the sentence?"

"I think money is a necessity," Dan said.

"Okay, I can see how it is necessary," Miz Nancy pushed her glasses up, "but don't forget that, as necessary as it is, it's important to make time for your wife. You can't work all the time. Who's next?"

Albert, the quiet, young black man, sat to the right of Dan. He had been in the first class I attended but usually said little and spoke so softly when he did speak that it had taken me weeks to learn his name. It kind of surprised me when he said, "I think money is a means to an end."

Eventually, each member present gave a response. One of the guys said it was important. Another said it was the root of all evil. I said it was nice to have around. Miz Nancy commented on a few of our responses, but mostly we just read them. Jake was last.

"I think money is a complication," he said.

"How so?" Miz Nancy wanted to know.

"Well, I wasn't sure when I wrote my response down how accurate it was," he explained, "but as I listened to the other guys, it became clear to me how complicated money makes things. For instance, in my relationship, I worked, and she worked, but I was financially responsible for everything. I'm sure some folks, or couples, have an easier time of it, but I would guess most relationships have problems because of money."

"You're right," Miz Nancy said, nodding her head. "Money and finances are in the top ten reasons for relationship problems in most cases."

As we discussed the next few questions, I once again realized how growing up with only Granny as an example was far from normal. After several questions had been answered, Miz Nancy asked Jake to read his response to number eight. The question wanted to know what the most difficult aspect of finances was to discuss with your partner.

"The hardest thing to talk about related to money is how to

spend it and who gets to decide how it's spent," he read from his packet.

"Top two," Miz Nancy said. "Does anyone else have a different answer?"

No one did, so we moved into our second and third page of questions. These pages dealt with how the household we grew up in handled the economic situation. Did the mom and/or dad work? Who had control of the money? After listening to the members explain how it had been where they grew up, I realized how many different ways a household could be set up economically. I wondered how Dottie and I should set up our household.

In the blink of an eye, and without thinking, I went there, and once you've gone there, there's no turning back. What had been a lovely little romantic interlude had suddenly and without warning become a serious, long-term relationship. I wasn't sure if I was ready for that. And if I was, I wasn't sure if I could do it. Whether I was ready or not, I suddenly realized that I very much wanted to spend the rest of my life with Dottie, and it scared the shit out of me.

I ran my hand through my hair and muttered to myself, "Holy shit."

"Something wrong, Hank?" Miz Nancy asked, snapping me back to reality.

I looked at her for a second, then shook my head weakly, "Nah."

When I looked at Jake, he raised an eyebrow and I shrugged. Miz Nancy was instructing the class to fill out their exit papers. I cleared my head and wrote: Tonight, I learned that there are many ways to set up a household economically. I learned that both husband and wife should be privy to the finances and agree on who will work and how the money will be spent.

My head was still in a fog as Jake and I left the center and headed for the Neon Church. I wondered if Dottie had feelings as strong as mine about our relationship. We stepped through the doors and started up the center and I nearly forgot about Sally.

She had reserved seats for us, and the discussion was in full swing. Jake slid into the seat beside her and I took the seat beside him near the center aisle. Brother Jim had pulled a chair up beside the podium and was seated facing the congregation.

"How do you sin against wisdom?" a man dressed in a black business suit asked.

"If you fail to follow God's instruction and you know His path is the wise direction to take," Brother Jim explained, "then you have sinned against wisdom."

"How do you know if the instructions are from God?" Mr. Business Suit asked.

That sparked a discussion between several of the church members. As I listened, I began to understand, or at least, I think I did. If a decision was to be made, one should pray about it and ask God how to proceed. An answer would come, and there would be peace in it. If a decision was made and there was no peace in it, then it probably wasn't God's wisdom which was being followed. I'm pretty sure that was the gist of things, but I figured I'd better run it by Granny tomorrow just to be sure.

The service ended with a prayer, Sally loaded up with Jake and they drove off, and I climbed into my truck and fired it up. Sitting there behind the wheel before I put it in drive, I closed my eyes and asked God what He thought about me and Dottie making a go of it. When I opened my eyes minutes later, I knew the path I was going to take, and there was peace in my heart.

WEEK 19—SEXUAL ABUSE AND MISTREATMENT

"If you walked out through a pasture, you know there's a good chance you're going to pick up a few hitchhikers along the way. Depending on the season, you might make it home with only a few stick-tights or a couple of cockleburs. Other times of the year, you can end up with chiggers and ticks." As I sat at Granny's table on Thursday morning, waiting for the coffee pot to finish, she talked as she fussed around, getting cups ready.

I had told her about the discussion at the church the night before and then stammered through the business of how my batterers class had made me realize how I felt about Dottie. I finished with how I'd kind of checked with God about His feelings on the matter. What I wanted was confirmation from Granny that I was on the right path. A simple yes or no would have been nice, but of course, that was never Granny's way, so I listened and waited.

"Do you understand what I just told you?" she asked, setting the cups down beside the coffee maker.

"No, Granny, you lost me," I admitted.

"You say you love this girl. You say you think you want to spend the rest of your life with her, she's the one." The coffee finished and she poured each of us a cup. As she set mine in front of me, she continued, "What are you going to do about the hitchhikers?"

"What hitchhikers, Granny?" I shook my head in confusion, wondering if she was entering the early stages of dementia.

"When you walk through this world, through life, temptations like stick-tights and cockleburs are going to try to stick to you. Women will make eyes at you. Friends will want you to go out drinking with them. You can't expect to go through the rest of your life and not pick up a few hitchhikers. You don't leave cockleburs stuck to your pants all day; you remove them as soon as you realize you have them. You have to be able to do the same thing with temptations," she explained, "Are you ready to do that for this girl?"

"Yes, Granny," I answered, "I am."

"Good," she said. "Now, let's talk about the chiggers and ticks."

By the time our conversation was over, I was more convinced than ever that I was ready for a serious relationship with Dottie. Granny had questioned me about what I would do if a woman threw herself at me, how I would handle a friend that wanted me to fish with him all the time, and what I would do the first time Dottie and I couldn't agree on something. Granny never did give me a solid yes or no, but I got the feeling she was onboard.

On Saturday, I picked up Luke from his mother's, and on the way home, I told him I had a girlfriend and asked him if he would like to meet her. I had already talked to Dottie, and while she was a bit uncertain about the possibility, she agreed to have dinner with us, depending on his answer. Nothing in the world could have prepared me for his response.

Instead of answering with a yes or no, he said, "You have a girlfriend?"

"Yes," I said. "Would you like to meet her?"

"You have a girlfriend?" he asked again and looked confused.

"Why do you keep saying that?" I asked.

"Because, Dad, I thought you were gay," he said and shrugged.

I nearly ran off the road, and I missed the turn to the house.

When I regained my composure and got turned back around, I asked, "Why would you think I was gay?"

"Well, you, well it's like this, well…" he seemed to have trouble putting it into words.

"Hey, it's okay, son," I said. "I'm not mad, just confused."

"Okay, then," he said. "For a long time, you didn't come around much. She doesn't anymore, but back then, mom called you the rodeo queen."

I felt my face turning red but kept my eyes on the road and drove. Part of me wanted to whip out the old cellphone and give her a good old fashion ass chewing. The new improved, wiser me remembered all the times I had called her a bitch and a terrible mother. It didn't hurt my ego any less, but somehow it made me realize I was growing.

"And," Luke continued, "ever since you've been back and I've been coming over, there's never been any girls around. Plus, Granny said you've been going to a class every week to help you get better. I just thought you were trying not to be gay anymore."

"Well, son," I tried to keep my voice low and calm, "I am not gay, and I've never been gay. I was a bull rider in the rodeo not a rodeo queen, and the classes I'm taking are to help me with my anger."

"Man, that's a relief," he said. "John Turner's dad is gay, and everyone makes fun of him. I sure wasn't looking forward to the guys finding out you were gay."

"I'm not gay," I repeated once again, "not that I have anything against gay people, but son I'm not gay."

Later that evening at the little burger shop in town, I introduced Dottie and Luke. Dinner went better than I could have expected. The two of them got along fabulously. By the end of the meal, I was almost feeling like a third wheel myself. Dottie followed us back out to the house and after a long visit, I walked her out to her Jeep and kissed her goodnight. She got in her vehicle and pulled away. As I started up the steps, I noticed the living room curtain move.

"You watchin' out the window?" I asked as I shut the door behind me.

"Yep," Luke admitted with a blush, adding, "I wanted to see if you kissed her."

"Why?" I asked.

"No reason," he grinned.

When it hit me, I grinned back, shook my head, and said, "I'm not gay."

We both laughed.

Sunday night, when I took him back to his mother, I told her about the rodeo queen discussion, and she thought it was funny. She laughed and wanted to know what had brought it up. When I told her about Dottie, she quit laughing.

"Get in the house," she nearly screamed as she pointed at the door and ordered our son in. As soon as the door closed behind him, she snarled, "You took my son to meet one of you slutty-ass girl toys without telling me. You fuckin' faggot."

"Hey, wait just a minute," I started to speak.

"No, you wait just a minute, motherfucker!" she punctuated the last word with an index finger inches from my nose, "I don't want my son around any… where the fuck do you think you're going?"

As I opened the door to my truck and slid in, I answered over my shoulder, "Home."

When I pulled out of the drive, she was still standing in the yard with her hands on her hips, and her mouth was moving. I couldn't hear what she was yelling, but I'm pretty sure I know the gist of it.

Halfway home, the adrenaline maxed out and I got the shakes. Two miles farther, tears filled my eyes and I pulled over. As the body heaves started, I could feel the anger welling up inside me, and I wanted to puke. I gripped the steering wheel with both hands, and through the tears, I stared a hole through the windshield and out into the night. Twenty minutes later, under control but completely spent, I pulled back onto the road and drove home.

Monday, I talked to Granny about it. Tuesday, I talked to Dottie about it. Both thought the language was inappropriate, but as to the mother's fear of her son being introduced to the caliber of women I usually dated, both of them felt it was founded. I had expected Dottie to be offended, but she simply explained that she was secure in who she was, and my ex-wife didn't know her.

I was in no better mood when I sat down across from Jake at the counseling center Wednesday evening. He looked pretty ragged himself but managed the usual, "How was your week?"

"Good, bad, and worse," I said, then asked, "and yours?"

"Just bad and worse," he answered.

Before we could compare notes, Miz Nancy called us to the front. Jake had beaten me to the center, so I didn't know if Sally had ridden with him or not. I found myself wondering if she was the bad, the worse, or both. The class topic for the evening was by far the most uncomfortable to date. Our packets consisted of four pages of facts and statistics about marital rape. There were no pages of questions.

Every member was required to read a section from the packet. Except for the one who was reading, everyone was completely quiet. It was almost like the oxygen in the room was limited, and everyone was afraid it would get used up if they moved around or even breathed too much. It was uncanny and uncomfortable. When the last section had been read, Miz Nancy explained that most states now considered martial rape the same as non-martial rape.

The class itself lasted the allotted amount of time, but it seemed like it was twice as long. I'm sure my need to talk to Jake was part of it, but the subject matter didn't help any at all. Finally, Miz Nancy dismissed us, and we handed in our exit papers. On mine I wrote: Tonight, I learned that rape is rape. It does not matter if you are married, if your spouse says no and you force her, it is rape.

Sally was in her usual seat and had ours saved. Brother Jim was deep in discussion with two members of the congregation when we sat down. I didn't get much from the discussion, I was curious and impatient. When the closing pray was finished, I told Jake I needed to talk to him a minute.

"What's up?" he asked as he walked with me to my truck.

I told him about my week, the introduction of Luke to Dottie, the blow up with my ex-wife, and the confusion I was feeling after visiting with Granny and Dottie. He listened intently. As I finished, it occurred to me that I had just dumped my load of problems in his lap and hadn't really thought about it ahead of time. It kind of embarrassed me. Jake must have picked up on it, because he smiled and said, "Good, bad, worse. That's pretty accurate."

"I don't know why I unloaded that on you," I admitted, feeling guilty.

"Sometimes, a fella just needs another fella to vent to and get it out of his system," Jake said. "Sounds to me like that's why."

"Yeah," I agreed. "I guess that was it. Thanks for listening."

"Anytime, Hank. One thing I've learned in life is things usually have a way of working themselves out. I wouldn't let it get to me too much, just give it a little time," he said and turn to go.

"Jake," I said, "what did you mean by 'just bad and worse'?"

He stopped, and for a minute, I thought maybe he wasn't going to turn back. When he did, he said, "Bad. Last week after we left church, I drove Sally home. We had agreed we would just be friends, but then when I dropped her off, she said she wanted more and got upset when I told her I couldn't do more. She wanted to know why, and I told her I was still in love with my ex-wife. Worse. I know my ex-wife has been dating again. I'd been told she'd been seen out with a couple of different guys. This week, I found out from one of my kids that she's been pretty much living with one of them at her house or his for some time now." When he finished, he shot me a sad grin and shrugged.

"Man, I'm sorry," I said.

"Thanks," He replied. "Actually, felt nice to vent a little myself."

We both chuckled, and he turned and headed for his truck. As I climbed into mine, I thought about my week compared to Jake's. I was in love with Dottie. I hadn't told her yet, but I knew I was, and I was pretty sure she had serious feeling for me. Even as bad as my week had ended, I still had the hope of a beautiful future ahead of me. Jake was still in love with his ex-wife. She was living with someone new. Jake's future seemed uncertain at best. I hated that for him, but it made me realize, as bad as my situation sometimes seemed, there are those who have it worse.

As I pulled out of the parking lot, I called Dottie. She picked up on the second ring, and the week's worries just seemed to fade away.

WEEK 20—CHRONIC MENTAL/PSYCHOLOGICAL ABUSE

There's an old brown tabby cat that stays out at the barn. From time to time she has a litter of kittens. When the kittens get big enough to wander off by themselves, they usually disappear. I figure the coyotes get them. So, Miss Lucy, that's her name, is the only cat we've ever had for very long.

On Tuesday afternoon, when I finished working and parked the four-wheeler in the barn, Miss Lucy was playing with a fairly large field mouse. If you've ever seen a cat toying with a mouse, you find yourself feeling sorry for the mouse. Not that folks usually have much love for mice. They're destructive little creatures, but it's the game the cat plays with them which makes the whole scene so dreadful.

After wounding the mouse, the cat will let it run off, even give it a head start. Just when the mouse thinks it might get free, the cat will pounce on it and either bite it once again or slap it with its claws. Once the mouse is exhausted and can no longer run, the cat will often toss it into the air repeatedly as if it were a play toy. Sometimes, the cat will then devour the mouse, and other times, she'll just walk away and leave it.

Wednesday night, as Jake read over the first page of our packet, I realized how much the mind games couples play are like the relationship between a cat and a mouse. First, one of the two wounds the other person, after which the real game begins. When Jake had finished reading, Miz Nancy explained how detrimental mental and psychological abuse can be to a relationship and to the people in it. She said that too often, when trying to counsel people in relationships where this type of abuse is occurring, the relationship takes priority over the individuals. In her opinion, the individuals suffer.

After giving instructions about the next couple of pages and the questions they contained, she left us to work on our packets. The first few questions were easy enough to answer with a couple of words, or at most one sentence, but the final two needed a paragraph. The next to the last question asked us to tell about a time when someone had psychologically abused us, and the last question wanted us to tell of a time when we had psychologically abused another.

"Who would like to share first?" Miz Nancy asked as she returned to the room.

Complete silence, not so much as a chair creaked or a paper shuffled. She stepped to the corner of the table and looked around at each member's paper. I found myself following along and looking myself. Every single one of us had written something down, but no one spoke, not even those who usually volunteered to go first.

"This is not unusual," Miz Nancy said. "It is not easy for men to admit that they have been mentally abused. It hurts their egos. And it's usually even harder for them to admit they have mentally abused someone else."

"I'll go," Gary said. "I'm a jealous person, and my last girlfriend knew it. When we would go out partying, if she got mad at me for something, she'd find some guy and dance really close with him."

"Yes, that's a good example," Miz Nancy frowned, "but didn't you tell us that, at one point, you were in relationships with three women at the same time? Was she one of the three?"

"Well, yes, but she didn't know it." He grinned.

"Goodness, Gary," she shook her head, then, "Someone else."

"My ex-wife would leave weapons lying around for me to find," Jake spoke up.

All heads turned to him. He sat staring down at the packet on the table. His shoulders and head sagged.

"What kind of weapons?" Miz Nancy wanted to know.

He raised his head and looked at her. "A steak knife on the side of the tub, a baseball bat wedged behind the headboard of the bed, rounds of ammunition and her revolver on the closet shelf."

"Did she ever use them?" Miz Nancy asked.

"No, after an argument or a disagreement, she would leave them out for a few days," Jake answered. "Then at some point, they would disappear. Once, I got angry about the bat and threw it into the woods behind the house."

"Did she know you threw it away?" was Miz Nancy's next question.

"Yes," Jake nodded his head. "We were arguing, and I saw it there and said I was sick of being threatened. I picked it up, went out the back door, and chunked it into the woods. I know I shouldn't have thrown it. I know that was the wrong thing to do."

"You're right, Jake," Miz Nancy agreed, "on all accounts. The weapons were psychological abuse, and you should have handled the situation in another way. It's good you realize that now. Someone else?"

Each of us was required to share. I was amazed at how many times cellphones were mentioned as weapons in mental abuse as one after another of the members gave examples of their experiences. It had become customary for Freddy to share last, but for some reason, when there was only me and Freddy left, Miz Nancy called on him first.

"Miz Nancy, I don't reckon, this here situation pertains to me," Freddy said. "In looking back, I can't think of a situation I've been in where I was abused like this or where someone or another did likewise to me. Situations like this just don't seem to be part of my history. And before you get after me in this here situation, I have thought hard about it, and I just cain't figure a single instance or situation like this in my past at all."

You would have thought we were watching a tennis match

in the seconds after he went silent. Every member's head swung from Freddy to Miz Nancy and back again. When neither one of them spoke, the heads swung back and forth once more. Finally, she just nodded at him and turned her stare at me without saying a word.

"Oh, okay," I said when the realization that I was supposed to speak finally hit me. "One time at a dance after a rodeo, my girl and me got into an argument. It was almost closing time, so I pretended to go to the bathroom and instead went and got in my truck and pulled it around the back of the building. When she figured out, I wasn't there, she flipped out. She called crying, and I pulled around and picked her up. It was a rotten thing for me to do, and afterwards, I felt bad about it. I'll never do something like that again."

"Okay, Hank," Miz Nancy said, "but we're still on the question of someone mentally abusing you."

"Yeah, well, you can't blame a fella for trying," I said and smiled.

Miz Nancy made me back up and tell how I'd been abused and then everyone else had to share how they had been abusive. Once again, cellphones played the biggest part. Second place went to men making their partners think they were leaving and not coming back. By the time it was all said and done, I was convinced that I had no desire to play mind games with anyone ever again.

At the end of the class, I wrote on my exit paper: I learned that mind games are never good in a relationship. I learned that mental and psychological abuse can be just as damaging and have just as lasting effects on an individual as physical abuse. I learned that I do not want to ever be in a relationship were abuse is occurring.

A warm south wind brought the smell of fresh cut grass from somewhere nearby as Jake and I walked from the center to the church. When we found our seats, they had already made it through the first twenty verses of Proverbs ten. The baritone fellow in the front row had just begun to read the last thirteen verses, so I flipped my Bible open and followed along. He finished, and my thoughts strayed back to the first part of the twenty-third verse: "It is as sport to a fool to do mischief." I thought it was interesting how that verse tied in with the lesson from earlier at the center.

At the end of the service, I walked with Jake and Sally out to his truck. We stood around for a few minutes, visiting and sharing our thoughts about the night's service, and then Jake opened the passenger door and Sally got in. He closed the door and I asked, "How're you doing?"

"Okay," he said and shrugged.

"You sure?" I pressed.

"I'm doing okay, really." He smiled. "It's nice of you to ask."

"Okay, then." I smiled back, but I could tell he wasn't okay.

WEEK 21—CHRONIC PHYSICAL ABUSE

Some weeks are seven days long. There are those who would even argue that every week is seven days long, to which I would have to call Bullshit. I know it's not true because this week itself has lasted a short eternity. After the cussing my ex-wife gave me two weeks ago, I expected I wouldn't be seeing my son the following weekend, but when I called again this past Thursday, I was hoping maybe the worst of it would have passed. Not so.

Liz let the answering machine pick up each time I called, and each time, I left brief message asking if I might see our son. On Friday, she finally picked up long enough to tell me no. I wanted to shout, to cuss, to really let her have it, but I simply said okay, and that I'd call again next week. Then I hung up before she could reply.

Granny says if she doesn't let me see him next week, I should call a lawyer. Dottie feels like she's to blame and thinks we should give the ex-wife some time. She says if it were her son, she would be concerned about who he was spending time with, and maybe when Liz realized that she was a decent person, she would come around. While I love Dottie, I tend to agree with Granny.

By the time Wednesday rolled around, I was feeling about as down as a fellow can get. When I got to the counseling center, I noticed Jake had driven his farm truck again and wondered if his good truck was still giving him trouble. Inside, I found Freddy in his usual corner but no Jake. I picked up a packet from the stack and plopped into my normal seat. Freddy had his packet in his hands and was mumbling to himself as he flipped through it.

Moments later, Jake stepped through the door. He appeared from down the hall where the restroom was located. He gave me a weak smile and asked, "How was your week?"

"Not so good," I answered as he pulled out his chair and picked up a packet, "and yours?"

"Likewise," he said. "Not good, not good at all."

Before I could ask him about it, several members strolled in and found seats. I busied myself reading through the material. There must have been something in the water or the air this week, because even the normally talkative members sat silently waiting for Miz Nancy to call us to sign in. I wondered how this weird phenomenon could happen. In my mind, I was questioning whether it was a seasonal thing or perhaps caused by the cycle of the moon, when Miz Nancy's voice floated down the hall.

I found myself in line between Dan and Jake. Moving slowly along, I looked at the wall, searching for new posters. It had been several weeks since any new ones had appeared. I thought perhaps it was because it was getting close to the time when school would be out, but I didn't know for sure.

"Just my luck," Dan turned and spoke to me.

"What's that?" I asked.

"Just my luck," he repeated. "My last night and everyone is man-struating."

I gave him a weak smile. "Yeah, I notice it too," I said.

I had been so caught up in my own funk that I hadn't realized how many members were present. As the room began to fill up, chairs were shuffled to make room. By the time Miz Nancy came in, there were sixteen of us stuffed in and around the table, and the room was beginning to get warm.

"How about a little more A/C?" Frank asked as she entered.

She picked up a packet and used it to fan herself. "It's on high and running full blast. I think it's about to go out. There's a technician coming to look at it tomorrow."

For a bunch of guys who mostly make their living working out in the heat, we sure can do a massive amount of bitching and moaning when we want our air conditioning. And sixteen men in the midst of man-struation without cool air is not a pretty sight.

"Good grief!" Miz Nancy chided. "I reckon y'all can handle an hour of heat. Now, let's get on with it."

Dan read first, and then one after another, each of the members read a paragraph or two until the body of the packet had been read. There was only one page of questions to answer. They asked about the physical abuse which occurred during the incident for which we had been ordered to attend the class. The last question asked us to describe that abuse.

Miz Nancy left the room, allowing us our customary five minutes to answer, and then she returned. The heat was getting worse and so was the whining. She began by stating that, due to the heat and the large class size, she would not require everyone to answer every question. She asked for volunteers, however, and insisted that everyone would be required to share on at least one question.

As the stories unfolded, I began to realize that in many of them, alcohol was involved. Only in Jake's case and one other had the cause not been related to drugs or alcohol. I began to reevaluate my own story. I hadn't had a drop to drink since they hauled me off to jail. I'd thought about it often, had even planned on it a time or two, but so far, it just hadn't happened. Now, I was beginning to think it was for the best if I never drank again. Somehow, the thought seemed odd, but it did not bother me. I think I'm alright with it.

Once all the questions had been discussed, Miz Nancy said, "Tonight is Dan's last night."

Rising from his seat, Dan nodded and said, "Thanks, Miz Nancy. What have I learned here? Well, I learned a lot more than I thought I would when I started. Not everything I learned pertained to my situation." He grinned and winked at Freddy who grinned back. "But even the stuff I learned that didn't pertain to me was still good stuff to know. I figure I might need it later on down the line. But the most important thing I learned did pertain to me and that is, never hit your partner. Walk away, leave, do whatever it takes to stay cool and calm, but don't hit'em."

When Dan had finished, Miz Nancy explained that, while time would heal the outward wounds caused by physical abuse, the mental and psychological effects would take much longer to mend. She said that often counseling was necessary, adding she knew all of us had physically abused someone because we were in the class, but that she knew many of us had also been physically abused as well. She encouraged us to get the help we needed and then told us to make sure she had our exit papers before we left.

On mine, I wrote: There is never a reason for physical violence. It should never happen. In the future, I hope that I will always remember this and walk away anytime trouble starts.

After class, Jake told me Brother Jim was out of town as we headed up the hall. Of all the weeks for the church to be closed, this was not the best one for it. He must have seen the disappointment in my face. Instead of getting in his truck, he hopped up and sat down on the back of the flatbed.

"So, what's got you down?" he asked.

I smiled and sat down across the bed from him. "My ex-wife still won't let me see Luke," I told him.

"I'm sorry to hear that." he said, "I'm sure it will work itself out. Once again, I'd advise patience. Women tend to come around in their own time."

"So, how's it going with you?" I asked. "You seem a little uptight yourself."

"Yeah, the kids aren't doing well with the ex and her new fella," he said. "It's hard on them."

"Hard on you?" I asked.

"If I'm honest," he cocked his head to one side and stared down at the asphalt, "yeah a little, but mainly I worry about the kids."

"Think she'll ever come around?" I wondered aloud.

"How do you mean?" he returned.

"I mean is there any hope for you and her?" I looked over at him.

He continued to stare at the asphalt for a long moment, then said, "No, I think that ship has sailed. Now that she's found someone new, it would never be the same."

"I'm sorry," I told him. He looked up and gave a weak grin and nodded.

We sat silent for a while, just two men sharing a quiet bit of misery. The sun began to fade in the west, and the orange and reds of sunset brightened the horizon. We left the parking lot before it completely disappeared. Nothing had changed in our lives, not our problems, not our worries, not our sorrows. But somehow, sitting on the back of that truck with that old man made everything a little better, made life a little more bearable, made hope seem a little more alive.

It was strange, but not something I was going to ever question. I called Dottie on the way home. By the time I pulled into the drive, I felt positive about the future once again.

WEEK 22—ABUSE OF ANIMALS AND WEAPONS

There is alone and then there is lonely. The two are not necessarily synonymous. On Friday afternoon, I took a four-wheeler and checked fences. In our north pasture, there is a large granite outcrop. With care, a person can make their way to the top. I eased the four-wheeler along the worn trail until I was sitting at the very edge of it. From there, I could see for miles in all directions. It is a beautiful spot and a good one for thinking.

I began to wonder if a man could sit high on a hill and look back over his life, what would he change? There were many things in my past I would like to change, but if I changed them, what would I lose? Would I get to keep my son? Would Granny still be here? Would my life be better or worse? If I could look into the future, what would I see? These questions brought me to the realization that being alone and being lonely are not necessarily the same.

In my life, I had spent very little time alone. I liked having people around, or thought I did. In the last nine months, I had spent more hours alone than I had in my entire life. But sitting on the top of my little knoll, I realized I was not lonely. I also realized that it was the first time in my life I wasn't lonely. I was alone, but not lonely. Before I had been lonely, but not alone. I liked the change.

That evening, I called Liz and asked about Luke. Her voice was like ice, but she agreed to let me pick him up the next day and keep him until Sunday evening. I maintained what I considered to be a dignified tone through the conversation, but as soon as I hung up the phone, I danced around, shouting like a kid at a party.

In the middle of my dancing, the phone rang. It was Dottie. I told her the good news and silence followed. I guess I was expecting her to be as excited as I was, or at least give me a hey, that's great, Hank, but there was only silence. I'm sure this is what it would feel like to be riding a roller coaster and have it jump the track and collide with a brick building.

"What's wrong?" I asked her, breaking the silence.

"I'm sorry, Hank," she answered. "I know you're excited, and I'm excited for you, but I guess I'm just concerned. I don't want to cause you or Luke any more problems." An hour later, with all our fears and concerns on the table, we decided I would spend the weekend with my son, but on Saturday night, me and Luke would pick up Granny and meet Dottie for dinner in town. The excitement I had felt earlier was replaced with a deep sense of calmness. I... we, had worked through an uncomfortable situation. This was new ground for me. In the past, I would have simply avoided it. Maybe I was becoming a better man.

* * * * *

On the ride back to my house from his mother's the next day, Luke said, "I'm sorry I didn't get to come over the last couple of weeks, Dad."

"I'm sorry too, son," I said. "I hope it's never this long again. I missed you."

"I missed you, too," he said, "and I don't think it will be this long again."

Shocked, I asked him, "Why's that?"

"I had a talk with Pops," he said. Pops was Liz's father, my ex-father-in-law. We'd always gotten along well.

"And what did Pops have to say?" I asked.

"Not much. He just listened to me. Then he talked to mom. I was outside, but I could see them through the window. She was mad, but she shook her head yes, and I knew she wouldn't keep me from seeing you again," he explained.

"What did you say to Pops?" I asked.

"Not at lot. Just that mom won't let me come to see you," he paused, looked down at the floorboard, then added, "and that I didn't think it was right, her getting mad 'cause of Dottie when she was always introducing me to her boyfriends and all. I also told him Dottie was nice."

The weekend went wonderfully. I could have kissed Pops, but I knew he wasn't doing it for me, he was doing it for his grandson. Still, I sure owed him a big one. It seemed like before I could turn around, I was taking my son back home. Liz was cold and silent when I dropped him off but not combative. I told Luke I loved him and drove home.

* * * * *

Wednesday came around before I knew it, and on my drive to the counseling center, I wondered if Jake was doing any better. I found myself hoping he was and knew that if he wasn't, I would feel guilty because my life seemed to be back on track. As I pulled into the parking lot, he and Sally were just stepping up onto the sidewalk in front of the church. Watching to see if he was going to give her a kiss when they parted, I nearly ran smack into a little red Volkswagen bug. I swerved hard, and when I looked back, she had disappeared into the church, and Jake was opening the door to the center. I swore under my breath and pulled my truck into an empty space.

The air was cool but pleasant when I stepped out of my pickup. I noticed that business at Suzie Q's seemed to have picked up. I wondered if they had more business during the spring or if it was just the birds and the bees and animals out in nature that became more interested in such exploits. Whatever the answer, a trio of giggling women passed me with little pink sacks as I headed for the door to the counseling center.

The first half of our packet was on cruelty to animals, or animal abuse. We read through it in the usual manner. It covered everything from the legal definition to the laws about hurting animals. The last section warned that those who abuse animals at a young age often become abusive in their relationships later in life.

The discussion that followed ended up being more about whether hunting was animal abuse or not. The general consensus by the end of the session was that if a person is hunting to provide food for someone, then it is not abuse. From there, we moved into how weapons are used in domestic abuse.

Of course, the main concern was bodily injury being caused by weapons, but I found the section on how threats with weapons can cause mental and psychological abuse very interesting. I had never considered how being threatened with bodily harm could put a strain on a person.

In closing, Miz Nancy reminded us that we were never to bring any type of weapon into her class. To the shock of some of the members, she said not even a pocketknife. No searches were made, but I'm thinking next week more than a few will be emptying their pockets before class.

Before handing Miz Nancy my exit sheet, I wrote: Tonight, I learned that people who abuse animals at a young age are more likely to abuse people when they are older. I also learned that weapons such as guns and knives can not only cause physical damage, but mental and psychological issues as well.

Stepping out the front door of the center, I got a surprise. A cold front had come down from the north, and the temperature had dropped several degrees. What had been a pleasant breeze now had a bite to it, and the air smelled like it might rain. Jake and I hustled down the walkway and hurried into the church.

I was so glad to be going to church that I practically skipped down the center aisle. Sounds kind of crazy, but in just these few short months, I had become very fond of the discussions. The night's discussion was based around the twelfth chapter of

Proverbs. Someone asked Brother Jim about the meaning of verse twenty just about the time we found our seats.

He read the verse aloud and then explained, "This verse, I believe, is explaining the different mindsets of those who have evil in their hearts and those who have love in their hearts. To the person who is deceitful and filled with evil, everyone seems to be out to get them or do them wrong, but to those filled with love, comes peace and joy."

After Brother Jim's closing prayer, Jake and Sally walked me to my truck. We stood around talking for a few minutes about what we had heard and about our week. I hated to leave them. The company was good, but it would be dark soon, so I said my goodbyes. On the way home, I called Dottie.

Life is so good, and it's beginning to scare me again. I keep waiting for it to go terribly wrong and praying to God that it won't. Funny thing is I don't even know what it is I'm worrying about and still I worry. I guess only time will tell how things will turn out.

WEEK 23—USE OF CHILDREN AS WEAPONS IN DOMESTIC VIOLENCE SITUATIONS

Mostly, when something goes wrong, there is a way to fix it. Occasionally, nothing will do but to give it time. I think possibly the only thing that will turn the events of this week around is time—well that and a lot of prayer.

On Thursday, I called Liz to see when I could see Luke. Still cold and distant, she said I could pick him up Saturday afternoon. Next, I called Dottie. We decided we would go out for dinner on Friday and have lunch with Granny after church on Sunday. Plans are great things to have, except when the shit hits the fan and all the planning ends up as one great big black fecal cloud floating just above your head.

Late Friday afternoon when I came in from the field, Shelby, the ex-girlfriend I had the fight with which landed me in jail, was sitting on my front porch. I guess she hadn't gotten the memo about me burning her letter. Now, Shelby is a little spitfire blonde and, as Uncle Toby would say, built like a brick shithouse. She is about five foot two and curved in all the right places. When I stepped out of my truck, she came off the stairs like a long-lost lover. Arms out and lips puckered.

"Hank!" she squealed and kept coming.

I put my hands out and then up as she hit me like a linebacker. It must have been a sight, me standing there with my hands in the air and her squeezing me like a giant, overstuffed carnival bear. "What's wrong with you?" she whined when she realized I wasn't hugging her back.

"I'm seeing someone," I said flatly, and she brought her knee up fast and hard.

The air left my lungs, my crotch exploded in pain, and I doubled over onto the drive. She stepped back, and from the ground, I saw her draw her booted foot back. Somehow through the pain, I managed to get a hand up and slap her heel away before it collided with my head. In doing so, I knocked her off balance, and she landed on her ass in the gravel. Through the fog, I heard a car turn up the drive, and I rolled over. Before I could get my hands under me and get up, Shelby launched herself from the seated position she was in, and the two of us went rolling.

Legs and arms intertwined and flailing, we came to a stop, and I scrambled to get untangled from the crazy blonde hellcat. She, on the other hand, tried to scratch my eyes out and started screaming like a banshee. By some miracle, I managed to get free and put a little distance between us before she regained her footing. My first thought was to flee, just take off and pray I could outrun her. Before I could move, she looked past me, and something in her eyes changed.

"So, you're the bitch that thinks she can take my man!!" she snarled at whoever was behind me.

"Who're you calling a bitch, bitch!!" came the response. It was Liz.

I was still trying to form an explanation when Shelby said, "Oh, you fucking whore!!!" and shot past me like a flash.

I turned in time to see the two of them collide in a fury of fists, hair, and dust. My first thought once again was to flee, just use the diversion to escape and run like hell. Somewhere along there, my conscious took over and I yelled, "Hey, knock it off you two!!" and grabbed Shelby from behind.

Liz got in one helluva free shot to her left ear, and Shelby used my body as leverage, planted both feet in my ex's chest and kicked out. Her body went airborne, and she landed on her ass several feet away. I swung Shelby around and was moving her away from Liz when something hit me just above and behind the right ear. I saw an explosion of red, and my sight began to blur. I let loose of Shelby and grabbed my head. When I brought my hand away it was covered with blood.

A car door slammed, and everything just seemed to stop. For several seconds, it was like time was frozen, and the only thing that moved was my eyes. Shelby was standing a couple of feet in front of me, still looking like a caged wildcat. Off to my right I could see Liz holding another rock like she was ready to launch it. Several feet to my left, Dottie was standing beside her Jeep with a bewildered look on her face.

"What the hell is going on here?" she asked in a voice barely above a whisper.

No one answered her.

"What the hell is going on here?" she repeated a bit louder.

Still no one answered. Before I could move, she opened the door to her Jeep, climbed in, backed out, and left. I stood watching her go and wondering what I should do, completely at a loss.

"Who was that?!!" Shelby yelled at me.

I turned and started for the house. Behind me, I heard Shelby yell, "And who the hell are you?"

I opened the door, stepped inside, shut the door, locked it, and left them to it. I had had enough. I got the bleeding stopped and took a shower. When I looked out the living room window a half hour later, they were both gone.

All day Saturday I tried to call Dottie. She didn't answer. I messaged her. She did not reply. Nothing.

That evening I drove to the Liz's house, and Pops meet me in the driveway. We had a long visit. I told him everything that had been happening over the last couple of months, ending with the fiasco in my front yard the day before. He sat silent for a long while and then said maybe it would be best if I waited until next weekend to take Luke. He understood my predicament, he said, and did not blame me, but sometimes things just needed to rest. I tried to call Dottie on the way home and still got no answer.

Sunday after church on the ride home, Granny asked, "What's bothering you, Runt?"

"I don't know, Granny," I answered, "I guess just life in general."

"Life, huh," she cocked an eye at me, "and not a bit of it has to do with that cat fight in your front yard, does it now?"

Why it shocked me I don't know. Granny always knew everything. It was like she was physic or something, more likely the or something. And the or something being a lot of busy bodies all over the county.

"Yeah," I shook my head, "that's a big part of it, I reckon. Now Dottie's mad and won't even answer my calls."

"Well, Runt," Granny grinned, "sometimes you just got to man up and face'em in person."

After a second, I agreed, "Yeah, I reckon you're right."

Fifteen minutes later, I turned up the drive to Granny's. As we pulled to a stop, she reached over, grasped my arm, and said, "Your Aunt Ellie heard those two exes of yours were going at it like a couple of old herd bulls. Is that true?"

I thought about it, smiled and answered, "Granny those two made bulls look tame, more like two bobcats with their tails tied together and hung over a clothesline."

She threw her head back and cackled. I laughed, too. Might as well get some good out of a bad situation.

* * * * *

When I arrived at the counseling center on Wednesday, I still had not found the time to drive to Dottie's. I had given up trying to call her and had left one last message saying I wanted to speak to her when she was ready. She had not replied, and I had decided that if I didn't hear from her by noon on Thursday, I was driving over.

The night's topic, using kids as weapons in a relationship, could not have come at a more appropriate time. As we read through the packet, I found myself making mental notes. I was glad that I was beginning to understand how all of this, if not handled correctly, could cause serious and lasting damage to my son.

After we'd all read through the material in the packet, Miz Nancy got on her soap box, as she put it. This was a subject she was very passionate about, and she let us know quickly that she did not think there was ever a time when it was appropriate to use kids as weapons in a conflict. She said, she saw it too often, and it was never good for the kids.

"Tonight, each of you will answer the questions as usual, and we will discuss them. I expect honesty," she stated flatly, turned, and left.

There were two pages of questions. The first dealt with our childhood and the second with how we handled our own children if we had any. I did the best I could answering the questions, but my mind was on Dottie. I wondered if I showed up at her place, would she even talk to me? Part of me said so be it; she was just another woman gone, but I knew somehow it was more than that, and I had to try.

I paid just enough attention to the conversation going on around the table to know when it was my turn to provide an answer. James was the one to answer the last question. When he finished, Miz Nancy stood with hands on her hips and stared around the room until she had everyone's attention.

"When is it okay to use your children as weapons?" she asked.

"Never," came the response from every member. I had never seen Miz Nancy look so serious. After we handed in our exit sheets, Jake and I walked out together.

"You seem a little distracted tonight," he stated, but it felt more like a question.

"Yeah, maybe a little," I said, stepping out into the night and heading for the church.

Jake stopped me. "No church tonight. Brother Jim's off visiting family."

"Oh, okay." I nodded.

"You wanna talk about it?" he asked.

We sat on the back of his flatbed, and I told him about my week. He listened, nodding occasionally. When I had finished, we sat quietly for a few minutes, then he said, "Was I in your shoes, I think I'd find that little lady and explain all that's happened. And then I'd tell her exactly how I felt about her."

The sun had long since dropped from the sky, and there was the beginning of a chill in the night air. I stared at the scuffs on the toes of my work boots and then past them at an oil spill on the pavement. Jake was the second person to tell me I needed to talk to Dottie in person, and both he and Granny were people I trusted.

"Yeah," I said, "I reckon I oughta do just that."

I thought a lot about what I would say to Dottie if I ever got a chance to speak to her again. On the drive home I missed talking to her, but I knew it would do no good to call her. As I pulled into the drive, I wondered if my ex-wife would try to use my son against me in the near future. It caused me to remember what I had written on my exit paper: Tonight, I learned that there is never a time when kids should be used as weapons in any conflict between a mother and a father. Kids should be encouraged by both to love and respect both parents.

WEEK 24—USE OF NON-VIOLENCE

Granny used to tell me, you can make some of the people happy all the time, all the people happy some of the time, but never all the people happy all the time. I'm sure she heard it somewhere herself and just changed it around to suit her own style. It seems that this week, I proved Granny's quote to be true.

I drove to Dottie's on Thursday evening after a day of mending fences while I tried to figure out all the perfect things I should say to win back her heart. When she stepped out on the porch, I couldn't remember one single thing I had rehearsed out in that pasture. I heard the screen door shut as I stepped out of the truck, looked up and there she was, just standing there as beautiful as a picture. Her long dark hair pulled back in a ponytail, she stood there barefooted, in a yellow sun dress with a floral pattern that reached to just above her knee.

Rounding the front of the truck, I said, "Dottie can we talk?"

As I stepped up onto the porch, she smiled and stepped into my arms. Her head against my chest, I could feel her crying softly as we held each other tight. We stood there for several minutes, just holding each other. Then she looked up and said, "Yes Hank, let's talk."

Once inside, she sat and listened while I explained who each of the woman were that she'd seen fighting in the front yard. I told her that I'd had no idea either of them was going to be there that day. I apologized for not answering her question when she asked what was going on and waiting so long to come and see her in person. When I finished, she asked me if there was any chance there would be anything like this in the future.

"Dottie," I explained, "I've lived a hard life the last several years. Looking back, I'm not proud of a lot of the things I've done, and there are people in my past who I'd say have every reason to hate me. Will there be fights like that one? I don't think so, but I can't say for sure. Many of the women I dated were scrappers. They'd fight at the drop of a hat and if need be drop the hat themselves. Will there be times someone says something or throws a nasty look my way? I'd say there's a good chance of that, but once again I can't say for sure. All I can do is be honest with you as things happen."

"I can't say I like it," her brow furrowed as she spoke, "but I like you, I like us, so as long as we're honest with each other, I think we could make this work."

When I rolled out of her driveway three hours later, I felt like a good amount of weight had been lifted off me. Dottie and I were good. It occurred to me for the first time how important it was to me that we were good. It also occurred to me that I had never cared whether any of my other girlfriends and I were good or not. Perhaps in the early days, I had cared a little about Liz, but not like with Dottie.

"You know there's someone else you need to go see in person," Dottie informed me an hour into our visit.

"And who would that be?" I asked.

"Your ex-wife," she stated sternly.

You could have knocked me down with a feather. It took her most of the next two hours to convince me it was the right thing to do. Because if Dottie and I were ever going to have a good relationship with my son, I was going to have to have a decent relationship with my ex-wife. By the time our conversation began to wind down, I was beginning to feel like Dottie should be leading a Batterer's Intervention Program.

* * * * *

Friday, I drove over to visit with Pops and ask him if he would mediate. He agreed and met me at Liz's house. It took no little effort and a threat of getting lawyers involved for her to agree to a sit down. With Pops's help, we managed to get through an explanation of who was who in the driveway battle. For some reason, the fact that Dottie had gotten in her car and left without a word made Liz like her a little.

"At least she has some sense about her," she said when I explained that Dottie was the one I was dating and the one who had left.

"Yes," I agreed, adding, "and for some reason, I seem to have more sense when she's around."

To which, she rolled her eyes and sneered, "Fat chance."

I let it go, and after another half hour of compromising and a generous amount of input from Pops, we managed to agree to a truce and set up regular scheduled visitation for me and my son. Liz even agreed to give Dottie a chance.

Saturday, I picked up Luke and kept him until Sunday evening. Monday morning, Granny handed me a list of things we would need to work the cattle and asked me to look it over. After I had, she sent me to pick up the items. Tuesday, I spent the whole day on the chute we used to work the cows. The last time we had used it, I got irritated because the release gate kept hanging when I would try to let a cow out. Like so many things on a ranch, the problem was simple, but the solution was a little more complicated.

The weld on the top of the right gate release had snapped, probably from cattle repeatedly leaning against it while they were being handled. The trailer with the welder on it was stored in the lean-to behind the big hay barn, and of course, one of the tires had gone flat. An hour later, after searching every inch of the workshop for the portable air tank, I remembered I had left it on the back porch of my trailer the last time I used it. A trip to my place to pick it up, and then back to Granny's, and by midafternoon, I had the chute working like a charm.

By the time I got to class on Wednesday, I was feeling good again. Jake was in his usual spot. James was seated at the other end of the table, looking over his packet, and Garrett, who I had learned was not a football official but an accountant, was scrolling through his cellphone. I picked up a packet, filled out the top of my exit page and scanned the room.

"Freddy must be running late. Missed last week. He's usually here early," I said to no one in particular.

"Yeah, kind of unusual," Jake nodded.

"Freddy's dead," James spoke from the end of the table.

"What?" I had heard him perfectly the first time, so why I ask him to repeat himself is beyond me.

"Freddy's dead," he repeated. "Fell off the wagon as they say. He overdosed. The shit got him after all."

It's strange how you can feel grief for someone you've only known for six months, for someone you barely know really. I guess because we were going through similar problems, I felt somehow connected with him. I sat staring at the tabletop in front of me and wondered why I felt like crying. It was a new experience, and I wasn't sure I liked it.

By the time Miz Nancy called us to sign in, several more members had shown up. Nothing more was said about Freddy, and I was glad. I was still having trouble with his death and had no idea how to express my feelings. When we were all seated, Miz Nancy explained that, before we could change our future, we must search our past. In doing so, we would identify trends and cycles and hopefully, then be able to formulate a plan for a better life moving forward.

The first page of our packets was a series of questions about ourselves. They ask everything: did we fight when we were kids? did we ever hit our parents? did our parents ever hit us? did we ever hurt animals? had we ever killed anyone? had we ever been wounded by a weapon? and, finally, had we ever been in a gang?

As we began to share and discuss each other's responses, it became clear that many of us had common experiences in our past. Some had seen more violence at a younger age than others, but everyone in the room, at some point in their lives, had been subjected to violence.

The final three questions wrapped up the session wonderfully. Who is responsible for how past influences control you? Can you define yourself as a male without violence? And can you create a nonviolent environment for your family?

My answers to the questions in simplified form: me, yes, and yes. By the end of the discussion, I found I had an even deeper resolve to build a loving, peaceful home in which to raise Luke, and perhaps even some brothers and sisters, eventually. On my exit paper I wrote: Tonight, I learned that studying my past mistakes can help me identify ways I need to change so I can have a more peaceful life and form lasting, loving relationships.

After class, Jake and I hurried next door to the Neon Church. I was surprised to find Sally wasn't there when we slipped in. The service wrapped up and Brother Jim ended with a prayer. As we walked out to our vehicles, I asked Jake about Sally.

"She's had a hard week," he said when we reached his truck. "This week was the anniversary of her husband's death," he explained.

"Really?" I said, then asked, "how did he die?"

"A drug overdose," he answered, adding, "just like Freddy."

We stood silent, each wrestling with our own thoughts and feelings. "Guess, I'd better be goin'," Jake finally said and reached for the door handle.

"Tell Sally, I said howdy if you talk to her." I turned for my truck.

"Will do," he said.

After Jake pulled out of the parking lot, I sat alone in my truck for a long while, staring at the neon sign in the church window. I thought about the damage drugs and alcohol do to a person. It dawned on me that the person using wasn't the only one affected. I had no idea how long ago Sally's husband had passed, but evidently, she still had some serious trouble accepting it. I'm sure Freddy had family who would be going through a tough time. It suddenly occurred to me, even though I'd never messed with drugs, that alcohol had played a major role in the wasted years of my life and the destruction of nearly all of my relationships.

As I put the truck in drive and pulled out of the parking lot, I made a promise to myself. My past would not define me. I was going to become a better man.

WEEK 25—CONCLUSION OF NON-VIOLENCE

There's something refreshing about spring. The smell of the air as new grass sweeps across the countryside, changing the background from brown to green; the rain washing the winter funk away; watching the fresh crop of calves grow as they frolic out in the pasture. Spring is a fresh start all around. After a long weekend and a busy Monday, late Tuesday morning, I rode the four-wheeler to the top of the granite outcrop and sat looking out over the land. It was beautiful; it was peaceful, and I drank it in.

With the first day of summer a couple weeks away, I knew it wouldn't be long until I was spending hours on a tractor, cutting, baling, and putting up hay for the coming winter. I made a promise to myself to always find time to take Luke fishing and to take Dottie on a weekly date, no matter how busy the ranch work got. It occurred to me, more and more, that I was planning a future with Dottie. A part of me wanted to let her know exactly how I felt about her, but something kept me from really going there. Oh, hell! There'd be plenty of time for that, right?

And there it was, a simple question really, a harmless assumption. And it hit me like a sledgehammer in the chest. The pain started behind my breastbone and rose up, escaping my throat in an unearthly combination of sob, scream, and shout. In the sob, I saw Freddy fidgeting in the corner and wanted to help him, knowing it was too late. In the scream, I saw myself wasting years in booze and bad relationships. I sobbed and screamed and shouted at the fear that terrorized me and kept me from seeing a decent life ahead.

"We aren't promised tomorrow, Runt," was all Granny had said when I told her about Freddy. In my mind I heard her words over and over again.

Freddie was gone. I was not promised tomorrow. I kicked the four-wheeler into gear, wiped the sleeve of my shirt across my eyes, and started back to the ranch. It was time I started letting people know how I felt about them.

* * * * *

Wednesday evening, I walked into class with a renewed sense of purpose. I would become a better man. The lesson for the week explained the difference between taking a time-out and walking away. After Jake read the first page of the packet, Miz Nancy asked if there were any questions.

"Not a question," Jake spoke, "an observation."

"Go ahead," Miz Nancy said.

"Altogether, my ex-wife and I probably spent a good two years in marriage counseling," he removed his glasses as he spoke, "and never once was the difference between these two things explained to us, nor were we ever given these rules."

"You mean, you were never told to take time-outs?" she asked.

"No, we were told to take time-outs," Jake answered, "but we were never told the rules, so what we actually did was walk away, and as the paper says, we spent the time blaming each other and planning our next strategy for winning the argument. It was not productive."

"I see." Miz Nancy nodded, looking around the table. "It is very important, while you are in a time-out, that you focus on what you can do differently and try to find ways the two of you can work together to solve the problem."

The exercise for the evening was two additional pages, front and back, of narratives and questions. As the group worked through those pages and began to understand a little better how a time-out should work, I found myself searching my past once again. Never once had I taken a time-out, but I had done a lot of walking away, and most of the time, when it came to that point, I just kept on walking, right out of the relationship. I thought of Dottie and the path we were on and realized I had unwittingly already taken what could be called a kind of time-out. The week after the fight between Shelby and Liz in my front yard when Dottie refused to talk to me was pretty close to a time-out, except neither of us had really agreed to it. I figured this might be a good idea to bring up the next time I talked with Dottie.

Miz Nancy wrapped the lesson up by saying, "The goal is not to win but to find a solution to the problems you and your partner are facing. If you remember this and use what you've learned in these classes, maybe I won't see any of you back in here."

Before I handed in my exit paper I wrote: Tonight, I learned I can't control anyone but myself, and it is important that I learn to have self-control if I want a chance at a real relationship.

On the short walk to the Neon Church, I found myself mentally searching for the right words to tell Dottie how I felt about her. I thought about asking Jake for help, but that just seemed awkward.

Where the discussion started, I don't know, but when we slid into our seats beside Sally, the congregation of the Neon Church was in a serious one about the meaning of two verses from Proverbs twenty-one. The first said it was better to hangout in the corner of the roof of a house than in the house with a brawling woman. The second verse said it was better to hang out in the wilderness than live in a house with a nagging woman.

I won't say everyone in the congregation was of one mind about the meaning of the verses. As I listened, it wasn't hard to tell who thought they only pertained to women and which members, especially which female ones, thought they were also relevant to men. In the end, Brother Jim asked for the floor and offered a few thoughts of his own.

First, he encouraged us to remember how life was lived in the time when the verses were written. He explained how, in a natural sense, in biblical times the wives nearly always stayed in the home, and their homes were not like those of today. Many of them had flat roofs, so a man could get on top of them. He said it would be kind of like a man today escaping to his shop or man cave.

"Perhaps, the verses are just an encouragement to men and women who live together not to let it get to the point in a fight or relationship where someone is being abused," Brother Jim offered. "Maybe they're just suggesting that people sometimes need a little space, a time-out."

I looked over at Jake. He was staring at me. I smiled and he chuckled. I don't know what he was thinking, but me, I was wondering if Miz Nancy and Brother Jim were somehow in cahoots. I found myself scanning the room to see if she had slipped in. She hadn't. Brother Jim closed with a prayer, and I followed Jake and Sally out to his truck.

"What's your thoughts on those verses?" I asked Jake.

His eyes narrowed, and he looked first to Sally and then at me and said, "I'd have to agree with Brother Jim, but I also think there is a spiritual message in them. In the first verse, the man is encouraged to go to the corner of the rooftop. In this position, he has put some space between himself and the earth. He has also moved himself closer to God. Now, he is in a better position to make good decisions. And in the second verse, he is told to go to the wilderness. Once again, the wilderness is a quiet place away from others, in this case a woman. In the wilderness away from the distractions and noise of the world, he is better able to hear God's instructions. Yeah, I'd say that about does it."

A light breeze pushed a plastic grocery bag across the parking lot. Jake reached down and grabbed it before it could sneak under his truck. He wadded it up, reached into the bed of his truck, took the lid off a five-gallon bucket, dropped the trash in, and replace the lid. Turning back, he smiled and said, "Better get Sally on home," and reached for the door.

Sally gave me an unexpected hug and thanked me before

she slid past Jake and into the truck. "What was that about?" I asked Jake after he shut the door.

"I told her you said howdy like you asked me too," he said.

"Okay." I must have looked confused and I was.

"She doesn't have a lot of friends," he explained. "Not too many folks care about her. When I told her, she cried. Happy tears."

"I see," was all that came to mind.

As the they drove away, I counted my blessings and reminded myself that I was going to do a better job of letting those I cared for know how I felt about them.

WEEK 26—PERSONAL ROADMAP/HISTORY OF VIOLENCE

Halfway through my court mandated classes; twenty-six weeks down and twenty-six to go. So, is the glass half empty or half full? Who gives a shit as long as the liquid in it is Jim Beam? Okay, with that comment, maybe I'm not as far along as I was beginning to think I was, but I sure feel like I've come a long way since I started this journey.

Tuesday night, I took Dottie to dinner at one of the finer local restaurants overlooking the lake. The weather was nice, so we ate outside on the veranda. That was Dottie's word for it, I just thought it was the back porch. We had a wonderful meal, and I asked her if she had given any thought to the future.

"I have," she said.

"And how do we fit in to that future?" I asked.

"Before I answer, I would like to know how you feel about us, about me." She smiled, but there was an uncertainty behind it.

Ain't it just like a woman to turn the tables on a fella? I couldn't remember ever being that nervous about answering a question. Granny would probably say it was because my relationship with Dottie meant more to me than just a roll in the hay. One of my old rodeo buddies used to say, "Nothing ventured, nothing gained". It was kind of a weird duo of thoughts all at once.

"I want to spend the rest of my life with you. I want us to make a home together," I spoke my mind.

"We've only known each other for a few months," she grew serious. "How do you know we are what you want?"

I was beginning to see that she wasn't going to make it easy on me. I looked down at my hands, thought about her question for a moment, looked back up into her soft green eyes and said, "I can't imagine my life without you. And if I'm honest, I'm not sure anymore what love is, but I feel like maybe this is it. And I can't remember a time when anyone made me want to be a better man, and you do. You make me want to be a better man, a better person."

After a second, she spoke, "Hank, it's been a long time since I let myself feel at all. Like you, I'm not sure anymore what love is, and I'm scared, but with that said, I think we're on the same page. I've given it a lot of thought, and the more time we spend together, the more I think about spending the rest of my life with you. I need you to promise me we can take it slow."

"Snail or turtle?" I asked with a grin.

"You pick, smartass," she answered with the most beautiful smile.

The memory of that smile surfaced as I drove to my class on Wednesday evening. I thought about our conversation and how glad I was that we had opened up to each other about our feelings. It seemed strange, that after being married and having had numerous relationships, the concept of honest sharing would be new territory for me, but that is exactly what it was—new territory.

Finding a spot in the parking lot at the counseling center proved to be a challenge. I wasn't sure if the additional vehicles meant the Neon Church congregation had grown or if there were going to be a bunch of newbies in the B.I.P class tonight. After a quick circle of the small lot in front of the building with no success, I slipped around the side and found a space in back of the store. As I stepped out of my truck, I noticed that Jake had parked in the back as well.

I did a quick check of his pickup and found that he had already gone in, so I made my way around to the front. Rounding the corner, I found Frank, leaning against the wall, smoking a cigarette. We each nodded a silent greeting, and I slipped through the door and down the hall.

"How was your week?" Jake nodded and grinned at me as I pulled a chair up to the table.

"Week was good," I said, then as James came through the door, "had to park in the back. What's that about?"

"I'm not sure," Jake answered. "I had to park in the back, too."

James chuckled as he found a seat at the other end of the table, "Suzie Q's is having a BOGO," he said and broke into a hard laugh.

"A what?" I asked confused.

Through the laughter, he explained, "You know, a BOGO. Buy one, get one half off."

I looked at Jake and he just shrugged. I guessed he didn't understand either.

Frank and Garrett came in from outside, both enjoying a good laugh. I was beginning to feel like Jake and I were the only ones left out of a really good joke. "You see it, too," James asked them as they found seats.

"You mean the sign?" Frank asked.

"Yeah," James answered.

"Yes, we saw it," Garrett said, "but that's not what's so funny. Man, we just saw a woman walk across the parking lot carrying two footlongs from Sonic."

"That's strange," Jake said. "Sonic is on the other side of town."

I thought James and Frank were going to fall out in the floor. Albert cackled as well. "Yep, clear across town."

"I don't get it." I was feeling a bit frustrated.

"Suzie Q's sells toys, Hank," Frank explained, "adult toys, like footlong adult toys. What better way to hide one of those toys than in a Sonic… well, you get the idea." The room exploded in laughter again. I looked over and saw that Jake had a big smirk on his face, and then I got it.

"So, if you pay full price for a footlong, do you get the six incher for free?" James wondered aloud, and we all had a good laugh.

Ten minutes later, the jokes exhausted and most of the members present, Miz Nancy shouted at us all to come to the front. Somehow, I ended up the last one called to sign in and pay. As I scratched my signature on the check in sheet, the front door opened, and a scruffy looking old man stepped in. A faded, green Carhart pocketed t-shirt tucked into a pair of raggedy, stained jeans that were held up with a plain brown leather belt a couple sizes too long covered the scrawniest frame I'd ever seen. Gray hair worn shaggy and matted on the top matched his unkept beard and mustache.

"Just 'bout gave up findin' a parking place." He grinned at Miz Nancy showing perfect white teeth. I'm not sure if they were dentures or his own natural ivories, but they seemed to be the only clean part of him.

"Back again then, Catfish?" she smiled up at him shaking her head.

"Yep," he answered and started pulling one dollar bills out of a dirty pocket.

Miz Nancy handed me a receipt, I nodded at the new fellow and headed down the hall to join the other members. Moments later, Miz Nancy followed Catfish into the room, and he found a seat just inside the door. I was very interested to know this new member's story.

"Some of you may remember Catfish." Miz Nancy motioned in his direction, "For those of you who don't, this is Catfish's third time in the program. He has successfully completed it once and was nearly through it the second time when he, well, let's just say, he's starting again."

And with no more explanation, she went into the night's packet. It included three parts, past, present, and future. For each part, we were required to write a half page story of our life. We were to include in the past what had landed us in the B.I.P.

program. In the present, she wanted to know where we were now compared to where we were when we began the program, and for the future, we were to write about what we saw as an ideal situation. Miz Nancy told us to get to it and left the room.

After a longer cigarette break than was customary, she returned and asked who would like to go first. When no one volunteered, she turned to Catfish.

"Oh yeah, throw the new guy under the bus." He stared around the room with a big grin.

"Come on, Catfish," Miz Nancy prodded.

"Alright, then," he looked down at his paper. "I grew up poor. I never finished school. My momma was a good woman, my dad was a mean-ass motherfu… sorry Miz Nancy, I've only been out a few days." Miz Nancy nodded with a stern look and he continued. "Dad wasn't very nice. He drank and liked to beat on momma and us kids when he was drinkin'. When he was sober, he loved to fish. I guess that's where I get my love of the river. I figure it's also where I get my temper and my love for cheap whiskey. The first time I was in this program, it was for slappin' my wife around. She left me. The second time, it was because of a girlfriend. I didn't finish because I caught a couple of guys runnin' my trotlines. I was lit, and well, shit happened. I ended up in county for a year. Now, I'm back and have to start at the beginning."

"So, what about the present and future?" Miz Nancy asked when he looked up as if he was finished.

"Oh, presently I'm sure glad to be out of a jail cell and lookin' forward to bein' back on the ranch. My old boss gave me a job. As for the future, I ain't even thought that far ahead. Can I get back to you on that one?"

Miz Nancy didn't answer but looked around the room and asked, "Who's next?"

"I grew up in a family who taught Christian values," Jake spoke up. "My childhood was filled with love and compassion. It is the values I learned in those early years and the support of my family that has given me the strength to make it through many of the problems I've faced in my life. As a young man, I blamed God for many of my failures instead of accepting the fact that He didn't make the bad choices, I did. Those choices led to three ex-wives and a great deal of heartaches and regrets. In the past, I did a lot of justifying my actions and trying to excuse what I'd done. By doing that, I allowed myself to continue in a failing relationship until I became frustrated and struck out at my wife. Years of poor decisions and bad choices lead to me being in these classes."

"Present and future, also," Miz Nancy reminded.

"Through my recent divorce, the whole court experience, and these classes, I now realize that, if I want to grow as a person and live a more peaceful life, then I must make some major changes. I feel like I've made some of those changes already, but I'm still learning who I am and who I want to be. Presently, my relationship with my kids is better than it has been in a long time. I'm all around better now than I've been in thirty years, but I know I've still got a ways to go." He paused, flipped his paper over and looked at it for a second, then continued. "In my ideal future, I'll retire and divide my time between writing novels and traveling around, taking photographs. But most importantly, I want to continue working on a better relationship with my kids and grandkids."

No mention of Sally, I noticed. I wondered how she would fit into his future. Miz Nancy pointed at Frank, who was seated to Jake's right. "Let's go around the table," she instructed.

One after another past, present, and futures were shared until it was my turn. I liked listening to the stories of the other members, but I still don't much care to share when it's my turn. I fiddled with my papers and tried to gather my thoughts. Miz Nancy cleared her throat and threw an impatient look my way.

"Granny raised me," I shrugged as I started. "Ain't much more to tell there. She is a good Christian woman. I can't blame her for the way I turned out. I had a good life as a kid. After high school, I started riding bulls now and then, mostly locally, and I helped Granny around the ranch. After a few years, I got married, and we had a kid. When he was two, the marriage went south, and everything kind of went downhill until I ended up in these classes."

"Really now," Miz Nancy said when I finished. "You think you can wrap up seven years of carousing in a single sentence?"

"I can sure 'nough try," I shot back.

"Should I ask questions," she asked, "or would you like to expound on why you're here?"

"Alright," I caved. "After my wife and I got divorced, I went crazy. I spent almost all of my time running from one rodeo to another. During my down time, I would make my way back to Granny's for a few weeks, and then I'd be off again. There are always girls around the rodeo circuit who want to sleep with bull riders, and so I'd hook up with one, and we'd spend a few months drinking and well… you get the idea. After a while, it always ended." I paused.

"Why do you think it always ended?" Miz Nancy asked.

"I don't know," I shrugged. "Maybe it just wasn't meant to be."

"Maybe it was the age difference and maturity level," she returned.

"Yeah, probably," I admitted.

"Present and future," she said.

"Presently, I'm doing pretty good. I'm seeing a girl who's my age," I raised an eyebrow at Miz Nancy, "and we're taking it slow. I'm full time at the ranch and haven't had a drink since before I started these classes. I guess I'm about as good as I've ever been as an adult. And what the future holds, I'm not sure, except whatever it is, it will happen on the ranch."

I guess either Miz Nancy was satisfied with my response, or I threw her off by admitting I was seeing someone, because she moved on to Garrett, who sat next to me. When we had gone around the table and the last member finished, she asked for our exit papers.

On mine, I wrote: Tonight, I learned that by examining my past and present, I can see how I am becoming a better person, and by thinking about my future, I can plan in it in ways that will help me be an even better person.

I was the last one to turn my sheet in. Jake was waiting for me when I got to the end of the hall. Catfish was just lighting a cigarette when Jake and I stepped out the front door. I nodded and we stepped around him and headed towards the church.

"Where y'all headed?" he asked as we passed.

"Next door to the church," Jake answered.

"Mind if I tag along?" he asked. "My ride'll be a while yet."

"Why not?" Jake said over his shoulder.

When we reached our seats, Jake motioned for Sally to scoot over one. He sat beside her and I ended up sandwiched between him and Catfish. I honestly couldn't tell you a single thing that was discussed or even what chapter was gone over. My mind was so busy wandering from Catfish to Sally to Jake that I got nothing out of the service. When it was over, Jake introduced Catfish to Sally, we shook hands all around and went our separate ways.

Suzie Q's was closed and the parking lot nearly empty when I pulled my truck around the side of the building and headed home. As I hit the edge of town, I called Dottie, and as we talked, I thought about the future. Was I ready for it?

WEEK 27—SOCIO-CULTURAL ISSUES & TRADITIONAL ROLES OF DOMESTIC ABUSE

Friday evening, my son and I were sitting on the back porch, enjoying the evening air, when a shadowy figure waddled around the far end of the barn and started out across the pasture. Even without seeing the white stripe, I would have known it was a skunk. I've heard weasels move like they do, but I've never seen a weasel in these parts, and besides, I'm told that they're much smaller than skunks.

"Dad, something's out there," my son said, pointing in the direction of the movement.

"It's a skunk," I told him.

"How do you know?" he asked.

His question kind of caught me off guard. I thought about it for a minute and then said, "Well, son, you see how the shadow moves a little funny, actually looks like it waddles almost. Around here there's no other animal I know of that moves quite the same as a skunk."

He was silent, satisfied with my answer, I guess. The skunk disappeared into the darkness and we sat. As I get to spend more time with my son, I'm starting to realize he's a lot like Pops. Like Pops, he doesn't talk much, but a lot of what he says makes sense and has meaning. Seems here lately, I'm listening more and talking less myself. So more and more, I find myself sitting on the porch with my son, just taking in the night sounds. I've really begun to love it.

My thoughts turned to my Wednesday night classes. The

more I learned in the classes, the more I understood how little I knew. It was a new realization to me, and I wasn't sure I liked it. Watching the skunk waddle out of sight, it suddenly occurred to me how anyone who paid any kind of attention could tell a skunk from, say, a cat or an opossum. I could tell the difference between a dog and a coyote at a mile, but ask me to pick a troubled woman out of a line up, and I'd mess it up every time.

I was pretty sure Dottie was a good woman, a good person, but then I'd been tricked more than once before. Part of me chalked the doubt up to cold feet. Now that I'd fessed up my true feelings, I was beginning to worry that I'd mess it up, and if I didn't, that Dottie would.

Overall, my life seemed to be running fairly smoothly. I was spending more time with my son. Dottie and I were moving in the right direction. Granny was happier than I've ever seen her, and for the most part, things at the ranch were going as scheduled. My ex-wife, while not exactly friendly, had been civil. And sometimes, I made it all the way through a day without looking over my shoulder to see what was going to derail my life.

* * * * *

The parking lot at the center was nearly empty when I arrived on Wednesday evening. The sign at the Neon Church was off. I figured no services tonight. As I stepped from my truck, two pickups pulled into spaces just down the row from me. A clean-cut young man in a Wrangler work shirt, Wrangler jeans, and worn boots got out of the closest truck and headed for the front door of the center. I got there first and held the door open for him.

As I eased into my usual chair across from Jake, I noticed Catfish kicked back in the corner. The new guy found a seat at the far end of the table and pulled out his cellphone. I picked up a packet from the center of the table and began to flip through it.

"Well, I'll be damned," a voice broke the silence, "if it ain't Tex."

147

"Tie me down and paint me yella," Tex smiled up from his cellphone. "How you been, Bo?"

"Not bad, and you?" Bo shot back.

"Cain't complain," came the response.

Tex reminded me of me only ten years younger. With his clean-cut face and his hair combed straight back, he looked like he could have just stepped straight out of a western movie. The only thing missing was the spurs. Bo, on the other hand, reminded me of a bearded Castello from the old Abbott and Castello movies. He found a seat across from Tex, and they began to catch up. As I listened to them visit, it wasn't hard for me to image the two of them doing the old Who's On First routine.

I picked up my packet and began to flip through it. The night's lesson concentrated on the characteristics of batterers. Before I got very far, we were called to the front to sign in. I was the last one to be called up, and once I finished, Miz Nancy followed me back down the hall to the classroom. Standing just inside the door, she asked for a volunteer to read the first page of our handouts.

After Jake finished reading, Miz Nancy explained that not all batterers have all of the characteristics. For instance, one batterer might have low self-esteem and be excessively jealous, while another might be self-confident and controlling. Our packet had a three-page list of the different personality traits associated with batterers and a questionnaire to help us understand which of the behaviors we might have exhibited.

Each time Miz Nancy explained a characteristic, I watched Jake make a note out to the side of his paper. As always, he was working hard to figure out what had gone wrong in his marriage. I didn't know exactly how to feel about that. On the one hand, I figured maybe it would give him some relief if he could make some headway, but on the other hand, I feared the more he learned, the more he would realize there wasn't much he could have done differently. But then who am I to say? After all, I'm still trying to figure my own self out.

When it was all said and done on my exit paper I wrote: Tonight, I learned there are characteristics that batterers exhibit which, once identified, can help them change the way they behave. I learned there were some behaviors in my past, that I must remove from myself and never use again.

It's funny how the more you get to know someone, the more comfortable you are around them. On the way out the front door, I asked Jake about the notes he was writing along the edge of his paper. I didn't even think twice about it.

"Oh, well, I reckon that was just me still tryin' to figure it out," he said.

"Well, did it work?" I asked.

"Maybe," he said and explained. "I know my ex-wife and I were both abusive to each other. I know what I did was wrong, and now I know what she did to me was wrong, also. When you're in the middle of a storm, it's hard to see anything but the storm. Once you step away from it, you start to see the rain and wind and lighting—hear the thunder. Making notes beside each characteristic we discussed allowed me to see some of the traits each of us had that lead to the storms."

"So, you think these classes are helping then?" I asked,

"More than I could have ever hoped for." He smiled as we reached his truck.

I'm still not one hundred percent convinced that these classes are all that helpful, but if they are helping Jake figure out mistakes in his past, maybe they will give me the information I need to keep from making mistakes in my future. One can only hope.

WEEK 28—COMMUNICATION TECHNIQUES

On Friday, my son and I rode four-wheelers out to the Granite Point. I rode the older one I'd had for several years, and he rode a newer one I'd bought for him at an auction earlier in the week. It really did me a lot of good to see how excited he got when I told him I'd bought it for him so we could ride together. I spent most of the weekend trying to convince him to do other things, but the new just hadn't worn off the four-wheeler, so I think we probably covered the whole ranch at least twice in the course of his stay.

Late on Sunday, as we made one last trip along the south side of the ranch, my four-wheeler kept trying to stall. It felt and sounded like it wasn't getting gas. At one point, we stopped, and I checked. The tank was still three quarters full. So, Monday evening, after all the ranch work was done, I went to work, trying to find the problem. Turned out to be a little plastic fuel filter in the gas line.

Tuesday morning, after checking the cattle, I made a run into town to get the part I needed to fix the four-wheeler. Once I got back, it took less than twenty minutes to change out the old filter with the new one. I took a test drive, and by the time I got back, I was convinced the problem was fixed. It's funny how a little piece of plastic, no bigger than a golf ball, can cause so much trouble.

As we got into our packet Wednesday night, my mind went back to that little piece of plastic and its importance. Miz Nancy asked for a volunteer to read the first page of the packet. Jake did the honors.

"A common problem with communication is the lack of a verbal filter," Miz Nancy said when Jake finished. She let her comment sink in a minute, then continued, "Too often, we speak before we think. Fill out the next page and then the questions on the last page." And she was gone back up the hall.

The next page had four sections. One for positive verbal communications and negative verbal communications at the top of the page and additional sections for positive non-verbal communications and negative non-verbal communications at the bottom. The questions on the last page walked us through our own style of communication and helped us analyze how our behavior, combined with our way of expressing ourselves, could help us prevent abuse in situations we found ourselves in at some point in the future.

"Okay, give me some examples of positive verbal communication," Miz Nancy said to no one in particular as she stepped back in the room.

"A calm, even, non-threatening tone," Jake offered.

"Using your inside voice," Tex spoke from the far end of the table. "At least, that's what the teachers use to tell me all the time."

"Which you never used," Bo chided, "even after they reminded you."

"So, you two went to school together," Miz Nancy quizzed.

"Yep, kindergarten through tenth grade," Bo said.

"You didn't graduate together then," Miz Nancy wondered.

"I dropped out," Tex spoke up. "Bo graduated. He's the smart one."

"Yeah, right," Bo laughed. "If I'm so smart, why am I here?"

"That's a good question," Miz Nancy said. "Since you and Tex came over when your counseling centers closed down, I didn't have either of you tell us why you were in the classes, but since you brought it up, why are you here?"

"Well," Bo's smile disappeared, "my wife and I had some problems, and the state took our kids. We're both having to take anger management classes, and I have to finish this program if we want to get them back."

"Was there physical violence?" Miz Nancy wanted to know.

"No, ma'am," Bo shook his head, "just a lot of screaming and cussing and throwing shit."

"And how 'bout you, Tex?" she asked as she turned towards him.

"Dammit, Bo." He glared across the table. Bo's smile reappeared. Turning back to Miz Nancy, he said, "Yes, ma'am, there was definitely violence with both me and my first girl. She's the mother of my son. But with the girl I'm with now, there's never been. Sometimes, we holler and fuss at each other, but no violence."

"Okay then, another example of a positive verbal communication," Miz Nancy redirected.

"A compliment," Jake offered another.

"Someone besides Jake," Miz Nancy ordered.

"Whispering," Catfish said with a sly grin in a whispered just loud enough for all to hear.

"Using sir and ma'am," Albert said.

"Saying I love you," Garrett suggested, a little hesitant.

"Which one did you say that to, Garrett?" James asked from across the table.

Garrett grinned. "Why, all three of them, of course."

When the laughs subsided, Miz Nancy moved us along to the negative side of the page. Some of the responses included; cussing, shouting, yelling, name calling, interrupting, and sarcasm.

"The more I think about it," Jake said, "whispering could be added to this list as well."

"How so?" Miz Nancy asked.

"Well, if you got really close in and whispered a threat into someone's ear, it could be somewhat scary and definitely negative," he answered.

"Good," Miz Nancy agreed. "How about non-verbal ways we communicate?"

"Smiling," Frank flashed the fakest smile I'd ever seen.

"Holding hands," Albert said.

"Kissing when you leave or return." Jake had one of those looks I hated to see. "That's if everything is good, I guess. If things aren't so good, that kiss can be a whole other kind of communication. Kind of like the whisper can be good or bad, I guess, the kiss can also be one or the other."

"The finger," Bo said and flipped Tex the bird across the table with a laugh.

I smiled and noticed Jake smiled too, but I could tell that it didn't reach all the way to his center. I was sure glad Bo and Tex had joined the class. It figured to be a more entertaining class with them in it. Miz Nancy wrapped it up by explaining the behavior behind the verbal or non-verbal communication is what makes it positive or negative. She used Jake's example of a whisper, saying it depended on how the whisper was used as to whether it was positive or negative. In addition, she used the bird Bo shot Tex, saying the same finger in the wrong situations could cause an all-out war. Several of the members shook their heads as she asked for our exit papers. On mine, I wrote: Tonight, I learned that the key to good communication is to have a positive attitude and do my best to never use negative verbal or non-verbal behaviors when I'm talking with another person.

When class ended, me, Jake, and Catfish made our way over to the Neon Church. After the service, the three of us and Sally stood around outside and visited. The coming weekend was the fourth of July holiday, and we were all excited about it. Catfish wasn't sure exactly where he was going to spend it. Jake had some of his kids and grandkids coming out to his place for a whole day of horseshoes, tag football, and fireworks. He'd invited Sally, but she wasn't sure she was up to a family as big as his.

"And besides," she said, "they might think there's something between us."

"Nope," Jake put her mind at ease. "I'm open and honest with all my kids and family. They know about you and know we are only friends."

Sally looked sad but tried to smile through it. I wondered if Jake would ever give her a chance. I know he's been hurt bad, but I really think she'd be good for him, and I know he'd be good for her. Like Granny says, best to keep out of affairs that don't concern you. So, I kept my mouth shut.

"Hey, that filter thing, Miz Nancy started the meeting with," I changed the subject, "it made me think about a fuel filter I had to change on one of my four-wheelers this week."

"How so?" Jake wanted to know.

"Well, that fuel filter is there to keep bad stuff from getting into the engine parts, and a verbal filter is kind of the same thing only, it's there to keep bad things from coming out of your mouth," I explained.

"That's pretty good." Jake smiled.

"What was wrong with the fuel filter?" Catfish wanted to know.

"It was clogged up," I told him. "Cost a couple dollars for a new one. I fixed it, no problem."

"Ever met someone who's been through so much that their filter seems to be clogged?" Jake asked.

"What?" Catfish asked confused.

"Sometimes, folks who've been through a tough time find it hard to talk to other people at all. It's like all the negativity they've been through has clogged the filter completely," Jake explained.

"I was that way," Sally smiled, "until Jake brought me out of my shell."

"You give me too much credit." Jake blushed.

"No, I don't," she returned.

My thoughts turned to Dottie. It had taken awhile before she was able to open up when we first met. Seems like she was much more comfortable visiting on the phone than in person at first. I'm sure glad that has changed. When our little group finally broke up, I got into my truck, and as I pulled out of the parking lot, I called Dottie.

WEEK 29—DEFINING THE USE OF NON-THREATENING BEHAVIORS

The Fourth of July was all I could have hoped it would be. Granny and Dottie cooked too much. Luke and I rode four-wheelers most of the day, and even though it was too hot, we fished for a couple of hours in the afternoon. We even manage to hook a couple of good size bass. Neither of us felt like cleaning them, so we released them back into the pond for another day.

When dusk finally arrived, I think I was more excited to get into the fireworks than Luke was. Granny and Dottie sat in matching rocking chairs on Granny's back porch and watched us set off fireworks one after another as fast as we could light wicks. When the last one had lit up the night sky, we built a fire and gathered around it. Granny disappeared into the house and came back with hangers, marshmallows, Hershey bars, and Graham crackers.

I wondered if Jake's family were doing s'mores at their gathering. At some point, Jake had told me that he had several kids and a bunch of grandkids. Sitting around the campfire, I wondered if I'd ever have more young'uns. Suddenly, I wanted more kids and a bunch of grandkids. Not all at once, of course, but in time. Jake and these classes were sure messing up my don't-give-a-shit, you-only-live-once, bachelor mentality. I guess I can't, in good conscience, blame it all on them, though. I'm sure Dottie is playing a big part as well.

The rest of the week and the beginning of the next week passed as usual. Luke spent the weekend with his mother since her family celebrated the holiday on Saturday when everyone could make it for a family gathering at Pops's place. It seemed I had hardly turned around before I was in my pickup headed back to the counseling center.

I knew the minute, I walked in the door Wednesday evening that something was eating at Jake. He tried to hide it with his usual greeting and grin, but there was no snap in the greeting and no depth to the grin. His face was flushed and there were dark circles under his eyes. Besides Jake, Catfish and Bo were also in the room when I arrived, so figuring out what was wrong with him would have to wait until later.

The night's lesson dived deeper into time-outs. In one of our past meetings, we had been taught the difference between time-outs and walking away. Tonight, Miz Nancy walked us through the right way to use a time-out. After explaining that both parties of a relationship must know about, agree to, and be willing to follow the guidelines for a time-out, she asked, "What are some things you do to relieve stress?"

"I like to go down to the park and shoot hoops," Garrett said.

"Me, too," Albert grinned.

"A long walk in the woods," Jake spoke up.

"I take a four-wheeler and ride to spot I like on the ranch," I said.

When each member had chimed in, Miz Nancy shook her head, "Good, so you all have a method for relieving stress. Now, when it comes time for a time-out, you use that knowledge. You don't just set around and stew. You go shoot hoops, Garrett, and you go for a walk in the woods, Jake. But you all spend time thinking while you're doing your thing. You should be thinking of solutions. Thinking about productive ways to better the relationship you're in."

Next came a list of things not to do. Alcohol and drugs, of course, topped the list. Others included: don't drive if possible, don't call people who encourage you to be angry, don't hit things or throw stuff, and don't leave without telling your partner. Miz

Nancy also reiterated that time-outs should not be used to punish your partner or as a way to avoid an argument.

"How long should a time-out last?" James wanted to know.

"That depends," Miz Nancy referred him to the last page of the packet, "at least a half hour but longer if needed. It's best if the two of you have a set amount of time, at the end of which, you can at least come back together even if it's just to let each other know you need a little more time. It's important that both of you are ready before you start a dialogue again."

"How will I know when I need a time-out?" Frank asked.

"We went over the physical, mental, and emotional signs you exhibit leading up to your abusive behaviors in a previous lesson," Miz Nancy turned to look at him. "Do you remember them?"

"Yes," Frank answered.

"For those of you who don't, you might look back on the notes you have from that lesson." She looked around. "And for those of you who haven't had that class yet, we'll get to it."

"Ain't much help, right now," Tex pointed out.

"You're right," Miz Nancy said. "Some of you help Tex out with some signs."

"At first, I get quiet and pace a lot," Jake said.

"I get sweaty palms, and my chest feels really tight," Frank added.

"Yelling and cussing," James said. "I get really tense and yell and cuss."

"Thanks," Miz Nancy said. "Any other questions?"

"Yeah," Jake spoke up, "the last time we talked about time-outs and walking away, I told y'all my ex-wife and I had never really done time-outs properly, but I'm wondering now, if you try using them and they don't work, then what?"

"And what if she just uses them as another way to screw with you?" James asked. "You know, like a mind game."

"Time-outs work well if both parties are willing to try. At some point, it may be too late for time-outs to work. At that point, you have to make some hard decisions," Miz. Nancy counseled. "If time-outs aren't working and you've tried everything you can think of and the relationship is still unhealthy, it is okay to walk away from it."

With that, she asked for our exit papers and dismissed us.

* * * * *

At the Neon Church I slipped into my seat between Jake and Catfish. Sally had nodded when we came in but then had quickly turned her attention back to the front.

"Matthew eighteen, the twenty-second verse tells us we are to forgive over and over and over again," Brother Jim said.

"Doesn't it actually say seventy times seven," a young man near the front asked.

"Yes, it does," Brother Jim agreed, "and if you want to do the math, it's four hundred and ninety times. Now, if you're anything like me, there is absolutely no way you could keep an accurate record of forgiveness from one to four hundred and ninety. I think the idea here is that we are supposed to forgive like our Heavenly father forgives us, over and over and over again."

The young man was silent. Something about Jake made me look over at him. Maybe it was the way his body stiffened at what Brother Jim said. Whatever it was, I saw a tear escape from the corner of his eye. He made no attempt to hide it or wipe it away. I turned my attention back to the front as it rolled down his cheek. Not sure what to do, I just sat there, but inside, I could feel my chest tightening.

The service ended when Brother Jim asked the young man near the front to pray. He did, and we found our way out to the parking lot. Jake was in his flatbed again, and before he or Sally had a chance to load up, I stepped up on the bumper and had a seat on the bed. Jake didn't act like he really wanted to, but he pulled himself up and sat also. Catfish excused himself, and when Jake offered Sally a seat beside him, she opted to stand, saying she had sat too long inside and needed to stretch her legs.

I didn't know how to broach the subject of what had upset him in church, and since Jake wasn't the kind to beat around the bush, I took a chance, and asked, "What's got you down?"

Jake stared at the pavement for a long time. At first, I thought he wasn't going to answer. Sally shifted from side to side nervously.

"Guess it might be good to get it off my chest," he said finally. "It's been a tough week. This week was my youngest daughter's birthday. She's expecting. Gonna have my next grandchild in a few months. Anyway, her mother was going to have a party for her on Saturday. Her birthday was on Thursday, and since no one was planning anything on her actual birthday, I had a party planned for her. When her mother and her mother's new fiancé found out, they gave her such a hard time about it that she got sick and couldn't attend."

"That's awful," Sally interrupted, then blushed. "I'm sorry."

"I got really angry," Jake admitted, "first at the ex-wife and her fiancé, then at myself."

"Yourself?" I asked, not following.

"Yes," he said, "myself. I thought I was in a place where she could no longer get to me. I thought I was safe, and then she hurt one of my children. I let her get to me through my children."

"So, who are you mad at now?" I asked.

"Nobody," Jake answered. "I'm not mad at all anymore. It's like Miz Nancy says, I make the choice. I can make the choice to let her get to me or the choice not to let her get to me. I can choose to be angry or not to be angry. I'm sure there are still going to be times when she gets to me, but if I can just remember that it's my choice whether or not I'm going to let her, then maybe, just maybe, well…"

After a moment, Sally asked, "So did you get to have birthday with your daughter?"

"Yes," Jake said. "I drove up to the city and had a wonderful dinner with her and her husband."

"That's good." Sally smiled.

"Tonight's service was really good for me," Jake said, "I guess I really needed to hear about forgiveness. Sometimes, it's not an easy concept to practice, but it was definitely a message I needed to hear."

"Man, you amaze me," I told Jake. "After the week you just told us about, forgiveness would be the last thing on my mind."

"You're still young." He glanced over at me with a smile. "Thanks for listening. It was good to get it all out."

"Anytime, Jake." I smiled back.

Jake asked Sally and I how our weeks went, and I told him all about my son and I shooting fireworks and making s'mores. He thought it was wonderful that I had been able to spend it with both Dottie and Luke. Sally had gone with a friend from work to a display of fireworks put on by one of the local casinos and said she was jealous since she hadn't been able to spend time with family. Dusk was creeping close when we finally climbed into our trucks and headed our separate ways.

Thinking about Jake, I recalled what I'd written on my exit paper: Tonight, I learned how to properly use a time-out. I learned there are times in an argument when two people need a breather. I also learned that sometimes a relationship is past saving, and if it has become unhealthy, it's okay to walk away.

I hope I'm learning enough from these classes to build a healthy, lasting relationship with Dottie. At the edge of town, I called her. She answered on the second ring, and we talked until I pulled to a stop in front of my trailer.

WEEK 30—CONCLUSION OF NON-THREATENING BEHAVIORS

I always hated Algebra. Simple math I can figure with the best of them but throw some random letter into the equation and tell me it's an unknown and I'm screwed. So, I did the math this week. Dottie and I started talking on the phone about five months ago. We met and started dating maybe four months ago. That to me is simple math, and I like simple math. But then there's always the higher math, the Algebra.

The first question on my mind is how long should we wait to have sex? Things are going great, and I'd love to move it to the next level, but I keep wondering if doing so will ruin it. On the other hand, I'm a little afraid she might be wanting to and be waiting for me. If so, will she get tired of waiting and move on?

Next question; Is it too early to start professing my love for her? Miz Nancy said you don't get to know who someone really is until you've been with them at least nine months. I don't know if I need to wait the full nine months to tell her how deeply my feelings run.

Relationship Algebra. Now, there's a class all guys should be required to take in high school. Of course, not one of us would or even could pass such a class at that age. Come to think of it, we would probably never pass it at any age.

Jake seemed better when I got to the meeting Wednesday evening. When I walked into the room, he was deep in a conversation with Catfish about the bait Catfish was using on his trotlines. Catfish was telling him about a caterpillar that feeds on the Catalpa tree leaves and makes excellent bait. I sat down across from the two and listened in.

"How was your week?" Jake asked when the conversation ended.

"Good," I answered, "and yours?"

"It was good," he returned.

Over the next few minutes, the rest of the members wandered in. Miz Nancy slipped in behind Albert, the last to arrive. As she handed out the packets, she explained that the copy machine was on the fritz, and she had just managed to get the night's lessons done. James said it wouldn't bother him one bit if it quit and we didn't have packets at all. Several others echoed his feeling. Miz Nancy just grinned, shook her head, and ordered everyone to the front to sign in.

The goal of the night's lesson was to create a plan, a plan we could use so, when things got out of hand, we would not become violent. Using what we'd learned in previous classes, we answered a page of questions. We identified our triggers and our pattern of escalation. Next, we created a three-level plan of defense against violence.

The first level of defense was against negative and distorted thinking. We had all identified our thought trigger. Our goal at this stage was to swap one thought for another. Miz Nancy asked for a volunteer.

"Instead of thinking I'm tired of this shit," Jake said, "I'd think to myself, what is the real problem here?"

"Good." Miz Nancy smiled and looked around the room for another volunteer.

"But what if the real problem is I'm tired of this shit?" Frank asked.

The guys chuckled but quieted quickly when Miz Nancy raised a brow. "Seriously?" she asked Frank.

"Yes, Miz Nancy," he answered, "seriously. I'm finding that more and more, I just get tired of the constant fight."

"I can't tell you how to live your life, Frank," Miz Nancy's voice softened, "but at some point, you have to decide for yourself if you really want the relationship to last. If you do, then you have to work at it. If not, then you have to walk away, but whichever you decide, you have to do it without violence."

When I looked around the table, Jake was staring at Frank and shaking his head. It was like he could see himself in Frank's situation, and I had to wonder if Jake had been through this class five years ago, would things be different for him now? Miz Nancy moved us on to level two.

The second line of defense had to do with cutting off our escalating behavior. For instance, in the past, my behavior went from withdrawing to pacing to raised voice to cussing. In a lot of my relationships, what followed was me walking out the door. I didn't want this to happen to me and Dottie, so the defense I wrote on my paper was to speak up, to actually talk about my thoughts and feelings when things weren't going well. I don't know how it will work, but it sounds good in theory. I guess time will tell.

The third part of our plan could just as easily have been placed in number one's spot. It was situational. In other words, we were supposed to list situations that we knew would cause stress on us or our partner. Most of the others listed holidays and family gatherings. When Miz Nancy called for us to share our answers, those were the two most popular answers.

"Anyone have anything different?" she asked.

"I guess I'm the odd man out here," I said. "Holidays traditionally are just me and Granny. I've never taken anyone home for a holiday, and we don't have what you'd call family gatherings. Once again, just me and Granny. But sometimes, in the past, some of the girls I dated were really jealous. It would get to the point that, if there was another girl anywhere around, they'd be all up on me. Made me feel, well, I guess odd, yeah odd."

"Odd why?" Miz Nancy wanted to know.

"I guess, because they didn't do it when we were alone," I shrugged.

"I used to feel the same way every time I had to check out

at Walmart, and there was a female at the register," Jake broke in. "I never knew when something I said or something the cashier said was going to set my ex-wife off."

"Some women do feel threatened by other women," Miz Nancy said, looked at Garrett, and added, "and some with good reason."

Garrett blushed and grinned.

"Yes, but I was a faithful husband," Jake said.

"And I was always faithful to whoever I was with at the time," I added.

"I can't tell you what a relief it was when stores put in self-checkout lanes." Jake shook his head, staring at the tabletop.

"You still use the self-checkout?" Bo asked from the other end of the table.

"Sometimes, but not always," Jake answered. "Funny thing is, it's been nearly a year now since I went anywhere with my ex-wife, and sometimes, when a cashier is nice to me, I still get that old sick feeling in the pit of my stomach. I have to remind myself it's okay to be nice back to folks."

The room fell silent, and after a moment, Miz Nancy asked for our exit papers. On mine I wrote: Tonight, I learned that it is important to have a plan established so that when relationships hit bumps in the road, solutions can be found without violence. I learned it is good to have more than one level of defense so that violent behaviors can be stopped.

The parking lot seemed to have more cars than usual when we left the counseling center. I wondered if Suzie Q's was having another sale as Jake and I walked next door to the church. It wasn't until we were inside that I realized Catfish wasn't with us.

We found Sally three rows back from our normal spot. There were several folks I had never seen before in attendance. I guess some folks would have been pissed having to give up their self-assigned pew, but here at the Neon church, our white plastic fold up chairs aren't exactly pews, and I for one was glad to give up my seat if it meant Brother Jim's following was growing. The discussion was centered around the twenty-sixth chapter of Proverbs. The eleventh verse hit home pretty hard, it read: "As a dog returneth to his vomit, so a fool returneth to his folly". The thought of an old, mangy mutt lapping up puke made me shiver, but the thought of going back to the man I'd been before made me sick to my stomach.

When the service was over, we hustled out to our trucks. No visiting tonight, a rare summer rain, while a welcome sight, made our usual discussion impossible. As I pulled out of the parking lot, my mind turned once again to relationship Algebra. Seemed to me at this point it's best to just keep things between me and Dottie simple. If things keep going, she and I will have been dating about a year when I finish these classes. I figure I'll be finished just before we ring in the New Year, and that's about five months away. Still, I can't help but wonder if I'm making a mistake. I sure don't want to lose her. Damn, getting serious is confusing.

I called Dottie.

WEEK 31—COPING STRATEGIES

I'm not the smartest fellow God ever put on the Earth, but it seems to me that most folks go through life with blinders on. I'm not saying I'm any better than the next fella and maybe even a little worse. Chalk it up to getting older or spending too much time alone or these classes, but whatever it is, I feel like I'm starting to notice things around me that I've never really paid attention to until now.

Dottie and I usually only see each other on the weekends. This week, we had a rare weekday dinner date on Tuesday. It was really very nice. The waitress came by our table, took our drink order, and hurried towards the kitchen, no smile, no pleasantries. Her eyes were a bit red and puffy.

As she walked away, Dottie said, "I wonder what upset her?"

"Yeah," I nodded, "looks like she's been crying."

We talked quietly about our day until the waitress returned with our drinks. She pulled out a pad and asked if we were ready to order.

"Yes," Dottie said, "but first are you okay?"

She bit her bottom lip and shook her head, "It's been a hard couple of days," she said. "Thanks for asking."

"If you'd like, we could pray for you," Dottie said.

"That would be nice," the waitress smiled.

Dottie reached out and took her hand, then as she bowed her head, she reached across the table and took my hand. There were only a few other customers in the diner, and by instinct, I looked around before bowing my head and checked to see if any of them were watching. No one seemed to notice us.

"Our Heavenly Father, Lord, we don't know what struggles this young lady is going through, but she does, and You do. We ask that you look after her, that you give her the courage to overcome whatever trials she is facing and help her to come through them stronger and wiser. Lord, we ask this in the name of your precious son, Jesus. Amen." When she finished the prayer, she released both our hands, smiled up at the waitress, and said, "I'll have the six-ounce Bubba Sirloin medium-well, a baked sweet potato with butter and cinnamon, and a salad with ranch, please."

"Thank you so much," the waitress said as she scratched on her pad.

I'd never experienced anything even remotely like that and wasn't sure what to say or do. My heart seemed to be swollen. When the waitress stopped writing, she turned to me.

"I'd like the ah…" I stammered. When I walked in the door, I knew exactly what I wanted, but now my mind was completely blank.

Dottie reached across the table and laid her hand on top of mine, and I looked into her smiling face. Sometimes, you hear of people having surreal experiences, but you have no idea what it's like until it's you. I smiled back.

Finally, I looked up at the waitress and said, "I'll have a nine-ounce Bubba Sirloin medium rare and a double order of French fries, please."

"Be right out," she said with a smile, turned and headed back into the kitchen. There seemed to be a little more spring in her step.

"I caught you off guard there," Dottie said when she was out of ear shot. "I'm sorry, I didn't mean to make you uncomfortable."

"It's okay," I said, "that was a really nice thing to do. I've never seen anyone do that before."

"When I was going through a rough patch in my life, people would say, 'I'll pray for you', but then they'd walk away, and I often wondered if they really remembered to do it. Somewhere about that time, I decided that instead of just saying it, I was going to do it. I figure when someone needs prayer, they need it right now, not when I'm saying prayers before bed, and they sure don't need to wait until I get to church on Sunday morning." She squeezed my hand under hers, "Thanks for being understanding."

I didn't know what else to say, so I said, "You're welcome."

Dinner arrived and we dug in. I had no idea if the problem the waitress was having was financial or not, but just in case, I dropped a twenty on the table as a tip. I held the door open for Dottie, and as she stepped through it, I reached down and took her hand. We walked hand in hand out to my truck. I'm sure the parking lot was paved but I'm not sure the soles of my boots ever touched the black top.

I was still floating pretty high Wednesday night as I walked across the asphalt toward the counseling center. Jake wasn't there when I walked in, pulled out my usual chair, and sat down. Catfish was visiting with Tex and Bo. The Catalpa tree bait Catfish was using was doing its job, and he was telling the guys about his biggest catch. I gathered a packet to myself from the pile in the middle of the table. Page one, front and back, listed ten ways to help you keep your temper under control. Following was a page of questions and then the exit page.

Several members arrived, but no Jake. I wondered what was keeping him. He still hadn't shown when Miz Nancy called us to sign in. As I paid my fee and signed my name, I asked Miz Nancy if she'd heard from Jake.

"He had an out-of-state family emergency," she said softly and just loud enough for me to hear.

The class crawled by slowly. The first thing on the list was 'think before you speak'. Tex said it was a hard thing to do when you're pissed off. The other guys agreed, and that sparked a discussion. My mind drifted off. I was worried about Jake. I told myself I was being foolish, that Jake was a big boy and could take care of himself.

Number two on the list was 'once you're calm, talk about your anger'. This made absolutely no sense to any of the members. Bo spoke out.

"If I try to tell the old lady why I was pissed off, it's just gonna start the fight up all over again," he said.

"Not if it's handled the right way," Miz Nancy said.

"And what would be the right way?" Tex wanted to know.

"How would you start the conversation?" she answered with a question.

"I'd say something like, I'm not mad anymore, but you really pissed me off when you did whatever she did," he answered.

"Okay, the 'I'm not mad anymore' is a good start," Miz Nancy nodded her approval, "but the follow up, that's likely to cause a problem. It's the wording, 'you really pissed me off'. Instead, you might try to lighten it up. Say instead, the reason I was upset was because I felt like you… See, that wording is not as abrasive?"

"Yeah, I guess," Tex said, but I wasn't sure he was really convinced.

Exercise, time-outs, using humor, relaxation skills, and knowing when to get help from outside were all on the list. Each was addressed, but mentally, I was elsewhere and didn't get as much out of the class as I could and should have. When Miz Nancy asked for our exit papers, I wrote: Tonight, I learned there are ways to cope with anger. I learned several strategies for keeping my temper in check. I plan to use what I learned in future relationships.

Jake's flatbed was parked beside my truck when I walked out of the counseling center. I hadn't planned to go to the Neon Church since he wasn't around, but when I saw the flatbed, I knew Sally must have driven it, and I decided to step in, just to see what was going on. Sally was sitting in the back row, as usual. I slid in beside her, and in a whisper, asked her about Jake. Before she could answer, Catfish sat down on the other side of me. It caught me off guard, and I guess I jumped a little. Catfish and Sally both stifled a giggle, and I blushed.

"Jake's grandmother had a heart attack. He drove his mother and father out to check on her. She lives out on the east coast," she whispered and then turned her focus back to the discussion. Brother Jim was explaining the seventeenth verse of the twenty-seventh chapter of Proverbs. The illustration was that like iron was used to sharpen iron, good friends could make you a better person. I thought of Jake and hoped he was doing okay.

After Brother Jim finished the final prayer and dismissed us, we wandered out to Jake's flatbed. We stood around visiting for a bit. As we parted, Sally said, "Y'all keep Jake and his family in your prayers."

"Sure enough," Catfish said.

I just nodded agreement. When I got into my truck, my mind returned to Dottie praying for the waitress. Before I put the key in the ignition, I bowed my headed and spent a few minutes praying for Jake and his family. I'd never done anything like that before, and I'm not sure I did it right, but it felt good.

On the way home, I called Dottie. We talked about Jake and prayer and our own grandparents.

WEEK 32—LONG TERM EFFECTS OF DOMESTIC VIOLENCE ON CHILDREN

Funk, that's what Granny calls it when someone is going through an unexplainable bad spell. This week I've been in a funk. I'm not sick. Everyone in the family is doing okay. Things are great between me and Dottie. I have no reason to be down or depressed. Life is good.

But then there's the funk. I'm an early riser. Usually, I don't even need to set an alarm. Years of working the ranch with Granny have trained my mind and body to roll out at five-thirty. Sleeping-in to me means getting up at seven. This week, I've had to force myself out of bed in the mornings. I feel fine, so it's not physical; I just don't seem to have the energy to get up.

I love working the ranch. Checking on the cows and riding fence line, looking for needed repairs has been one thing I've enjoyed since my early childhood. Sitting a horse with Granny is one of my earliest memories. This week, I found myself doing whatever I did because it was what I was supposed to do. On Monday, on my way in from the back pasture, it occurred to me that I'd been in a funk for the past several days.

Wednesday evening, on my ride to my batterers' class, I thought back over the weekend, and I realized that I really hadn't been very good company for either Dottie or Luke. We'd hung out, of course, but in hindsight, I don't think I was exactly what you'd call a joy to be around. I wondered why neither of them had said anything.

I arrived earlier than usual at the counseling center, parked, and once inside, found Jake already seated at the table. No one else had arrived yet. He had dark circles under his eyes but the usual smile on his face.

"How was your week?" he asked.

"It was different. I've been in a funk here lately," I said and wandered why it was so easy to express myself to Jake. "I don't know exactly how to explain it. Anyway, funk is what Granny calls it."

"I know what a funk is," Jake returned. "My momma's folks use the same word. I've been in one more than once in my lifetime." He grinned knowingly.

"I'm sorry," I said. "I haven't asked about your week. Sally said your grandmother had a heart attack. Is she okay?"

"Yes." he answered with a nod. "She's quite a story, that one. Be ninety-eight this December. Threw a fit when she was told she could no longer live by herself in her own house."

"I'm sorry to hear it," I said.

"Oh, it's for the best," he explained. "It was a hard decision for Dad and my uncle, but her staying by herself just isn't safe."

"What's not safe?" Catfish asked as he cleared the doorway and realized Jake was back. "Hey, now, how's Jake?"

"Jake's fine," Jake said, "and leaving my ninety-seven-year-old grandmother in a house by herself isn't safe."

Catfish laughed, "Wonder if I'll ever see ninety-seven?"

The conversation turned to age. As each member arrived, it grew and turned into a weird kind of contest. What was the oldest any member of your family had been? Bo had a great uncle who had seen ninety-two. Frank said, as far as he knew, no one in his family had ever made it to eighty. Jakes' grandmother was by far the oldest known living relative of anyone in the room. The conversation made me realize that I knew very little about my family's history. That didn't set well with me, and I decided I need to get with Granny and fix it.

When Miz Nancy stepped to the door, Tex asked her, "What's your oldest known relative, living and dead?"

She looked at him like he'd lost his mind. "Y'all come and sign in," she ordered and headed back up the hallway. Tex threw his hands up, and we all laughed.

The night's material reminded me a lot of the material from one of our earlier classes. This one went into more detail at each stage of a kid's life, starting with how being exposed to domestic violence effects an infant. Each age group, infant, preschool, elementary age, preadolescence, and adolescence, was defined and discussed. As before, the whole idea of me and my ex-wife arguing and fighting and maybe screwing up my son somehow made me cringe inside. I wish I could go back, but as Granny likes to say, sometimes in life, there are no do-overs.

There was quite a bit of overlap as we moved from one age to the next. Often, an indicator that started in preschool would still be present in elementary and might even remain into adolescence. One of the problems I'd never thought about before was that some kids end up having physical problems caused by the mental stress of being around the violence. In other words, medically, there is no reason for them to be sick, but the stress of the situation causes illness. I couldn't imagine putting a kid through that kind of hell and hoped nothing I'd ever done made my son physically ill.

The last page of the packet gave signs kids might show if abuse was affecting them. It also listed a few possible ways to help children through it. I tucked the information away and planned to keep an eye out for any of the signs in my own son. I wasn't exactly sure of the best way to begin a conversation with him about how me and his mother's past arguments had affected him, but I knew I needed to figure it out and find a good time to talk to him.

At the end of the class, on my exit paper, I wrote: Tonight, I learned that domestic violence can have devastating physical and mental effects on kids. I learned that, for my son's sake as well as my family's and my own, I need to make sure I never put myself into another domestic violence situation.

Bo and Tex followed Catfish, Jake, and me out to the parking lot after our class. As had become our habit, we dropped our class folders in our vehicles and grabbed our Bibles. When we started for the church, Bo and Tex wanted to know what we were doing. After a quick explanation, the two fell in with us, and the five us headed for the service.

Sally saw us coming and started scooting farther down the row, leaving enough seats for everyone. She whispered to Jake when he was seated and he in turn passed the information on to me. They were discussing the twenty-fourth verse of the sixteenth Proverb. Tonight, we were supposed to be in the twenty-eighth chapter of Proverbs, so how the discussion had ended up in the sixteenth, I don't know and didn't bother to ask. Opening my Bible up to the right place, I read 'Pleasant words are as an honeycomb, sweet to the soul, and health to the bones.' A young woman in a brown uniform spoke up and told how a man in the checkout line at a local store had been kind to her. She said it wasn't so much what he said as the way he said it. She'd been having a bad day and it made her feel good.

Several others gave similar testimonies. Brother Jim wrapped it up by saying we could all probably think of at least one time in our lives when a kind word had come at just the right time. He said we never know when an act of kindness on our part will help someone who is down, so we should do our best to be kind at all times. Christ lived His life as an example for us, he said, and if we follow His example, we can help others live a better life. After a prayer, Brother Jim announced there would be no service next week because he would be out of town.

By the time Jake, Sally, and I got outside, Catfish and Bo were already in their trucks and pulling out of the parking lot. Tex was standing behind Jake's truck and seemed to have something on his mind. The four of us stood in a rough circle and waited.

"What'd you think of the service?" Jake finally asked.

Tex looked up. "I don't know," he said. "I'm not much of a church kind of fella, but…" he hesitated.

"But you felt something?" Jake asked.

With a shrug, Tex answered, "Maybe. I don't know. Could be I just haven't been to church in a long time."

"We try to catch the end of the service every Wednesday after classes," Jake told him. "You can come any time you want."

"Thanks, maybe I will," Tex said, nodded, and headed for his own vehicle.

When he was gone, I asked, "What was that all about?"

"The Lord works in mysterious ways," Jake said. "I think Tex wasn't sure how it all works and just needed an invitation."

"To church?" I asked.

"Yes," Jake answered, "but more than that, he wasn't sure about what he was feeling, and he need to verify that it was real. Maybe, instead of invitation, a better word would be validation. He needed to know he wasn't crazy."

Fifteen minutes later, our conversation wrapped up, and I headed to my pickup truck. As the lights of town faded behind me, I called Dottie. It didn't occur to me until I hung up and stepped out of my truck at home that something was different. It took me a minute to figure it out. When I did, it was like a weight lifted. The funk was gone. Where it came from, I don't know. Why it came, I don't know. Why it left, I don't know, but I was sure glad it was gone.

WEEK 33—DEFINING PARENTING IN THE CONTEXT OF DOMESTIC VIOLENCE

"Are you attracted to me?" Dottie asked from the passenger seat as we drove to town for our weekly dinner date.

"Yes," I answered, "very much so."

She sat silent. I look over at her. She was wearing one of her sundresses. It had spaghetti straps, at least, I think that's what they're called, and a yellow background with tiny little blue flowers all over it. Her hair was down, and she looked beautiful.

"So, why haven't you tried anything?" she asked, turning in her seat to look at me.

"Like what?" I asked in return.

"Like sex?" she said.

There it was. Caught off guard, I kept my eyes on the road and drove. When I found a place to pull over, I eased the truck off the black top and put it in park. For a long minute, we both sat in silence.

"I like you, Dottie," I said, turned, and looked into her eyes. "I mean I really like you. I'm not real good at this, and I'm scared to death that I'm gonna mess things up for us. It's not that I haven't thought about it. It's just that I want us to last, and I don't want to do anything to ruin it."

"And you think us having sex will ruin it?" she asked.

"I don't know," I stammered. "I just…"

"It won't," she said, and I believed her. I don't know why. Maybe it was the way she said it, or maybe it was the look in her eyes when she said it, but whatever it was, I believed her.

"Okay," I nodded.

"Good," she smiled. "I'm really not all that hungry," she said. The smile got bigger, and she wiggled her eyebrows.

"Okay," I repeated.

"I think you should take me back to your place," she said. "I think we've waited long enough."

I put the truck in reverse, looked both ways, eased onto the blacktop, and headed home.

* * * * *

Wednesday found me mentally in a bit of a fog. I made it to the counseling center later than usual and found there were already several members seated around the table. Jake paused in his conversation with Catfish long enough to greet me as I picked up my packet. I nodded a greeting in return and began to look over the material for the evening but Miz Nancy called everyone to the front before I made it through the first page.

Tex and Bo wandered in halfway through the sign in process and got an ear full for being late. Red-faced, they made their way to the back of the line, enduring mock rebukes from several of the members they passed. If Miz Nancy heard, she didn't respond, probably figured they'd earned whatever they got.

The objective of the evening's packet was to make us aware of what we teach our children when we engage in domestic abuse. Children learn from what they see and will live out in their lives what they have learned. Miz Nancy pointed out that children raised in homes where domestic abuse took place were far more likely to enter abusive relationships when they were older.

After we had read through the packet, Miz Nancy instructed us to answer the questions on the last two pages. Our responses were to come from our observations of our own kids. The members who did not have children were told to use children they knew who had or were living in homes where domestic violence was a problem. When Miz Nancy started up the hall, everyone started writing. It surprised me that every person in the room knew a kid who lived with domestic problems.

I answered each question as honestly as possible but realized quickly that I had little idea about what my son thought. It made me angry, made me want to go all "Fight Club" on my own ass. It also made me realize that I had to do a much better job of being a father.

Miz Nancy returned, and one by one, we shared our responses. As the discussion moved around the table, I noticed Jake staring at the tabletop, lost somewhere deep in his own mind again. When the third question made it around to him, he missed his cue, and the room went silent.

"Jake?" Miz Nancy spoke.

His head came up and he looked at her.

"You, okay?" she asked.

"What?" Jake said. "I guess I drifted out. What question are we on?"

"Three," Miz Nancy answered.

Jake looked at his paper and then said, "To be honest, I've written a lot on each of these questions, but what really bothers me is that now I can see how my actions affected my kids and it's too late to fix it. My youngest graduated from high school just this last year and all of my older children are grown and out on their own. Most of them have kids, my grandkids. I can't go back and change the past. I wish that somehow I could have known all this earlier. Wish I could have taken this class before instead of after."

Miz Nancy's eyes softened. "It's never too late to pass on what you learn here."

Jake smiled and nodded. The discussion moved on, and as I listened, I was glad that I was in the program at this point in my life. That's not to say, I'm at all happy about having to take these classes, but I realize the information I'm learning is going to be useful in the years ahead of me.

When Miz Nancy called for our exit papers, I wrote:

Tonight, I learned that the way I live my life will greatly influence the way my son lives his life. I want to make sure that I am setting a good example for my son to follow.

After counseling, Jake and I walked out to his truck. The parking lot was nearly empty, and the Neon Church was dark. I had forgotten about Brother Jim being out of town until Jake reminded me. Catfish, Bo, Tex, and James stopped on the way to their vehicles, and we all stood around for a bit visiting. One by one, the guys drifted away until it was just me and Jake.

"Had a good week, did you?" he asked as soon as Catfish was out of earshot.

"Yes, I did," I admitted with a smile, then noticed the knowing smile on Jake's face.

"What are you grinning at?" I asked.

He chuckled, "Nothing."

"Is it really that obvious?" I wanted to know.

He just chuckled again, "I've raised a bunch of kids, been around the block a time or two myself, and well… let just say at my age, yeah, it's obvious."

I grinned, then said, "I'm still a little scared that this will ruin our relationship."

"Only if you base the whole relationship on it," he said, "and only if you let it."

With that, he gave me a pat on the shoulder, said he needed to get on down the road, and climbed into his pickup. I watched him go and wondered if my life would have turned out differently if I'd had a father like Jake in my life.

Taking a chance, I called Liz and asked if I could tell Luke good night. She said yes. It was nice to talk to him, even if only for a couple of minutes. When I hung up with him, I called Dottie. We talked until I pulled into the drive at home.

WEEK 34—VICTIM PERSPECTIVE

The meeting room was empty when I arrived tonight. Miz Nancy was in her office with her door open, so I eased down the hall. This was the first time I'd walked into an empty room. It was a little eerie, and I wandered how Jake did it every week. I sat down, grabbed a packet, and waited for someone to show up. I spend hours on a four-wheeler roaming the ranch all by myself, so why sitting in a room alone bothered me, I don't know, but it did. After what seemed like an eternity, but in reality was less than ten minutes, James slipped in, grabbed a packet, and found his usual seat at the end of the table.

"Where's everyone?" he asked as he scooted his seat away from the table.

"Don't know," I answered. "Guess they're runnin' late.

Slowly, over the next fifteen minutes or so, members filtered in one or two at a time until everyone was there except Jake and Catfish. Bo and Tex were discussing the best way to go about getting a medical marijuana card, and James and Frank were deciding which day would be best to get together to work on Franks' truck. When Miz Nancy called us to the front, neither Jake nor Catfish had arrived yet.

The line slowly dwindled as one member after another paid and signed in until it was my turn. I laid my money and my verification sheet on the counter and scribbled my signature on the appropriate line. Miz Nancy signed off on my sheet, wrote a receipt for the cash, and handed them back to me.

"Thanks, ma'am," I said then asked. "Heard from Jake or Catfish?"

"No." came the short, curt answer, and she motioned for the next guy in line.

The lesson for the night covered domestic abuse from the victim's point of view. After reading over three pages of terms, definitions, and legal policies, we answered questions which attempted to help us understand what it was like to be the victim in situations like the ones that landed us in these classes. I had a hard time staying focused. I won't say I was worried, but I was wondering about Jake's and Catfish's absence.

Over the weeks I'd been in class, it has not been uncommon for a member to miss a night here and there. We are allowed seven misses as long as we didn't miss more than two in a row. We are supposed to call in any time we have to be absent. It never bothered me much when the other guys missed, but Jake being gone? Well, I didn't like it. And while the feeling wasn't as strong where Catfish was concerned, I knew it was bothering me a little.

Miz Nancy guided us through the lesson, and some of the guys seemed to have a hard time with it while others grasped it with no problem. Frank said he completely understood and had talked at length about the domestic abuse he had put his wife and kids through, not only with counselors in prison, but also with his wife who had stuck with him through it all. James also had no trouble talking about how he really messed up his relationship with his first wife and had nearly done the same with his current spouse. The two of them were still having a hard time of it, but he thought it might last. As Frank put it, both he and James had come to terms with the assholes they had been and were working on being better husbands.

Bo and Tex, on the other hand, were not buying in. Tex felt like he had been as victimized as the girl who landed him in the class. Bo figured the system was being used against he and his wife. At the end of the class, Miz Nancy managed to make nearly everyone in the room understand that those who had been on the other end of the domestic situations which had landed us in the class were victims. As such, besides the physical wounds, they had emotional and mental damage which would take time to heal. She explained that a part of changing our attitudes about domestic abuse was understanding that we had caused our victims injury, not only physical but also mental.

When she closed and instructed us to fill out our exit papers, everyone sat quiet. Miz Nancy had already disappeared up the hall, and no one seemed to know exactly what to write. Finally, Frank picked up his pens and began to scribble. One by one, the others did the same. On mine I wrote: Tonight, I learned that in my domestic abuse case, I hurt the girl I was seeing, not only physically but also mentally. I understand that I made her feel like a victim, and I never want to put another person in a position like that again.

I walked out the front door of the counseling center and found Sally waiting beside my pickup. She was crying, and it took me a minute to get her to tell me what was going on. Jake had not picked her up. She usually arrived early when he came to the B.I.P. meeting and helped set up the chairs at the church. When he didn't show up, she tried to call and text him. When he didn't answer either, she had a friend bring her over. After Brother Jim started the service, she got a text from Jake's phone. She took out her phone, pulled up the text, and handed it to me.

The text read: This is Jake's sister. Jake asked me to let you know he is in the emergency room at the hospital. He told me to tell you everything was okay. He said to tell you he is sorry for not letting you know sooner.

"Sounds like everything's okay," I said trying to ease her mind, but a sinking feeling was beginning to grow in the pit of my stomach.

"Somethings not right," she wiped at her eyes with an already damp wad of tissues. "I can feel it."

I could feel it, too, but had absolutely no idea what to do. My thoughts went to Dottie. Why, I couldn't begin to say, but they did. I held up a finger to Sally, and said, "Give me just a minute."

I called Dottie, explained the situation, and asked her what she thought I should do. I had not been invited to the hospital. I did not know if Jake wanted me there, and I sure didn't know if he wanted me to bring Sally. Doing nothing seemed wrong, but I just wasn't sure if going was the right thing to do.

Dottie listened to me ramble, then said, "Take Sally to the hospital. If Jake wants to see either of you, fine. If he doesn't, at least, he will know you cared enough to come and were thinking about him. I'll say a prayer for him as soon as I hang up. Call me and let me know how things go, please."

"Thanks," I said, "I will."

On the way to the hospital, Sally thanked me repeatedly for taking her. Truth be told, I should have been thanking her for letting me know something was wrong with Jake. It didn't occur to me until later how worried I was and how bad I would have felt if I hadn't known he was in trouble. Even now, trying to wrap my mind around those thoughts and feeling leaves me at a loss.

When we finally found Jake, he had been admitted and was in a private room. A distinguished looking gentleman and a lady with a sweet, if a bit worried smile, were with him. I would learn later that Jake had two younger sisters, and that this one was the older of the two. It was evident that she had been crying. I introduced myself and then Sally and started to explain who we were.

"We know who you are," the man smiled and stuck out his hand, "It's nice to meet you. I'm Will, Jake's dad, and this is Jake's sister, Ellie. Jake has told us about both of you. It's very nice of you to stop by. Come on in. He's awake."

I shook his hand as Ellie stepped to the bed side and said, "Jake, you have some visitors."

I followed Sally to the other side of the bed and stood looking down at him. I had never seen anyone so pale. He lay perfectly still, hands at his side, face staring up at the ceiling.

"He's weak and having trouble moving," Ellie explained.

"Hello, Jake," I said.

His eyes met mine and he tried to smile, "How was your week?" escaped his lips as little more than whisper.

I smiled back.

Sally asked, "What do they say is causing this?"

"They don't know yet," his dad told her. "He's been spiking a hundred and four to a hundred and five temperature for the past thirty-six hours. By the time he called us and let us know he was sick, he was already too weak to drive himself to the hospital. I drove down and picked him up myself. The doctors are running tests now, trying to figure something out. So far, they know it's not the Flu."

When his dad finished talking, I looked back down at Jake. He was looking up at Sally, and she was trying hard not to cry. "It'll be okay." Jake whispered.

"Yes, it will," his sister said.

We stood there a moment in silence. Thoughts crisscrossed my brain like a runaway tornado. I'd start to say something, think about it, reject it, and move on. What do you say to a man who is not your father but who has become a father figure to you? It occurred to me that his children would be coming to check on him, his real children. Part of me felt like a phony, like I shouldn't be there. Part of me wanted to stay until he was well.

"Dad," Jake groaned and there was an urgency in his face.

"You'll have to step out," his dad said, and motioned towards the door. "Thanks for coming."

Ellie followed us out into the hallway and pulled the door shut. She explained that Jake was having bouts of severe chills, and he didn't like anyone to see it. From behind the door I could hear Will's voice and metal rattling. Ellie offered to walk us out, and as we started towards the elevator, I realized the rattling was the rails of the hospital bed. Jake's chills must have been really bad.

At the elevator, Ellie wiped away her tears and said, "Thanks for coming. It means a lot to Jake, I'm sure. He's been through a lot this past year."

"If there is anything I can do, just holler," I said and then realized that Jake didn't have my number. I said as much and the three of us exchanged numbers all around.

I dropped Sally at her apartment with a promise I'd pick her up the next day and take her to the hospital to see Jake. I called Dottie as I was pulling away from Sally's and told her what was going on. My voice broke when I told her how bad Jake looked, and before I knew it, I was sobbing and apologizing and trying to find a place to pull over.

When I finally got it under control and pulled back on the road, Dottie asked if I wanted her to take the day off tomorrow and come with me to see Jake. I said yes, and we talked until I reached the house. I couldn't tell you a single thing we discussed, but I was sure thankful that she was there for me. Sleep would be a long time coming. I was worried about Jake.

WEEK 35—PERSONAL AND FINANCIAL RESPONSIBILITY

Thursday morning, I dropped by Granny's to let her know what was going on and tell her I'd be away most of the day. She listened silently, then insisted I have breakfast before I left. Half an hour later, I was rolling towards Dottie's house with a full stomach and wondering how Jake was doing. Dottie was waiting on the porch when I pulled into her drive. She climbed in, pushed the center console up, and scooted over to sit beside me.

On the way to Sally's, I asked Dottie about her own parents. Her dad had never been in the picture, and her mother had passed away from leukemia when she was ten. Her grandmother had raised her. Neither of us could imagine how we would ever function without our grandmothers, and that led to funny stories about each of them.

Sally was waiting out front when we pulled up. Ten minutes later, we were walking down the hallway towards Jake's room with Sally in the lead. I found myself marveling at the strange circumstances behind our friendships. For me and Jake to meet, we had to both end up in B.I.P. classes at the same time. For me and Jake and Sally to meet, she had to being attending the Neon Church, trying to find a relationship with God again after her husband passed. And even stranger was the way Dottie and I had ended up together. Now here we were.

We found Jake sitting up in his hospital bed. His older sister, Emma and one of his daughters, Renea, were watching over him. Right away, it was easy to see that Emma was a bit sassy and

Renea was reserved and shy. After introductions, his sister began to explain what had happened during the night.

Before she got very far, Jake interrupted, "In case y'all weren't aware, I'm doing better and capable of talking for myself."

"Oh, hush up, you ol' bear," Emma sassed back, then to us, "As you can see, he thinks he's all that just because he made it to the bathroom using his walker this morning."

"I don't know about thinkin' I'm all that," Jake smiled at Sally, "but I am feeling much better, and I did make it to the bathroom all by my little ol' lonesome."

"Yeah, and nearly wore yourself out in the process," Emma fussed.

"It's good to see you doing better," I said. "You really gave us a scare last night."

"Gave myself a pretty good scare if you must know," Jake admitted. "I'm still a bit weak, but nothing like last night. I guess whatever they put in this IV must be working."

We spent an hour visiting. Jake seemed to enjoy the company but grew weaker and weaker the longer we stayed. Finally, Sally suggested we should let him get some rest, and we slipped out. On our way to the elevator, we met Jake's dad and mom, Louise. Another round of introductions was necessary, after which Jake's mom excused herself and headed for his room. His dad looked like he hadn't had much sleep. He walked us to the elevator and thanked us for coming.

Leaving the hospital, the conversation was about how weak Jake looked, and then Dottie asked Sally, "So what's with you and Jake?"

"I really like him and would like to move our relationship to another level," she said, "but he says I'm too young, and he hasn't gotten over his ex-wife."

"Jake says he's not over his ex-wife, or you say he's not?" Dottie wanted to know.

"He's pretty clear on it," Sally shook her head. "Says he doesn't think he could ever love somebody like he loved her, and it wouldn't be right to put someone in a position where they'd be second in his heart."

"So how old are you?" Dottie was just full of questions, and I couldn't think of a single question to move the conversation in another direction.

"Thirty-nine," Sally answered.

"And Jake is?" Dottie looked over at me.

"Fifty-two," Sally said before I could answer.

"That doesn't seem like that much to me," Dottie stated.

"Me either," Sally agreed, "but he has a daughter who's thirty-one, and he says I'm closer to her age than his."

"Y'all wanna get some lunch?" I asked, which began a discussion about which restaurant sounded good.

Friday evening, we returned to visit, but on Saturday I received a text message from Jake saying he had been released and was back at home. Worried he was staying by himself, I called to check on him. He assured me that his youngest son was staying with him through the next week, and all was well.

The weekend flew by, as did Monday and Tuesday, and on Wednesday, I drove to the counseling center for class. Jake's pickup was in its usual spot in the parking lot when I pulled in. Inside, Jake greeted me as usual. He looked frail but seemed to be in good spirits. I asked him how he was feeling, and he said he was still weak but feeling much better.

"Better than what?" Catfish asked as he came through the door.

"Jake was in the hospital and missed last week," I explained before Jake could, "and where were you last week?"

"You okay?" Catfish asked ignoring my question.

"Still a little weak, but okay I guess," Jake told him.

Catfish wanted to know what happened, and somewhere in the process of Jake catching him and me up on what the doctors had said, I forgot all about wanting to know where Catfish had been. Whether by accident or design, Catfish managed to keep the focus on Jake as the other members filtered in. He was still asking questions when Miz Nancy hollered for us to come sign in.

The night's lesson was on personal and financial responsibilities, and I figured we'd be discussing actual cash; instead, it was an emotional bank account. After reading over the first two pages of the packet, we had to make a list of emotional deposits and withdrawals on page three and fill out a series of discussion questions on page four. Miz Nancy instructed us to fill out page three and disappeared up the hall.

Looking around the room, I was glad to see that I wasn't the only one who was lost. Several of the guys were looking first at the paper in front of them and then around the table. Jake was busy on his list. Frank started to write something, shook his head, and look over at me. I shrugged.

Finally, I said, "Jake, we could use a little help here."

Jake looked up at me and then around the table. Everyone was staring at him.

"Okay, first, on the left side under where it says deposits, put all the nice things you do for your partner. Like I put cook, dates to movies, cards, poems, stuff like that. You got it?"

Everyone said they did, and he continued, "On the right side, under withdrawals, you put the bad things you've done. Like I put yelling, screaming, cussing, throwing things. Got it?"

We had it, and by the time Miz Nancy returned, most of us had the left side filled up. None of us had the right side even half filled.

Miz Nancy circled the table, looking over our shoulders. When she had completed a round of the table and was back standing at the door, she asked us why we thought we had less withdrawals than deposits. After a brief discussion, it was generally decided that we all did a lot of good things in our respective relationships.

I think we were all feeling pretty good about ourselves, and then Miz Nancy informed us that, as a rule, for every withdrawal, it took at least twenty deposits to get out of the red. So, for every one of the bad thing we did, it took twenty good things to offset them. I looked at my list of twelve good deeds and my list of seven bad behaviors and realized that I was pretty far in emotional debt.

Looking across the table at Jake, I realized how lucky I was to be at the beginning of my relationship with Dottie. Jake was looking down at his list and shaking his head. Like me, in his previous relationship, he'd gotten too far in debt. Unlike me, he wasn't willing to try again. I wondered if he ever would.

When Miz Nancy called for our exit papers, I wrote: Tonight, I learned that for every bad behavior I do in a relationship, it takes twenty good deeds to overcome them. I learned it is better to make emotional deposits on a regular basis and, if at all possible, to never make a withdrawal.

After class, Jake and Catfish and I slipped over to the church. Sally had our seats saved, and we caught the last half of the night's discussion. During the final prayer I bowed my head and thanked God for seeing Jake through his hospital stay and asked Him to watch over him as he was regaining his strength. It was sure good to have everyone back in church after such a hard week.

Jake was feeling worn out by the time the service was over, so Catfish and I walked him and Sally out to his truck and said goodbyes. As Jake pulled away, Catfish turned to me and said, "I was in jail last Wednesday. They got me for an outstanding warrant, I didn't even know about, and it took me a couple of days to get it figured out and post bail. I didn't want to say anything in front of Jake. He's got enough on his mind right now, and I think sometimes he worries too much."

"Okay," I said, not knowing exactly what else I should say. I stuck out my hand. He took it, we shook, and each headed for our own vehicles.

On the way out of the parking lot, I called Dottie.

WEEK 36—CONSEQUENCES OF DOMESTIC VIOLENCE

Friday morning after a check of the ranch, I stopped by Granny's house. I found her out in the backyard, tending to her chickens. One of her favorite hens had been pecked nearly to death by the rest of the flock. I asked Granny why.

"Could be a number of things," she said, cocking her head to the side. "Chickens have a pecking order. Every chicken has its place, and once its place in the flock is established, it's hard for that chicken to move up in the order. Now down, that's another story. I figure this chicken probably wounded herself somehow. Birds are bad about picking at one that's hurt. If I hadn't found her when I did, she'd be dead."

"Where was she in the pecking order?" I asked.

Granny stared around the yard at the other hens as they pecked and scratched the ground. "Fourth, I think. The big red hen over there is definitely number one, and the speckled hen by the barn door is number two. That solid black biddy right there was always fighting with her, and most of the time she backed down, so yes, I'd say number four."

"What will happen to her now?" I asked.

"She'll get better or she'll die. If she gets better, she'll have to reestablish herself in the pecking order," Granny answered.

As I pulled away from Granny's a half hour later, that damn chicken was still on my mind. It seems to me, as much as we like to think we're so much better than other animals, we sure act a lot like them. Let one of us make a mistake and just like the chickens pecking one another, our fellow humans begin to judge us, slowly breaking down our self-esteem, our self-worth, and our self-image. It's not bad enough that we are crucifying ourselves; the world lines up for its pound of flesh as well.

The weekend with my son and Dottie went smoothly. The ex-wife, while not friendly was at least civil during our brief encounters. The herd was growing and the ranch was running smoothly. For the first time in my life, I felt like things might be going well.

Wednesday night, I rolled into the parking lot of the counseling center feeling better than I could ever remember. Jake greeted me as I entered the room and found my place at the table. He looked much better. One member after another wandered in and the room began to fill up.

"Thirteen weeks right down the drain," Garrett complained loudly as he found a place at the far end of the table.

"What the hell are you belly aching 'bout?" Catfish asked him.

"I've got to start over," Garrett shot back, "Last week was my eighth miss. I was on the golf course when I realized I was already forty-five minutes late for class. I knew it would be over by the time I got here. So, now I have to start over again. I've been in Miz Nancy office going through the initial entry process again. Thirteen weeks and nearly five hundred dollars gone—just gone."

Catfish laughed, "I feel you brother. This is my second time around, too."

The lesson for the night, after the normal procedure of signing and paying, was an in-depth discussion of how domestic violence had affected us. Miz Nancy let it be known how much she disliked it when a member had to start her program over because of stupidity and then read through the first two pages of the packet. It included the states definitions of domestic violence and domestic abuse and the fines and jail time which could be enforced against anyone who was found guilty of the crime. It also included the number and statute which required attendance in a Batterers Intervention Class.

The following two pages had questions for us to answer about how domestic violence had affected us personally. The first page dealt with our emotions, and the second concentrated on how it had affected our place in society. Once again, I found myself thinking about Granny's chickens.

When Miz Nancy came back from her smoke break, we started with question one on page one. "Who would like to go first?" she asked.

The question asked what our mood was like before the domestic abuse incident and what our mood was now. I'm not sure why, but I spoke up. "Before, I was pissed at the world, and I guess, at myself and the girl I was with, but mainly probably myself. And now, I'm pretty much okay. I still have some problems and doubts, but for the most part, life is good"

When I finished, I looked over at Jake. He smiled at me and said, "I'll go next. Like Hank here, when I was in my past relationship, I stayed angry all the time. I was angry with her, angry with life, angry that I couldn't fix everything, but mostly angry with myself. Now, since it's over, I'd have to say I've become somewhat of a hermit. I go places, but I avoid people and relationships except for my own kids and family. And I am overly cautious where women are concerned."

I thought of Sally and a part of me wanted to shout hallelujah. One by one, each member said their piece, and then we moved on to the next question. The general consensus was that moods, behaviors, and relationships had been bad before and during the domestic abuse and had since been slowly getting better. Questions four, five, and six asked about happiness, self-esteem, and the future. Miz Nancy said that for time purposes, we would each answer those three together.

Since I had started, she asked me to answer first after explaining what she wanted. I looked over my answers and said, "Happiness. I can't remember being happy for a long time before or during, now I am the happiest I've been in years. Self-esteem. I guess I never had a real problem with self-esteem. My future.

Until I ran into this problem and this class, I never thought much about the future. Now, I think about it a lot."

One after another, the guys answered, and then it was Jake's turn. I had been in my own little world until he started. "Looking back, I wasn't happy in the relationship. I wanted to be, and I wanted her to be, but it just never seemed to happen. Now, it's up and down. Some days I'm very happy; others, not so much. My self-esteem bottomed out when the abuse happened. I was angry at myself for what I'd done and for not being able to fix all the problems we were having. Now, it's getting better, but I figure I still have a ways to go. As for the future, I have a bad habit of planning a long way ahead. I used to tell my wife… I mean my ex-wife, I wanted us to sit on the back porch in our rockers and look out over the land when we got old. Then when it all went south, I had trouble seeing from one day to the next. Now, I'm kind of in between. I can see past tomorrow, but I don't try to plan for the next fifty years."

"Cause you'll be dead in fifty years," Catfish interjected with a grin, and several of the guys chuckled including Jake.

The second page took us through how our spouse, children, extended family, and social life had been affected by our domestic abuse charges. To say it had not been helpful in any arena of our lives would be a massive understatement. We also discussed how it had affected us financially. The lesson forced us to think of how our mistake had affected every aspect of our lives. When Miz Nancy asked for our exit sheets, I wrote: Tonight, I learned that the domestic abuse mistake I made has affected every aspect of my life. I learned that no matter what, domestic abuse is never worth the problems it causes for yourself or for others involved. I learned that I never want to be involved in domestic violence again.

Jake was still weak, but he insisted on attending the Neon Church after class, so Catfish and I followed him next door. We managed the last half of the service. After a quick goodbye to Jake, Sally, and Catfish, I headed home. As had become the custom, I called Dottie on the way.

WEEK 37—PERSONAL GOALS AND SAFETY PLANNING

Friday morning, I ran into town to get feed and stopped at the gas station to fill up. As I stood in line waiting to pay, the man in front of me had a problem with his bank card. I don't know if it was the card or the reader, but by the end of the scene, the man had decided to pay with cash and had given the poor lady behind the counter an earful.

I watched him storm out the front door and get into a little red sports car. As he tore out of the parking lot, I stepped up to pay and couldn't help but notice the woman was still visibly shaken. Not knowing what to say, I handed her my money, nodded, and smiled. She returned the smile, but it was a bit weak.

Two miles outside of town, the same little red sports car was pulled to the side of the road. The man from the gas stations stood behind it with his hands on his hips. As I eased past, I could see that his rear driver's side tire was flat. *Karma's a bitch*, I thought to myself as I smiled and waved.

On the way home, I stopped by Granny's to let her know I'd picked up the feed. During our conversation, I told her about the man in the sports car and how he'd got what was coming to him.

"What goes around, comes around," Granny said, "Or another way you'll find it in the Bible is you reap what you sow."

I thought about my life and the Wednesday night class. "So, am I reaping what I sowed now, you reckon?" I asked.

After a moment of thought, she answered, "In a manner of speaking, yes."

Granny never was one to hold back. I smiled at her, and she asked, "So, how are those classes going?"

"Good," I answered.

"Learnin' anything?" she wanted to know.

"More than I ever thought I would," I told her.

She raised an eyebrow. "You keepin' a journal?"

"Didn't you tell me I should keep one?" I grinned back.

"Yes." She raised both eyebrows, and we both laughed.

Monday morning, I was reading my Bible and came across a verse in Proverbs. It warned that a person who digs a pit will fall in it, and someone who rolls a stone will have it return to him. The pit digging, I had come to terms with, and I knew I had dug the hole I had fallen into with my own stupidity. Then I thought about that stone. Even though I hadn't realized it, I'd been rolling a stone for the better part of my adult life. Maybe all young people think they are in control of the stone they are pushing; I know I did. Talk about a wakeup call when it rolls right back over you.

Tuesday evening, when I got back to the house, Dottie was waiting on the front porch. She smiled as I stepped out of my truck.

"Everything okay?" I asked.

"I hope so," she said her cheeks flushing red. "I was gonna call ahead, but then thought I'd surprise you."

"Surprises are kind of nice," I said.

"You really think so?" she asked smiling. "You really don't mind?"

"Not at all," I smiled back.

"Good, then I have another surprise for you." She stood, took my hand, and pulled me towards the front door.

"Another surprise?" I asked as she swung the front door opened.

She turned, pulled my head down, whispered in my ear, "I'm not wearing anything under this dress," and, giggling, fled to the bedroom.

An hour later, she was sitting at the table, dressed in one of my white t-shirts and a pair of my long socks. As I scrambled eggs in a bowl, bacon sizzled in a cast iron skillet. I could feel her eyes on me while I stirred around gathering up plates and utensils.

"I could get use to this," I said as the toaster ejected the toast.

"You could get used to cooking?" she joked.

I gave her my sternest look, and she laughed. "You don't scare me, big boy."

"I'm trying to be serious," I said, "I really could get used to…"

She cut me off. "Hank don't rush. I'm not doing this to pressure you. I want this to last just like you do, but I'm fine with taking our time."

"So how long should we take?" I asked.

She tilted her head to the side, laid her index finger against the corner of her mouth, raised her eyebrows, stared at the ceiling, and pursed her lips, as if deep in thought. Then she looked at me with a grin and said with a deep southern drawl, "Oh, at least two weeks, darlin'."

* * * * *

Wednesday night, I found Garrett sitting at the table with Jake and Catfish when I walked into the classroom. Each of them was looking through the night's packet; only Jake looked up and greeted me. I returned the greeting and picked up a packet. The first page explained the importance of having goals for not letting people anger you and why accomplishing those goals would be made much easier with a safety plan.

After the usual procedures, we began to discuss our goals. The first step was to identify the individual or individuals who made us angry. Miz Nancy asked for volunteers.

"Ex-wives," Jake said.

"Which one?" Miz Nancy asked.

"Well, I guess the last two," Jake said. "I have no idea where the first one is, so she seldom ever makes me angry anymore."

"Next." She motioned to Catfish who was sitting beside Jake.

One by one, everyone told who it was that made them angry. When it was my turn I said, "Lately, no one has made me angry, but if I had to guess who it would most likely be, it would be my ex-wife, the mother of my son."

When the discussion came back to Jake, the next question we had to answer was what situation or situations would most likely cause us to be angry? Jake adjusted his glasses, looked down at his paper, then back up at Miz Nancy. "You know, I've finally found a little peace in my life, and so it's hard to think I'll ever let anyone take it away from me, but for purposes of this question, I'd say holidays, kids' birthdays, and maybe sporting events. Those are the only times I can think of that I'll have to be around any of my exes."

"Are all of your kids married?" Miz Nancy asked.

"Hadn't thought of that one," Jake admitted.

Once everyone had pinpointed who and when it was that they would most likely become angry with, the rest of the class dealt with a review of triggers. Behaviors, thoughts, and physical sensations from prior classes were identified from previous class packets.

At the end of the class, we filled out a comprehensive safety plan sheet, which included our triggers, positive coping skills, steps of intervention, and the names and phone numbers of our support personal. Of course, Granny was at the top of my list, but I also listed Dottie and Jake. I wasn't sure if I was supposed to list someone who was in the class with me, but somehow, he had, at least mentally, become an important part of me turning my life around.

* * * * *

After class and the church service, the usual crowd met at Jake's truck. He seemed to be recovering well. He told us that he still ran out of steam by the end of the week, but he was getting stronger every day. When the others finally left and it was just Jake and me, I caught him up on my relationship with Dottie, leaving out the part about our sex life.

"Sounds like everything is going well," he said.

"I think so," I told him, "but how do you really know?"

He stood silent for a moment, then answered, "You pray about it. Then you do whatever God puts in your heart. That's your part. Once you've done your part, you put the rest in God's hands."

As he drove away, and I pulled the door shut to my truck, I thought about what I'd written on my exit papers: Tonight, I learned it is important to have a plan. It is important to know who the people are that will likely make me angry. It is important to follow the steps of my safety plan so that I never again become violent.

It occurred to me as I put the truck into gear that there are some things you can plan for and others you cannot. Knowing the difference between the two is, perhaps, the most difficult thing for a person to learn. I called Dottie, and we discussed it as I drove. When I parked my truck and got out, I was standing in her driveway. I walked to the door, knocked, and held my breath.

When she opened the door, I smiled and said, "Surprise."

She stepped into my arms laughing and said, "I love surprises."

WEEK 38—PERSONAL STRENGTHS AND ABILITY TO MAKE CHANGES

The fall just before I turned sixteen, I was helping Granny and the hired hands work cattle when I got too big for my britches. I thought since Granny owned the land and cattle, it was okay for me to order folks around. Eventually, Granny got wind of it and called me over to the edge of a big, galvanized water trough we kept up near the corral.

"Runt," she said pointing at the water, "stick your finger down in there."

The tank was full, brownish green in color, and stagnant. I looked at the water and then back at Granny. She shot me one of her famous raised eyebrow glares that meant now, so I stuck my right index finger until the second knuckle broke the surface.

"Now, when you pull it out, the hole that's left equals the amount of authority you have earned on this ranch," she explained. Then she ordered, "Pull it out."

I pulled my finger out, and the water naturally filled back in the space it had displaced. I looked up from the surface of the trough, thinking the lesson was over, but it was never that simple with Granny.

"Now, put the finger in your mouth." She said.

I shook my head and stammered, "Granny, no, I don't want to, that's…"

"Disgusting?" Granny finished for me. "One might even say distasteful?"

"Okay," I said, "I get your point. You don't want me ordering the hands around."

"That's only half the point," she explained. "Yes, I want you to stop ordering the hands around. Most of these guys have been helping me out since before you were born, and for them to take orders from you is not right. But more than that, I want you to understand that ordering people around does not make you big or powerful or respected. I want you to grow up to be a good person, a respectful person. Do you understand?"

"I think so," I answered.

It's crazy the way a memory comes back to you out of nowhere. Friday evening, sitting on our four-wheelers high on a hill overlooking the southern half of the ranch, Luke and I watched the cattle grazing lazily below. It wouldn't be long before he was grown. I felt like I'd lost so much time with him already, and I want to make sure he grows into a good person, a respectful person - a better person than I have been.

* * * * *

At class on Wednesday, we discussed our values in an effort to identify our strengths and work towards the changes we needed to make in our lives. The topics were family (other than marriage), marriage or intimate relationships, parenting, recreation and relaxation, spirituality, friendships and social relationships, work or career, community, and physical health. Miz Nancy explained that it was important to know our thoughts in each of these nine areas. She said knowing how we felt about them could help us make better decisions in the future.

"Let's begin with family," she opened the discussion, "not immediate family, but extended, say your mother and father, brothers and sisters, the big family. What should these relation-ships look like, are you contributing, and what are you contri-buting? Who wants to begin?"

"I'll go," James said from the far end of the table. "To me, family has always meant being close-knit. Like, all of my family, except, a couple of cousins, live within a short drive of each other.

We all grew up together. We have big get-togethers nearly every weekend, and we all support each other. I figure I contribute as much as anyone else in the family. If anybody needs help, I'm on it, and I make sure I contribute my share of the beer on the weekends."

His last comment brought smiles all around the table and several invites to the other members' gatherings the following weekend. Miz Nancy grinned, too, but then moved on.

"I can't say I've been very good at contributing to extended family," Jake spoke next, "My family extends like a series of circles. My dad, mom, and sisters all live within fifty miles, but then my aunts, uncles, and my only living grandmother lives anywhere from a day's drive to all the way to the coast. I think the ideal family relationship would be for everyone to be open and honest with each other and to keep in touch. With social media, like texting and Facebook, there's really no reason not to reach out more than twice a year. A lot of the older generation is passing on, and I don't feel like I've done a very good job of keeping in touch with those who are still with us. I need to work at this area of my life."

"That happens in a lot of families," Miz Nancy said, and several of the guys nodded agreement. "I'm just as guilty as you."

One by one, each of us gave our take on family. Mine was short and sweet. I had Granny and a couple of distant aunts and cousins I did not know much about. I wondered how extensive Dottie's family was and decided I needed to ask her. I was kind of hoping she had lots of family. I figured our kids needed a bigger family than I grew up around.

Marriage came next, and it had been discussed so often in so many of the other classes already that it seemed mainly to be a lot of repetition. All agreed that the ideal intimate relationship had to start with trust. Equality, honesty, along with give and take, also made the list. Answers to the question of whether each of us was contributing to our relationships varied greatly, but all agreed that we could definitely do more than we were currently doing.

Jake opened the section on parenting. "I think the role of being a parent is to be open and honest with your kids. Hiding things from them only causes problems in the long run."

"Kids are very perceptive," Miz Nancy agreed. "We think they don't know what's going on, but often we are only fooling ourselves. Jake, as a parent, how would you like your kids to describe you?"

"Honest, fair, and loving," he answered.

When we got to spirituality, Miz Nancy grinned and said, "Hank, I think you should start us out on this one."

"Well, now," I said and grinned back at her, "spirituality to me means having a good relationship with God. As for is it important to me? I'd have to say it has become more important to me since I've been coming to these classes. I'm afraid, as Granny would say, I've been a backslider for years, but I'm working on it. And do I feel like I'm doing enough? Definitely not, I've got a long way to go."

At the end of the discussion, Miz Nancy asked, "What did we learn here tonight?"

"I learned I didn't know myself as well as I thought I did," Garrett answered.

"How so?" Miz Nancy followed.

"Well," he gave it a few seconds, then said, "these lessons are making me really think about who I am and what I want in so many different areas of my life. I've never really slowed down long enough to figure out who I am and what I want, and now, I'm being forced to do it."

"Good." Miz Nancy was all grins. "I hope everyone is feeling the same. Now, fill out your exit sheets and have a good week."

On mine I wrote: Tonight, I learned that I need to be contributing to the many different relationships that make up my life. It is important to me, first and foremost, that I am a good father from here on out. And I want to do all I can to build a great relationship with the girl I'm currently dating.

* * * * *

When we slipped into our seats at church, Sally slipped a card to Jake. He blushed and slid it into his Bible. Brother Jim and the congregation were going through the last chapter of Ephesians. I tried to follow the discussion, but my mind kept slipping back to the question of spirituality from class. Never in my life had I felt a deeper need to build a better relationship with God. I looked around the little congregation and realized I wasn't the only one. This little hole-in-the-wall church was being attended by those looking for the same thing I was.

Outside after Brother Jim dismissed us, Jake took the card out of his Bible. As he opened it, he shook his head and asked Sally, "How'd you know?"

"Your baby sister," she giggled. "We're friends on Facebook, you know?"

"Yippee." Jake rolled his eyes and kept shaking his head, but I could tell he was enjoying himself.

"So, how old are you, Jake," Catfish asked.

"Fifty-three this last Friday," Jake answered.

"Man, I'd have never guessed it," Catfish looked shocked. "I thought you were maybe forty-five."

After congratulations all around, Jake and Sally headed off. I visited with Catfish until the sun sank below the horizon and then headed home myself. Dottie's birthday was at the end of this month, and I wondered what I should get her. Mine was the middle of next month. Thinking about it, I realized how blessed I was. I couldn't think of a single thing that I wanted or needed at the moment. I had Dottie, my son, Granny, the ranch, and a great life, and it had been months since I had felt like it was all gonna fall apart. I smiled. Maybe I was getting better. I called Dottie and just kind of floated home.

WEEK 39—DEFINING RESPECT

"Runt, how long are you gonna wait before you make an honest woman of Dottie?" Granny asked as we sipped coffee on her back porch Thursday evening.

"We're not rushing it," I answered honestly. "Neither of us is in a big hurry."

"Well, you two may not be," she cocked her head around at me, "but I'm no spring chicken, and I'd like to see some more babies in this family before I go see my Jesus."

I couldn't help but grin. There it was, and just like Granny, straight forward and to the point. I took a sip of coffee, shook my head, and watched from the corner of my eye as Granny turned back towards the pasture, staring off into the twilight.

Friday morning after my normal routine, I rode out to the south pasture. I'd been contemplating a building site for a new house for the last couple of months and had just about settled on one. If all went well, once it was built, I could sit on the front porch and look across the way at my favorite granite outcrop. Several times, I'd parked the four-wheeler and sat quietly. It's hard to explain, but there, surrounded by oak and hickory and mountain cedar trees, listening to the wind and the birdsongs, something would just wash over me. A calmness, a peace, a knowledge that this spot was home. And not just a for-a-while home. This was the place where I would build our home, my family's home.

Dottie and I have been spending more and more time together. On weekends when I don't have Luke, Dottie usually stays with me. We are slowly becoming more and more comfortable with each other. I think we're both waiting for the first major difference of opinion to hit. Part of me is dreading it, but another part of me, the part that thinks these classes are making a big change in me, is ready to see how it goes.

Saturday morning, when I came in from checking the cattle, Dottie was just putting breakfast on the table. Fried eggs sunny side up, sausage, homemade hash browns, and biscuits and gravy covered the dining room table. She was dressed in blue jeans and a long-sleeved red plaid shirt with the sleeves rolled to the elbow. A pair of my long winter work socks worn over the top of the jeans completed the ensemble. Three places were set at the table.

"Expecting company," I asked on my way to the sink to wash up.

"Granny should be pulling in anytime," Dottie answered, adding, "I called her just after you slipped out."

"Guess, I didn't do a very good job of slippin' out," I chuckled. "I was planning on letting you sleep in."

"Yeah, well, I was planning on breakfast with Granny," she smirked.

"Guess I should warn you," I toweled my hands off, "Granny's been pushin' for more young'uns around here."

"Well, if she brings it up, I'll tell her we been practicing a lot." She reached out and took the hand towel from me.

The sound of Granny's truck roaring up the drive put an end to the banter. Dottie shot me her best 'I win' grin and said, "Better let Granny in."

After breakfast, Granny helped Dottie clean up, then said she had business in town. As she eased out the front door, I saw her throw a wink at Dottie. Dottie winked back. The whole morning kind of warmed my heart and made me feel even better about life.

On a whim, I talked Dottie into a four-wheeler ride and took her out to the spot I had picked to build our house. She had put her hair back in a ponytail, grabbed one of my old caps, slid her hair through the snapback, and climbed on behind me. It was the first time we had ridden double. It was an excellent ride.

I pulled to a stop, killed the engine, and offered her an arm to hold onto as she swung off. We stood together, looking out over the land. My granite point rose up out in front of us. She came closer, picked up my arm, threw it over her shoulder, and put her arm around my waist.

"So, this is it," she said.

"This is what?" I asked.

"The spot where we're gonna build our home," she answered.

If you had hit me square in the forehead with a sledgehammer, I don't think it would have had nearly as great an effect as those eight words did. I had not told anyone, not even Granny, about this spot or my plans. How could she know? I opened my mouth to ask her, then shut it again. I should say something kept going through my mind, but for the life of me I couldn't think of what that something should be.

Finally, she asked, "Am I right?"

I pulled it together. "Yes," I answered, "but I haven't told anyone, so how did you know?"

"Hank, we haven't been together long, and I know there is a lot more I need to learn about you, but one thing I already know is that everything you do has a purpose behind it," she explained.

"Well, it has been more than two weeks since you said we had to wait two weeks," I said, "So, what do you think?"

She chuckled, then with a squeeze, answered, "I love the view, and when the time is right, I think it is the perfect place to build our home."

"Still not in a hurry, then?"

"No hurries." she laid her head against the side of my chest. "Let's just let it happen as it happens."

* * * * *

Wednesday afternoon, the neighbor's bull found another weak spot in the fence and came a callin'. Running him back over wasn't much of a problem, but mending the downed wire nearly made me late to class. By the time I arrived, everyone but Bo and Catfish had signed in. Miz Nancy gave me the stink-eye when I eased through the door and stepped to the end of the line behind Catfish.

The night's lesson focused on the difference between respect and fear. After the introduction had been read, we were all asked to tell about someone in our lives we respected because they frightened us in some way. Then we were asked to talk about those people in our lives whom we respected without being intimidated by them. During the discussion, I began to see that there were different levels of respect, some good, some bad.

Good healthy respect was the kind I had for Granny. I realized that in my life there had been too few people I had that kind of respect for, and it bothered me. I thought of Dottie, and after giving it some serious consideration, decided I felt that kind of respect for her.

At the end of the lesson, all members agreed that it was better to be respected than feared. I looked around the table and was amazed at how much growth was evident. Besides Jake and me, Frank and James had the most weeks in, and from all appearance, the classes seemed to be really helping them.

When Miz Nancy asked for our exit papers, I wrote: Tonight, I learned there is a difference between being respected and being feared. I would like to be a respected person. I do not want fear to ever be involved in that respect.

At the front door, Jake informed us that there was not a church service tonight because the forecast was calling for severe thunderstorms. We all shook hands and stepped out just as the first wave of rain hit. Even at a dead run, I was soaked by the time I got into my truck and slammed the door.

A quick check of the radar on my phone told me if I hauled ass, I could get home before the really bad stuff caught up to me. I threw it in gear, called Dottie, and headed for the hacienda.

WEEK 40—UNDERSTANDING RESPECT

"You know, Dad, I've got a birthday coming up at the end of the month," Luke said.

Not sure whether it was a question or a statement, I waited. We were sitting on our four-wheelers, looking out across the pasture. I had been counting cattle and had kind of zoned out when he spoke. Finally, I said, "Yep, I know."

"Well, what's the plan?" he asked.

The plan? I hadn't thought about it really. I hadn't been much of a father for the first nine years of his life. I remember his first birthday; it was the last time I actually saw him on his birthday. Now, I wasn't sure what was expected of me and had no idea how to answer his question.

"Son, I'm sorry, I haven't been much of a father to you," I told him. "I really want to do things right from here on out, but some of this is all new to me, so you may have to help me a little along the way."

"It's okay, Dad," he grinned. "I'm glad you didn't already have plans because I wanted you to take me and Dottie and Granny out to eat at Dairy Queen for my birthday."

"Okay, I can do that," I said. "Anything else?"

"Well, since you asked, afterwards, can we build a big fire, roast marshmallows, and make s'mores again?"

"I reckon I can make that happen," I grinned.

"Good. Okay," he said, then, "I counted fifty-seven head, not counting their calves, and I think that old knot head by the granite outcrop has hers hidden behind that big rock just to her right."

I had no idea he had been watching me or even that he knew what I was doing, but he nailed it. One day, he was going to make a helluva rancher. I could feel my heart swell in my chest. "Well now, that's a mighty good eye," I told him. "You keep it up, and you're liable to turn into a rancher someday."

"That's my plan," he grinned, "a rancher just like you."

There are moments in a person's life that are priceless. They are rare. This was one of mine. If I had any doubt left in me that I would mess up again, it disappeared in that instant. I had not always been the best example for my son, but I knew I would be for the rest of my life. I knew it like I'd never known anything before in my life.

* * * * *

Somewhere along the way, I had lost all respect for myself. How or when it disappeared, I couldn't tell you, but Wednesday's class made me realize it had been a long time since I'd had any self-respect. After the first two pages of introductory material, Miz Nancy instructed us to answer the questions on the following two pages and then disappeared up the hall.

Five minutes later, she strolled back in with papers in her hands. In a quick round-the-table session, we discussed the questions we had answered, and then she handed each of us an additional page. It was a letter of respect. The beginnings of nine sentences were given and we were required to finish each.

"Take your time," Miz Nancy smiled as the assignment began to sink in. "Think carefully about what you are going to write. Each of you will read your letter out loud and then hand it in for me to look over."

She disappeared once again. When she returned, most of us had finished our letters. Mine read as follows:

210

Dear *Liz,*

When I was a little boy, what I learned about respect was that *everyone deserves to be respected, and I should be respectful to everyone.*

I used to think respect meant *if a person respected me, they would be nice to me.*

Now I know *no one is nice all the time, and respect is something you earn.*

I am sorry for *the way I treated you. Especially, the way I spoke down and cursed you.*

In the future I will *try to be respectful and do a better job of communicating with you about our son.*

I want you to know how much *I appreciate our son and that I am very thankful that you are a good mother to him.*

I want our son to learn from me *that respect is something you always give to the mother of your children.*

I respect you for *the way you have raised our child, for putting up with me as long as you did, and for the way you have handled this last year of me trying to get to know our son better.*

I respect myself for *the improvement I have made in myself and my life since I started the B.I.P. classes.*

Sincerely,

Hank

When Miz Nancy returned and asked for a volunteer, I said, "I'll go first," and began to read. As soon as I finished and before Miz Nancy had even had time to prompt, Bo started reading his. Bo finished and Tex read, then Garrett, then James, and so on. Not once did Miz Nancy have to asked someone to read. I began to realize that this exercise was allowing each of us to express something from deep down inside that we all felt the need to express but, for whatever reason, could not. Catfish read and then the only one left was Jake. At first, I thought he didn't know he was the only one left. Then he picked up his glasses from the table and put them on.

As Jake read, I watched his face across the table. The last time we talked he still hadn't had any contact with his ex-wife. It was very likely, he would never again talk to her. It was like he knew this was as close as he would ever come to actually telling her how sorry he was for the pain he had caused and how much he appreciated her as a mother. When he finished, I looked down at my own letter, afraid if his eye met mine we'd both start bawling. Now, wouldn't that be a sight, a bunch of full-grown men in a B.I.P class blubbering like a bunch of saps?

On my exit paper, I wrote: Tonight, I learned that just because you give respect doesn't mean you will always get respect. Respect is something you earn. And that I should always do all I can to be respectful.

Catfish was waiting just outside the center doors when Jake and I stepped out. He knocked the cherry from the end of the cigarette he'd been smoking and fell in with us as we started for the Neon Church. Our class must have run longer than usually, because we were barely seated before Brother Jim started wrapping up the discussion on the fifth chapter of Matthew.

After the church service, I caught Jake and Sally in the parking lot.

"Jake, my son's birthday is coming up, and I was wondering if you could help me with an idea of what to get him," I said.

"Really, now that's interesting," Jake smiled. "My youngest son has a birthday coming up as well. So how old is yours going to be?"

"He'll be ten," I answered.

"Well, every boy is different, so you'll have to decide for yourself," he said, "but I bought my boys their first rifles and a good hunting knife when they turned ten. Does he like to hunt?"

"He likes the outdoors. I don't know if he'd want to hunt or not. Until these classes are over, we can't be around guns, and I sure can't buy him one," I reminded him.

"You're right," he shook his head. "Maybe another year on the gun then, but the knife and perhaps a good hatchet."

I thought about it for a minute and I liked it. I thanked him and headed for my truck. On the way out of the parking lot, I called Dottie. We were still discussing the pros and cons of giving a ten-year-old a hatchet and knife when I pulled into the drive.

WEEK 41—CONCLUSION OF RESPECT

"Hank, I'm not getting any younger," Granny stated in her usual matter-of-fact tone. "It's time for me to hand over the reins."

Bright yellow egg stain on the empty white plate in front of me was the focal point my eyes fixed on. I nodded to let her know that I had heard and understood, but inside of me, an emotional cyclone was threatening. When she had called early and asked me to come to breakfast after morning chores, saying that we needed to talk, I figured it had something to do with buying and selling this year's calf crop. I was not prepared.

It is one thing to think about what you would do if you were in charge, it is another thing entirely to actually be in charge. I guess I figured that I would feel all grown up and somehow superior. I didn't. I felt unsure. I felt unready. In that moment, I realized my Granny was the strongest person I'd ever met. When my grandfather died, she had just picked up the reins and ran with them. Never once did I see her cry. Never once did I hear her complain.

"I appreciate it, Granny," I said when I finally found my voice, "but are you sure I'm ready?"

"Runt, you're ready," she answered quickly, then smiled. "You know I've been waiting for years now, waiting for you to be ready. I almost handed it all over to you when you got married, but something told me to wait. After your divorce, you went kind of crazy for a while there, so I guess it's a good thing I waited. Things are coming together for you, and I think this ranch is the final piece that's missing. It has always been yours. Now, it's time for you to take full responsibility for it."

"Granny, this place will always be yours in my heart," I told her, "and I'm glad you think I'm ready, but I'd sure like to be able to run things by you. If that's okay?"

"I wouldn't have it any other way." She picked up her plate, stood, leaned over and kissed me on the top of my head, and headed for the sink.

The knowledge that I was now in charge of the ranch just didn't seem real to me, so I kept it to myself. I spent the weekend doing my usual routine. I spent time with Dottie, spent time with my son, but found myself stopping by Granny's more often than normal. It was a strange week, and when I pulled into the parking lot at the counseling center for class Wednesday night, I still hadn't told anybody about my conversation with Granny.

The night's lesson concentrated on helping us build a normal, healthy family. After some of the usual reading materials, we discussed the ways each of us had been disrespectful to the person whom we had harmed to get placed in the class. Several of the guys posed questions about the disrespect they had suffered at the hands of those they had abused. Miz Nancy was quick to explain our focus should be on ourselves, and that continuing to use other's actions as an excuse for what we had done was not going to help us grow.

The final page of the lesson was a list of twelve characteristics a family should have to be healthy. Most of the attributes were worded in a very formal manner. As we went through them, I started a list of my own in the margin. My list was somewhat simplified. It read:

1. Everyone has what they need, physically, mentally, and spiritually.
2. Everyone gets to make mistakes.
3. Everyone gets to express their feelings.
4. Problems get fixed so they don't keep coming back around.
5. Within reason, everyone's feelings, needs, and wants are respected.

6. Boundaries are clear but flexible.
7. Everyone has the right to ask for help.
8. Everyone is accountable for his or her own actions.
9. No talking behind each other's backs.
10. If it ain't your problem, leave it alone.
11. Give advice when necessary, but let'em figure stuff out themselves now and then.
12. Don't be afraid of asking outsiders for help if it's needed.

It was a good list, and I decided that when I got the time, I'd do a better job of it and find a place to hang it in the house. I figured if I had it close to refer to, maybe I wouldn't make as many mistakes along the way. On my exit paper, I wrote: Tonight, I learned there are some common qualities that normal, healthy families share. I learned what they are and am now planning to do my best to make them a part of the family I am in the process of building.

* * * * *

Sally had our seats saved when we slipped into the church. Brother Jim was responding to a question from one of the members. While he was doing so, Sally leaned around Jake and, in a whisper, explained that the discussion was over the twentieth verse of Proverbs thirteen. I flipped my Bible open to it. It seemed pretty simple to me. If you run with a bad crowd, trouble is gonna find you; if you hang with the smart guys, you might just get a bit smarter yourself.

Throughout the service, my mind kept drifting back to my visit with Granny. I was still at a loss as to what she saw in me that made her think I was ready. Brother Jim ended with his usual prayer and dismissed us. I wandered out to the parking lot with Sally and Jake. The other guys shook hands and disappeared.

"Something on your mind?" Jake asked.

"That easy to tell?" I asked in return.

He chuckled, "Son, you've been distracted all night. Yes, it's easy to tell. Want to talk about it?"

I thought about it for a minute, then said, "Yep, I think I do." I took a deep breath and poured it all out to him. He and Sally listened, each nodding now and then, until finally I had spilled it all. The ranch, my feelings about it, my fears, and how they were the first ones I had told about it.

When I finished, Jake smiled and said, "First, let me say, congratulations. Then I'd like to say I think your Granny is a very wise lady. I've known you nearly a year now, and I've watched you grow and change. I would trust you with my place, and I'm not a real trusting person, so I believe your Granny is right to think you're ready."

Sally waited until he finished speaking, then with a huge smile of her own, said, "Hank, I'm so proud for you, and happy for you and Dottie. Congratulations."

"Thank you both for listening." I felt like a great weight had lifted. It made no sense to me at all. I guess it still doesn't, but I'm learning that not everything always makes sense.

"So, what did you think of the service tonight?" Jake asked, changing the subject.

The question caught me off guard and I stammered, "I didn't get as much out of the service as I should have, but I guess it's like Granny says sometimes, if you root with the hogs, expect to get some mud on you."

Sally giggled, "My grandpa used to say something similar about dogs and fleas."

"I've read that verse many times," Jake said, "heard it preached on quite a few times as well, but tonight, I had a different thought on it. Usually, the verse is taken as a warning to be careful not to be running with the wrong crowd, but the part about a person who walks with the wise becomes wise really spoke to me. We all have people we influence. People we are an example to, like my children and your son. It made me wonder if what my children are learning from me is wisdom."

I didn't know what to say when he finished talking, so I just nodded in agreement. Sally was doing the same. A few minutes more and we shook hands. I called Dottie on the way out of town and asked her if she was up for a surprise. She told me she was, and I headed for her place. It was time to tell her about the ranch, and as I drove, the excitement grew.

WEEK 42—DEFINING SUPPORT AND TRUST

There have been so many times in my life where I simply walked away to avoid a possible bad situation. For reasons beyond my understanding, my ex-wife decided to invite us to Luke's actual party. We had already celebrated with him at the Dairy Queen and Granny's house, and I wanted to politely decline the invitation, but Granny would have none of it. So, as Granny, Dottie, and I pulled to a stop in front of the local trampoline/pizza place birthday party combination warehouse, I felt a bit of my old self rear up, and if it hadn't been for my son, I might well have hightailed it. The thought of disappointing him kept me from doing anything stupid.

Granny was as giddy as a five-year-old, but I could tell that Dottie was as nervous as I was, and I couldn't really blame her. The first and last time Dottie had laid eyes on my ex-wife, she had busted my head open with a rock and was in a standoff with my ex-girlfriend. Not exactly someone the normal person would be overanxious to meet again.

"Come on you two slow pokes," Granny hooked an arm in each of ours and headed for the door, "we're gonna miss the party if y'all don't get a move on."

We were twenty minutes early, so being afraid of missing the party was a bit of a stretch, but that's Granny. At the door, we were met by Pops who directed us up a set of stairs. They led to a hallway, and off the hallway were three doors. The last door had a big sign with Luke's name and a bunch of balloons attached to it. Granny headed down the hall like she was gonna miss out on the cake and ice cream. There was nothing for Dottie and me to do but follow.

As soon as we stepped into the room, Liz turned from the table where she was laying out napkins. Granny never missed a step. She walked right over and gave her a hug and asked how she was doing. Before I had a chance to speak, Granny turned to Dottie and motioned her forward.

"I don't think you two have been properly introduced," she said. The next thing I knew, I was being shooed off to find the birthday boy.

As the door closed behind me, I heard Dottie ask, "What can I do to help set up?"

The party went off without a hitch. I spent most of it visiting with Pops while the two of us watched the kids do various acrobatic tricks on the numerous trampolines. By the time everyone was called back to the room for pizza, presents, and cake, I was nearly worn out from just watching.

Dottie and Granny insisted on helping clean everything up. Pops and I were appointed as party pack mules and hauled everything out to his truck that was to be transported to Liz's house. When everything was packed and a last check had been made to ensure nothing was missed, Liz stopped me.

"Hank, she's a keeper," she said indicating Dottie with a nod of her head, "Try not to screw it up."

"I'll do my best," I promised.

On the way back home, Granny spoke, from the back seat, "Well, I thought that went pretty good."

"Yes, it did," Dottie agreed. "I think everything is going to be okay."

I nodded but kept my thoughts to myself. I figured one good birthday party did not a perfect relationship make, but I was hopeful. I was also wondering how Jake's son's birthday would go. If I understood Jake right, it was just a couple of days after my son's.

* * * * *

Miz Nancy read through the first page of the night's lesson as we followed along. She was dressed to the T. Her button-up-the-front silk blouse tucked neatly into a pair of form-fitting, dark gray slacks was enough to shock the bunch of us when she stepped out of her tiny office and called us to the front to sign in. Her usual Nike runners had been replaced by a pair of black flats that clicked as she had walked around the table handing out our packets, and the sound reminded me of one of my high school English teachers. But the most noticeable difference was the way her hair framed her face. It was the first time we had seen her with her hair down. I think maybe she had on makeup, too, but if she did, it was the just enough to enhance her cheeks.

"Damn, Miz Nancy," Catfish spoke aloud what we were all thinking as we lined up.

Miz Nancy spun around and gave us a look that nearly melted us where we stood. "Next person who says something gets to go home, and I'm counting it as an unexcused absence," she announced with a look that dared anyone to try her.

"Sorry, Miz Nancy," Catfish stammered. "Just wondering what's up?"

"I had a meeting with the big bosses," she said, rolling her eyes and shaking her head. "It ran late, and I didn't have time to go home and change."

When she finished reading, she gave her usual instructions to answer the questions on the following pages and disappeared. The questions were designed to make us think about what made us trust someone, or what made us not trust someone. By the time I'd finish both pages, Miz Nancy still had not returned. I placed my pen beside my packet, leaned back, and looked around the table.

Bo had finished and was waiting patiently. Everyone else was still working. Jake seemed off in his own world again. I had to wonder if something had happened to him this week. When he finished, he caught me watching him, shot me a weak smile and raised an eyebrow.

Catfish was the last one to finish. He laid his pen down, looked past me up the hall, and then in a half whisper said, "Miz Nancy looks hot as hell tonight, huh?"

Several of the guys chuckled. Before anyone could respond, the sound of her flats clicking on the tile floor silenced the room. There was no way she heard anything Catfish said, but he was blushing like a twelve-year-old boy who'd just got his first kiss when she stepped back through the door. This brought on a bout of snickers.

For the next twenty minutes, we answered the questions in no particular order. When we reached the last of them, there was still time left. I thought perhaps we would get to the church a little earlier tonight, but then Miz Nancy told us to turn our papers over to the back and write, in our own words, what we had learned about trust. Without any additional instructions, she turned and left the room again.

I looked around the table. No one seemed to know what to do. Everyone sat staring at the blank page in front of them. Finally, Jake picked up his pen and began to write. Slowly, everyone else followed suit, until everyone was scribbling away.

Fifteen minutes later, Miz Nancy came through the door. "Who wants to go first?"

Without hesitation, Jake started, "I pictured trust as a liquid. If you think of a person as a glass bottle, then the more you trust someone, the more liquid there is inside. But if something happens, say like a crack in the bottle, the trust starts to leak out. With time and effort, the bottle can be repaired, like maybe with supergluing, or the trust can break down, the cracks continue to widen, and eventually the bottle can't be repaired, so all the trust just runs out."

"That's pretty good, Jake," Miz Nancy smiled. "Anyone else?"

"Well, I don't know nothin' about trust in a bottle," Catfish laughed. "I prefer whiskey in my bottles, but I did write some stuff here about trust."

A half hour later, when everyone had spoken, Miz Nancy released us. On my exit paper, I wrote: Tonight, I learned that trust is hard to get back once you've lost it. I learned that there are times it is possible to find trust again once it has been lost and other times when it is not possible. In my future relationships, I want to do all I can to ensure there is always trust.

As soon as our papers were turned in, we hustled to the Neon Church. Once again, our class had run so long, that we made it into the church just in time for the final prayer and dismissal. Sally filled us in on what we'd missed while the rest of the congregation filed out. Brother Jim stopped by and asked us how we were doing but seemed in a hurry himself, so we all headed towards the front. Outside, I asked Jake how his son's birthday went.

"It went well," he said. "Took him out to dinner on his birthday, and then he had some of his buddies over on the weekend. How did it go with your son?"

I told him about the party and how the ex-wife and Dottie had gotten along. He listened and smiled.

"I'm a little worried though," I admitted. "I'm new at all this, and I'm afraid it won't always be this easy."

"That was a statement," Jake said after a minute, "but it sounded like there was a question in there somewhere."

"Yeah," I grinned.

"Wish I could tell you it would always be all peaches and cream, but that's never been my experience," he shook his head. "I am glad everything is going well for you and wish you all the best, though."

"Yeah," I said, "that's kind of what I thought, too. So, how's everything with your situation?"

"About as good as can be expected," he said. "My latest ex and her new fiancé have decided that my kids need to decide whether they want a relationship with me or them. It's kind of hard on the kids."

"The fiancé?" I raised an eyebrow. "Been in the picture, what, six months?"

Jake laughed, "Something like that, but you know I can't really blame him. Twenty years ago, I was in his shoes. He thinks he's saving her from me, just like I thought I was saving her from her first ex-husband."

In the time we'd been talking, the parking lot had cleared out. The only vehicles left were mine and Jakes. I suddenly realized that Sally hadn't followed us out to Jake's truck.

"Where'd Sally go?" I asked.

Jake smiled. "Brother Jim gave her a ride tonight."

My look must have said it all, because he began to chuckle, "Sally and I were only ever going to be friends. She was too young for me, and I'm much too old to sweep in on a white horse and save the damsel in distress."

"But Brother Jim is older than you are?" I said, still confused.

"Yeah," Jake said. "He's just giving her a ride home. She's actually seeing someone now, and I didn't feel right taking her, knowing how she feels about me."

"So, you knew she was interested?" I grinned.

"I'm old, Hank," he laughed, "not stupid."

We stood there chuckling, just two men who were finding a little peace in a world that had not shown them any peace in quite some time. I'm not sure if I can even explain the change I saw in Jake, but I was sure glad to see it.

On the way out of the parking lot, I called Dottie. I told her about Jake and Sally and the change I was seeing in him. I talked to her all the way home.

WEEK 43—USE OF SUPPORT AND TRUST

On Friday, I hauled seven yearling steers and an old cull cow to the auction. I'd planned to unload and head home. The front office is good about sending any checks that haven't been picked up out with Monday's mail and, I was in no hurry to get paid.

I unloaded, tossed my receipt in the console, and was making my way out of the gravel parking lot when I spotted Jake's old flatbed. Why it surprised me I don't know, but it did. I found a place to park clear out by the edge of the road, locked the truck up, and meandered in and out between trucks and trailers towards the front doors.

Inside, I found Jake leaned back against the wall on the top set of risers. He saw me coming and broke out in his usual smile.

"How's your week going?" he asked when I slid in beside him.

"Pretty good," I answered, then asked, "What are you doin' here?"

"Window shoppin'," he chuckled.

"What?" I shook my head.

"Window shoppin'." He motioned to the cattle being moved through the arena. "Just lookin' at what I hope to buy someday."

"You in the market for cattle?" I looked from the arena to him, not sure if he was being serious.

"Not just yet," he admitted. "I'm just lookin'. I put a bid in on the place I'm renting. If it goes through, I'll own eighty acres. There's another three hundred adjacent to it I think I can lease in another six months, so I'm window shoppin'."

"When you're ready, let me know," I suggested. "I could help you find some stock."

"Thanks, Hank. I'd appreciate that." The next bunch of cattle came into the arena and he turned his attention back to the auctioneer.

I hung around a little longer, watching, then shook his hand and eased through the growing crowd. Outside, I found my way back to the truck and headed home. Somehow, Jake as a rancher had never crossed my mind. It occurred to me that, as much as we knew about each other, we really didn't know each other all that well. I knew he was an educated man and he worked inside. In my mind, he sat at a desk most of the day. He was near retirement from what I could tell, but I never imagined him as a cattleman.

I stopped and picked up Luke on the way back to Granny's. He had a hundred questions about the gooseneck I was towing behind the truck. I answered each question as he asked them, but each answer seemed to bring one more question. It was surprising how many questions he had and even more surprising that I was able to answer them all. I began to realize how much I actually knew. Not that I had ever considered myself a total moron, but I never went to college. I'd spent all my years since graduating high school, helping Granny run the ranch when I wasn't off chasing rodeos and riding bulls. I guess that somewhere along the way, I had gleaned a little knowledge.

The weekend went great but seemed to end way too soon. I spent Monday and Tuesday checking fences and clearing away trees at the site I'd picked for the house. Before I knew it, Wednesday slipped up on me, and I was pulling back into the parking lot at the counselling center.

The night's lesson was over all the ways trust can be destroyed in a relationship. As we went through the lesson, it became clear that controlling personalities were not healthy for a good relationship. Miz Nancy read the two-page introduction and then asked if anyone felt they had been controlling in their relationships.

"Yeah," Garrett spoke up, "I use to check my ex-girlfriends' odometer and go through her cellphone."

"And how'd that work out?" Miz Nancy gave him a pursed-lip raised-eyebrow look.

"Yeah," he responded, "not so well. She's the reason I'm here."

If possible, the eyebrows raised even higher, "Who's the reason you're here?"

"Oh man, I didn't mean it like that Miz Nancy," Garrett crawfished. "I just meant…"

"I know what you meant," Miz Nancy scolded. "Be careful."

"I think, in my relationship, we were both controlling." Jake drew Miz Nancy's attention, and Garrett breathed a sigh of relief.

"How so?" Miz Nancy asked.

"Well, I know she was constantly checking up on me. She went through my phone, would time my trips to the store, go through my laptop. Since we've been divorced, I've even had people come to me and tell me that she was texting and calling them, trying to find out if I was doing something wrong," he explained, "and as for me, there towards the end, I'd asked to see her phone, and I'd tell her if I couldn't leave, neither could she."

"And how'd that work out?" she repeated her earlier question.

"I'm divorced and she hates me," Jake shrugged.

"And how 'bout you?" Miz Nancy asked. "Do you hate her?"

"Nah," Jake shook his head with a weak smile, "I don't hate anyone. I've moved on. I'm at peace."

"Good for you," she smiled.

As the discussion continued, one by one the other members gave examples of how they had either been controlling themselves or how their partners had controlled them. The most common controlling behavior seemed to be going through the other person's cellphone. It kind of made me wonder what people did fifty years ago before they were invented. I was the last to share. I didn't feel like I had ever really been controlled and I was never a controlling person, my problem had always been being too quick to walk away. Miz Nancy must have been tired because she didn't push me like I figured she would, but simply told us to make sure we handed in our exit papers before we left.

The church was dark and quiet when we left the counseling center. I asked Jake about it, and he said Brother Jim was out of town again. He didn't know where or why.

"You serious about what you said in there?" I asked, indicating the center with a nod of my head.

"About what?" Jake returned.

"Being at peace?" I clarified.

"Yeah," he answered, fell silent for a few seconds, then added, "yeah. I'm at peace. God has been very good to me this last year. There are still times when I wish things had turned out differently. I figure there will always be times I feel that way. But, now, I know our relationship was slowly destroying both of us, and I have found peace in the fact that being apart was the only way for us to heal. I pray every day that she is happy with her life."

On the way out of the parking lot, I recalled my exit paper. I had written: Tonight, I learned you cannot hope to ever trust someone by controlling them. You must let them be themselves and work together. Trust grows when two people love each other and work together to build a relationship.

I was nearly home, lost in thought, before I realized I hadn't called Dottie. She picked up on the first ring.

"I'm sorry, I forgot to call you when I left the center," I stammered.

"Why are you apologizing?" she asked.

"Well, I usually call, and I forgot," I answered.

"And then you remembered and now you're calling," She laughed.

I chuckled, "Yeah."

"So, how'd it go?"

I was still talking to her when I parked my old truck and headed for the front door.

WEEK 44—CONCLUSION OF SUPPORT AND TRUST

Sunday morning, Granny pulled into the front yard just as Luke and I stepped out the door. She had decided to meet us at my house and ride with us to church. As I drove, the two of them kept up a running dialogue. I'm sure it was important and meaningful, but my mind kept slipping back to the conversation I'd had with Jake. How did he know he was at peace?

When we pulled into the church, all conversation stopped. At first, I thought it was simply because we had arrived. Then I saw Dottie step from her Jeep and start toward us. Granny was grinning from ear to ear. All I could do was shake my head.

"Surprise !!" Dottie grinned as she wrapped her arms around my neck. "Hope you don't mind."

"Not at all," I said. "I've been meaning to ask you how we were going to do the church thing and just didn't know how to start the conversation."

"Is that your idea of a proposal?" she feigned disgust.

"Oh, I'm sorry." I did my best to look shocked and flustered as I started to lower myself to one knee.

Dottie grabbed my arm and pulled me up, "You get your ass up right this minute," she demanded. "I was just joking, and you know it."

"Swearing at church and on a Sunday," I raised an eyebrow. "Guess we better get you inside quick."

All my life I've heard folks say 'God works in mysterious ways'. After the opening prayer, announcements, and several hymns, the preacher took the pulpit and preached on the peace that comes from following Jesus' example and God's will. I don't know how much anyone else got from the sermon, but for me, it could not have come at a better time.

* * * * *

By Monday afternoon, I'd cleared away all the trees necessary to get started on the new house. What could be used as firewood was stacked neatly between two nearby trees, and the rest had been hauled down to a gully that needed to be filled in. The day's work through, I backed the pickup to where I figured the front porch was going to be, dropped the tailgate and sat looking out over the valley.

I thought about what Miz Nancy had been teaching us. I thought about what Jake had said. I thought about what the preacher had preached. And slowly, I began to put the pieces together like a jigsaw puzzle. Now, I'm not claiming to have the whole puzzle figured out, but just to be able to see a small portion of it, well, for me, that's saying something.

The way I figure it, peace is something you choose. You either have it or you don't, but either way it's your choice. Looking back over my life, I could see that I'd spent a lot of time blaming others for my lack of peace. I'd blamed my folks for not being there for me. I'd blamed my ex-wife for not sticking by me through the hard times. I'd blamed anyone and everyone but myself, and I come to find out, I'm the only one who can choose peace for me.

Sure, others can try to take away my peace, but whether I let them or not is my choice. So ultimately, my peace is what I make it. Now, add that to the preacher's sermon, and you have an even better, more precious peace that comes from having Jesus in your life, and once again, my choice. So really, if I'm not at peace, then the blame goes to the fellow I see in the mirror every morning.

Life is too short to live without peace. It's high time I had peace in my life, and I decided right there on the back of that old tailgate that from then on, I was gonna choose peace.

* * * * *

"Tonight, we're going to get personal," Miz Nancy stated, to begin our class on Wednesday.

She had just finished reading the introductory materials for the evening's lesson and was looking around the table. It was another one of those weeks where everyone seemed to be in a bit of a lull. Except for Jake, I don't think I'd seen anyone smile since I walked into the building. So, we all just sat there staring at her.

Finally, she continued, "On the back of your packet, I want each of you to write at least two things you are presently having issues with in the area of trust."

"Miz Nancy," Jake spoke up frowning, "I'm not in a relationship, so I don't currently have any trust issues."

"Really, Jake?" She responded by lowering her head as a sarcastic little grin spread across her face. "It wasn't very long ago that we were talking about you not trusting yourself to have a relationship."

"Okay, then," Jake matched her grin, and Catfish chuckled beside him.

Miz Nancy left us to our work and returned well before the usual time. I'm not even sure she was gone long enough to smoke an entire cigarette. The thought crossed my mind that maybe she was trying to quit.

"Catfish, you're up first," Miz Nancy said as she came through the door.

"Me?" he asked and then before she could respond, "I got a pretty good relationship going right now, but I guess I don't trust it's gonna last. That's what I put down."

"And why don't you think it's gonna last?" Miz Nancy wanted to know.

"Well, I ain't ever had a relationship that lasted yet," Catfish shrugged.

"And why do you think that is?" Miz Nancy wasn't letting him off easy.

"I reckon it's because I only pick crazy women," he shrugged again.

Several of the guys chuckled, and more than one nodded their heads in agreement. I caught Jake's eye, and he grinned and shot me a 'here-we-go-again' look. Miz Nancy took a deep breath, let it out, and then to my surprise, turned to Jake.

"Jake, you're next." And the grin disappeared from his face.

"Well, to be honest, with you Miz Nancy," Jake said, "I'm with Catfish on this one. I wrote two things, the first one was I only pick crazy women. Now, before you lose it, let me explain. I know we've talked about how men and women are equally crazy, but I seemed to be able to pick the… well, how should I put it? My first wife was a shoplifting pathological liar, my second wife was a drinker, and my last wife was over the top controlling. But my issue is not with them, it's with myself. I don't trust myself to make a good choice for future relationships."

"Okay," Miz Nancy pushed her glasses up, "so, what do you need to work on then?"

"I guess I need to trust myself more," Jake said, "which leads to my number two. I haven't dated in nearly thirty years. I mean, I've been out with my wife, but not like dating dating."

"So, you don't trust yourself to date?" Miz Nancy asked.

"Like riding a bicycle," Catfish chimed in.

"Oh, really," Miz Nancy shot him a look.

"What?" he shot back.

"And how did the dating go with the relationship that brought you back here?" she adjusted her glasses once again.

"Now, Miz Nancy, that's not fair," he whined. "You know that wasn't no relationship, and it wasn't dating either."

Catfish squirmed in his chair while we all sat watching. Miz Nancy stood across the table. Once again, like watching a tennis match, our eyes traveled from one to the other and back again. Finally, Catfish broke eye contact with her and look around the table.

"A buddy of mine called me and said this woman had called him and needed a ride," Catfish explained. "His truck was broke down, and he wanted to know if I could pick her up. She'd just gotten out of jail. I said no problem and drove two counties over and picked her up. One thing led to another and well… it didn't end well. But it wasn't dating." He looked back up at Miz Nancy.

"Like riding a bicycle?" Miz Nancy mocked, and the room erupted in laughter.

Catfish turned red, and Miz Nancy turned back to Jake.

"So, once again, Jake, you don't trust yourself to date?" Miz Nancy said.

"Not really," Jake said, "but right now, it's really not a problem, because I'm not sure I'll ever want to date again."

"Jake, you're still young," Miz Nancy offered.

He held up a hand, "I know, Miz Nancy, but I've got a bunch of kids and grandkids, and at my age, any woman who would be interested in me would probably also have kids and grandkids. It would be pretty complicated."

Miz Nancy laughed. "Jake, we're talking about a date. You need to slow your thought process just a bit."

"Yeah, maybe," he agreed.

Member by member each discussed their trust issues until it was my turn. On my paper, I'd written that I was having trouble trusting myself to be able to run the ranch. That was my biggest issue, and my second, like many of the others, was trusting myself to maintain a lasting relationship. Overall, I was beginning to feel like, for myself, trust was something that was just going to take time and effort. Looking back over the months since I'd started the class, I could see how much improvement I'd made and how much more I trusted myself now than I had in the beginning. I figure, in time, I might trust myself completely, but as they say, only time will tell, and I'm not holding my breath on that one.

When Miz Nancy dismissed us, I wrote on my exit paper: Tonight, I learned that it is important for a person to trust themselves. I cannot truly trust others if I am unable to trust myself.

* * * * *

The Neon Church was still going when we stepped out of the center. Catfish, Bo, and Tex had all headed for their vehicle, so it was just Jake and I that wandered over. Inside, Sally was seated beside a fellow, so Jake and I found seats across the aisle and listened to the discussion. It's crazy how you get used to something in your head, and then when it changes, your mind doesn't want to accept it. Jake and Sally had never really been a thing, but in my mind, they were, and probably in Sally's mind as well. Now, Sally was in a relationship with someone other than Jake, and I was having a hard time with it.

I didn't get anything out of the evening's discussion. I couldn't even tell you where they were at in the Bible. I kept turning the situation over and over in my head. I told myself that Sally wasn't being unfaithful to Jake because they had never been a couple, but it just wasn't ringing true for me. By the time Brother Jim dismissed the congregation, I'd given up arguing with myself.

"Jake, Hank," Sally said as we stepped into the aisle, "I'd like to introduce you to Dan."

Dan stuck out his hand and Jake took it, "Very nice to meet you, Dan."

"Nice to meet you too, Jake," Dan said. "Sally speaks very highly of you."

Jake just smiled, and Dan turned and stuck his hand out to me. I shook it and nodded. Sally and Dan walked out in front of us. I walked with Jake out to his truck and visited for a few minutes. When I asked him if he was okay with Sally and Dan, he just chuckled.

"I'm okay, Hank," he said. "I'm in a very good place in my life right now. I'm happy for them."

"Okay." I didn't know what else to say, and nothing I said or thought seemed to be going right tonight.

On the phone, Dottie and I discussed my crazy thought

patterns as I drove home. I hung up with her as I pulled into the drive. I turned the engine off and sat in the truck until the lights went off. Staring at the dark figure of my trailer, I wished that Dottie was inside.

235

WEEK 45—DEFINING HONESTY AND ACCOUNTABILITY

Thursday morning, as I was putting the coffee on, Luke called, "Hey, Dad, I know it's short notice, but can you pick me up for a little while this evening?"

Trying to remain calm, I said, "Sure bud, is everything alright?"

He must have heard the worry in my voice, "Oh sure, Dad, nothing like that. It's just that this weekend is Halloween, and since I'm at mom's this weekend, I'm gonna go hang with some of my friends, but I really wanted to do something with you, too."

"What time should I pick you up?" I asked.

"How 'bout five o'clock?" he answered after a few seconds of thought.

"Sounds good," I agreed, "see you then."

It wasn't until after I hung up that I realized I hadn't asked him if he had cleared it with his mother. I thought about calling her to check, but somehow wasn't quite comfortable with the idea. In the end, I decided if I showed up and if he hadn't cleared it, I would smile, apologize, and leave. Something one of my bull riding buddies used to say ran through my mind. It's better to ask for forgiveness than for permission.

As it turned out, he had cleared it with his mother, and when I picked him up, she said even though it was a school night, he could stay out until ten o'clock. By ten o'clock, I started to tell them, I was usually in bed and asleep myself, but then I caught myself. No use having them think I was old. Thinking about it later, I chuckled at the change the last year had brought about, not only with my mindset, but also with my lifestyle.

When I asked Luke where he wanted to go, he told me he wanted to go to Granny's house. It caught me off guard, but when we pulled into the yard and I saw Dottie's red Jeep, I knew I'd been set up again. This was beginning to become a habit with the three of them, a good habit.

We had a wonderful evening. Dottie had picked up a fresh box of Graham crackers and several Hershey's chocolate bars. Granny brought out the marshmallows left over from the last time we had made s'mores. After dinner, me and Luke built a fire, and we laughed and cut up until time for me to take Luke back to his mother's.

* * * * *

Wednesday night's counseling session shed light on more good habits. In this case, habits that were changing my life. Miz Nancy read through a list of ten components of accountability. Each component forced us to accept responsibility for our own actions, thoughts, and feelings.

When she came in from her smoke break, she opened the discussion by asking, "Are there any of the ten components you disagree with?"

No one seemed willing to step out on that limb. Everyone sat quiet, waiting for someone else to put their foot into that bear trap. After a minute of silence, Miz Nancy realized what she was asking, and a chuckle escaped. I'm not sure who it surprised more, us or her.

"It's okay," she said. "I'm not gonna bite your heads off. It's important that you know where you are with these components."

"Number six," James spoke from the end of the table.

Most of us were still not convinced it wasn't a trap, so after a quick look at James, every head swung back to Miz Nancy. She was looking down at her packet and read aloud, "Because my thoughts, actions, and feelings are a choice, I cannot be provoked." When she looked up, she gave James a smile then said, "That one gives a lot of people a problem."

Feeling more comfortable, James shrugged. "The idea that I can't be provoked is hard for me. My ole lady knows how to push my buttons, and sometimes, I think she does it just for fun. It says I can choose not to be provoked. I ain't so sure about that."

"I'm with James on this one," Bo spoke up, "and number seven says when I received consequences, I was the only one responsible, not the court, the police, the district attorney, or my partner. Well, that's a hard one for me to swallow, too. I still think the D.A. has it in for me."

"Catfish, you're awful quiet tonight," Miz Nancy observed.

"Just tired, ma'am," he grinned, "and I reckon I agree with all of them."

"Really now," Miz Nancy wasn't buying it. "None of them seem wrong to you?"

"No ma'am," he said. "I know I'm the one to blame for where I'm at, and I know I'm the only one who can fix it."

Miz Nancy looked around the room. "Well, this has to be a first. Anyone else feel this way."

"Yeah, I do," I said aloud as Jake raised a hand across the table.

"Seriously?" her surprise was genuine.

As I looked away from her and around the table, I realized that the rest of the guys were having as much trouble accepting what we were saying as Miz Nancy was. The discussion moved from one member to another, and I found myself doing an internal check. Did I really buy into the idea that I had a choice in every situation? Was I solely responsible for my thoughts, actions, and feelings? I went back over each of the ten components and found that I was at peace with all of them.

When the class ended, I wrote on my exit paper: Tonight, I learned that I am solely responsible for my actions, thoughts, and feelings. I learned that trying to control someone else is never good. I never again want to be in a relationship where I am controlling or where someone is trying to control me.

* * * * *

Neither Sally nor Dan were at the Neon Church when Jake and I slid into our seats. The discussion was over the verses in the seventh chapter of Matthew where Jesus was telling about the strait and narrow gate. Brother Jim was visiting with a young man on the front row. As I listened, it occurred to me that this young man was struggling with an addiction. He wanted to know how to find this strait gate and narrow path so he could overcome it. Brother Jim was trying to explain to him that Jesus was the way. For some reason, it wasn't taking; he wanted something more.

By the time Brother Jim finally dismissed the congregation with a prayer, the sun had sunk below the horizon. I walked out to the parking lot with Jake. At his truck, I asked, "Were you really okay with everything we covered, tonight?"

He answered without hesitation, "Yes, I was. I think it has a lot to do with being at peace with yourself, and I'm there. How 'bout you? Were you really okay with it?"

Just like Jake to throw it right back into your court. I grinned, "Yes. I don't know if it's the B.I.P. classes or the Neon Church or something else, but I'm at peace with myself, for the most part and most of the time, anyway."

"Good." He smiled and climbed into his truck. "Have a good week, Hank."

"You, too," I returned.

WEEK 46—USE OF HONESTY AND ACCOUNTABILITY

"So, Dad, do you know how to propose?" my son asked me on Friday night as we placed wood into the fire pit behind Granny's house. Granny and Dottie were inside getting everything ready for s'mores.

A quick look towards the house and I half whispered, half hissed, "Yes, I do."

He dropped another stick of wood on his side of the fire we were building, looked up at me with a big grin, and half whispered back, "Just checkin'. You seem to be takin' your own sweet time. You know you ain't getting any younger."

"That does it," I shot him my best back off glare, "you've been spending too much time with Granny, I'm thinkin'.

The back door opened, and his grin grew even bigger. When Granny and Dottie reached us, I was sure glad we hadn't lit the fire yet. Leave it to a ten-year-old boy to make me blush.

I'm not sure who liked the weekend visit more, but I'm pretty certain that Granny is the one who enjoyed the s'mores the most. She likes to act like it's all about Luke, but I've been watching, and she usually matches him one for one while sneaking little bites of chocolate bar when she thinks no one is watching.

Dottie has been spending more and more time at the ranch, even on the weekends Luke is there, but she always goes back to her house for the night. Sunday mornings, we can always be found in the pew alongside Granny, and after church, we treat her to lunch, her choice. This week, she wanted to go to Dairy Queen following the service, but I apologized and told her we had plans.

"What plans?" she wanted to know, and it was clear she was not happy about it.

"I'm sorry, Granny," I apologized again, "Luke has a birthday party he has to go to, and Dottie has to go get her Granny from church today."

"Well, I'll be," she fussed but climbed in the truck.

Halfway back to her house, I pulled the truck to the side of the road. Granny had been in a full-blown pout and hadn't said a word to me or Luke. As, I stepped out of the pickup, she looked past Luke and asked what I was doing.

"I thought I saw the engine light flash on a minute ago," I explained. "Just a second. I'm gonna take a look at the engine."

Five minutes later, I shut the hood and climbed back in beside Luke.

"Well?" Granny asked.

"Didn't see anything," I answered. "I'll keep an eye on it."

She went back to sulking, and I eased the truck along checking the instrument panel now and then. Half an hour later, we pulled up in front of her place, got out of the pickup, and started for the house.

"And just where are you two going?" Granny asked.

"I thought we'd see you inside," I answered.

"Y'all get along," she ordered. "Y'all have places to go, and I can make it up the steps without any help. I'm not that old you know?"

"Oh, come on, Granny, don't be like that." I countered, "You know we love you. Just let us see you inside, and we'll skedaddle."

As Granny stepped through the door and into the living room, Dottie and Mrs. Walters shouted, "Surprise!" from the dining room, as did Luke and I from behind her. Before she had time to react, Dottie came through the door with a birthday cake in her hands, followed by her grandmother.

"Well, I'll be," Granny said, but this time, there was a smile on her face and a twinkle in her eyes.

"We didn't know how many candles to put on it." Dottie giggled as she held the cake out for Granny to see.

"Ain't something you need to know," Granny laughed. "All you need to know is I'm still young at heart."

I don't think I can remember a more perfect afternoon. After lunch and cake, Granny and Mrs. Walters ran me and Dottie and Luke out of the house, saying they could handle the cleanup themselves. I figure by the time we made it back to the house from our walk, the two of them had pretty much planned out the rest of mine and Dottie's lives.

* * * * *

By the time I made it to the counseling center on Wednesday, I had thought of a hundred different ways to propose to Dottie and discarded every one of them. It was important to me that I got it right this time. With Liz, well… I suppose you could call how it happened a proposal. Liz and I had been seeing each other whenever I was in town for nearly a year, and one night after a rather rowdy romp, she curled up on my chest and I said, "I wouldn't mind doing this every night."

"Is that a proposal?" Liz asked.

"If it was, what would you say?" I questioned.

"You first," she demanded.

"Sure, then," I said. "I guess it is."

"Well, it ain't exactly how I pictured it, but what the hell," she sighed, "yes."

And two months later, we were married.

I was beginning to think maybe I didn't know how to propose. As I pulled out my chair and sat down, Jake looked over, and with his usual smile, asked, "How was your week?"

The smile I returned was somewhat half-hearted, "I'd have to say my week was great, but…"

No one else had arrived yet. Jake laid the packet he was reading down, placed his glasses on the table beside it, and asked, "Want to talk about it?"

In the five minutes before James walked in, I walked him through the conversation with my son, my failed attempt at trying to figure out the best way to propose, and my frustration with myself at not being better at such things. He listened and nodded occasionally. When James came through the door, I picked up my packet and started to read.

Jake turned to James and asked, "How was your week?"

"Huh?" James looked over at him, then answered, "Um, okay, I guess."

Looked like I wasn't the only one having problems. Slowly, the other guys filtered in until the room was full, and Miz Nancy called us to the front. As we lined up, I found myself thinking we were getting close to Thanksgiving. The crazy season was almost upon us. Perhaps that was why everyone seemed a little uptight.

"Last week, we concentrated on blame," Miz Nancy said to get the session started, "Tonight, we're going to look at denial and minimalization. Would someone please read the introduction?"

Jake began to read. When he finished, Miz Nancy instructed us to answer the questions on the next two pages. As her footsteps faded up the hallway, I looked around the table. If the weather held and nothing unexpected happened, I had six more weeks of class after this one. Suddenly, I wasn't so sure I was ready for it to end. I had gotten used to the routine of coming here on Wednesday nights, and well, if I was honest, I was getting a lot of help. In addition, I was going to miss some of these guys.

"So then blame, denial, minimalization," Miz Nancy looked around the table as she returned to the room, "Which is your choice of defense?"

A moment passed, then James said, "Minimalization."

"And give me an example of how you minimize," Miz Nancy directed.

"Well, my wife and I got into it this week," he explained. "It was a pretty bad argument. I caught her going through my phone again, and I lost it. I grabbed her phone, and when she refused to give me her pass code, I chunked it. I keep telling myself it's okay because the phone didn't break, but I know I should do a better job of controlling my temper, and I shouldn't have thrown her phone."

"So, does she have reason to doubt you?" Miz Nancy inquired.

James looked down at the table. When he looked up again, he answered, "Yeah and no. A few years ago I fuc . . I mean, I messed around on her. We split up for a while. I've been faithful since we got back together."

"It sounds like there's still some healing to do where she's concerned," Miz Nancy suggested.

"Yeah," James agreed, staring down at his packet.

"Someone else," Miz Nancy said.

"Blame," Jake spoke up. "My big defense was if she didn't push my buttons, I wouldn't have gotten angry and started screaming and cussing in the first place."

"So, your defense was to blame her," Miz Nancy summarized. "And did that work out for you?"

"Well, it ruined my relationship with her," Jake answered, "and until I started being honest with myself and my kids, I didn't have much of a relationship with them either. Once I was able to admit I was in the wrong, I began to feel better about myself and my relationship with my kids got better."

"Then at this point, you no longer blame your ex-wife?" Miz Nancy seemed doubtful.

"I'd be lying if I said I don't have trouble sometimes," Jake confessed. "There are times when I have to really step back and re-evaluate myself. I have a tendency in my mind to fall back into old bad habits. I guess you could say I'm a work in progress."

"We all are," Miz Nancy smiled. "Next?"

"Denial," Frank spoke from the end of the table. "I hate it that for years I told myself that because the bedroom door was shut, the kids didn't know what was happening. Like the door was soundproof, and they couldn't hear the filth that was coming out of our mouths or the sound of us hitting each other. Every time I think about it, I wonder how I could have ever been such an asshole."

One by one, we all told which of the three ways we were most likely to use to avoid accountability. When the last member had spoken, Miz Nancy asked us each to turn our papers over and write the blame at the top, minimalization in the middle, and denial at the bottom.

"Now, under each, I want you to write one sentence about a time when you used each instead of being accountable, and below that sentence, write a sentence explaining what you should have done."

She gave us a few minutes, and then each of us shared. The first set of sentences varied from one member to the next, but the revelation came with the sentence explaining what should have happened. Everyone, in one form or another, wrote: I should have manned up to what I had done wrong and accepted the blame myself.

At the end of the class on my exit paper I wrote: Tonight, I learned that it is not okay to use blame, minimalization, or denial as a means of avoiding accountability. I learned that when I do something wrong, I need to do the right thing and man up and admit I was in the wrong.

* * * * *

The Neon Church was letting out as we left the counseling center. Jake and I stood on the walk and watched the congregation leave.

"So, about this proposal?" Jake looked down at the pavement.

"I don't know," I admitted. "You've been married, what, three times? Any advice?"

245

He chuckled, the chuckle turned into a laugh, and I found myself laughing with him. When he finally got control, he smiled and said, "Nope. None at all. Looking back, I really sucked at proposals, and as for anything to do with marriage, I'm the wrong fellow to asked. Sorry, Hank."

"Well, thanks for listening anyway," I smiled. "I reckon I'll figure it out somehow."

"I'm sure you will." He started towards his truck, then turned back. "Maybe one bit of advice. Don't forget the ring," and he turned and walked away.

The ring. I'd been so busy worrying about how to propose that I hadn't even thought about a ring. Well, one thing at a time. Note to self, start looking for a ring.

WEEK 47—CONCLUSION OF HONESTY AND ACCOUNTABILITY

An old cowboy once told me that trying to read a woman's mind was like crawling on a bull and thinking you knew exactly what he was going to do. When I asked him how that was, he just chuckled and said, "He'll throw your sorry ass every time."

On my way back from the feed store on Thursday, I stopped into the jewelry store. When I walked in the door, I realized the jeweler's wife was going to be on the phone as soon as I left. Now, I'm standing just inside the door, trying to decide how to broach the subject of a ring without letting the whole town know I was planning on proposing, when she came around the counter.

"How can I help you today?" she smiled.

"Well, I . . ," I stammered, "I, I need a wedding ring."

Her smile widened, "Just a wedding ring or a set?"

"What?" I asked, realizing I was in way over my head.

"Just a wedding ring or an engagement ring, also?" The twinkle in her eye said this wasn't the first greenhorn to wander into the store.

"Oh, I see," I nodded. "I'll need both."

"Okay, this is the counter you need to be looking at," she pointed me in the right direction. "Do you know what she would like?"

I looked down at the selection and then looked back up at her. I could tell she was trying not to laugh. I just shook my head.

"Maybe, I should come back another time," I said sheepishly.

"We'll be here whenever you're ready," she returned, and I headed for the door.

I spent the weekend mulling it over in my mind. It was my weekend to have Luke, so he and I spent quite a bit of time running around the ranch on four-wheelers throughout the days and hanging out with Granny and Dottie in the evenings. Life had become a slow, easy routine, and I had fallen in love with it. But for the life of me, I couldn't figure out how to ask Dottie what kind of rings she wanted without ruining the surprise of a proposal, and I still didn't know how I was going to propose.

By Tuesday, I'd come to terms with the fact that I was going to have to elicit some help. I stopped into Granny's for breakfast. As she moved around the kitchen, getting eggs and bacon ready, I sat at the table, and we talked about the cattle and the ranch. When she had everything on the table, she sat down across from me.

"You bless the food this morning, Runt," she said and bowed her head.

Caught off guard, it took me a minute, but I stumbled through a prayer and even remember to include thanks for the food. When I finished and looked up, Granny was grinning across the table at me.

"So, Runt, what's really on your mind?" she asked and reached for a biscuit.

"What makes you think something's on my mind?" I returned.

She buttered her biscuit, took a bite, and looked across the table at me as if to say, "I'm waiting." I'd seen the look to many times in my life to mess with her. I laid my fork and knife down.

"I need some help with a wedding ring," I told her.

Without a word, she pushed her chair back, got up, and left the room. I sat looking down the hallway where she'd disappeared and wondering if she was coming back. After several minutes, she reappeared at the end of the hall. When she sat down at the table again, she passed a little, black velvet ring box across the table to me.

"That was my mother's, your great-grandmother. I think Dottie would like it," she explained.

I opened the box. Inside was a very simple gold engagement ring with a diamond set into the top, and beside it a matching gold wedding ring. I took them out and looked them over, placed them back, and set them in the center of the table between us.

"Okay, I'll look for something like them," I said.

"Or you could just get those sized," Granny suggested.

I didn't know what to say, so I ate. When Granny finished eating, she pushed her plate away, and leaned back.

"Dottie will want something simple," she stated. "She also likes things that have meaning and history. You could go buy her a new set of rings, and she'd like them fine, I'm sure, but she'd rather have these."

"And how do you know all this?" I pushed back my plate and asked her.

"I asked her," she grinned.

"Why?" flustered, I asked, "why would you ask her?"

"So that when you asked me, I could tell you," she answered as if it should be obvious.

"What made you so sure I would ask?" I wanted to know.

"Oh, Runt!" she laughed. "Oh, Runt!"

I waited, but that was all the answer I would get for that question, so I asked, "Granny, why didn't you bring these ring out the first time I got married?"

She scoffed, "Really, Runt. I figure if you proposed at all to her, you were buck naked and thinkin' with the wrong head." I felt myself blushing, but she wasn't finished. "You were young, and I wasn't sure it was going to last, and I didn't want to lose my grandmother's rings."

"So, how do you know this one will last?" I asked.

She smiled, "I just know, Runt," and that was that.

By the time I left her place, it had been decided that I would take the rings to the jewelers and have them cleaned up. When I asked Granny about proposals, she told me she couldn't do everything for me. Somethings I would have to figure out myself. I dropped the rings off on my way to the counseling center.

The lesson for the night was designed to help us move away from making excuses for our bad behavior and towards becoming more accountable. By understanding we are responsible for our actions, we are more likely to stop unwanted actions. Miz Nancy was suffering from a headache and a cold, so the discussion was held to a minimum, and we got out of class in time to attend the last half-hour of the service at the Neon Church.

On my exit paper I wrote: Tonight's lesson reaffirmed what I have learned over the last couple of weeks. I am responsible for my own actions, thoughts, and feeling. Blaming others and refusing to accept responsibility for my actions will only keep me from growing and becoming the person I want to be.

* * * * *

At the Neon Church, the discussion for the evening revolved around the thirty-third verse of the tenth chapter of John. Sally was seated by herself when we entered. I was in the lead, so I slipped into the row she was in. Leaving a seat between us, I sat down. Jake sat beside me. Sally smiled, whispered greetings, and then turned her attention back to Brother Jim who was talking about tribulations.

"So, what you are saying is having Jesus in our lives will keep us from having problems?" someone near the front asked.

"Not at all," Brother Jim clarified. "We are all going to have troubles and tribulations. There is not a day that goes by that I don't want a drink, but I know I would never stop with one drink. That is one of the temptations I face daily. Before I asked Jesus into my life and learned to lean on his help and grace and mercy, I was never able to overcome the temptation. Now, with Christ's help, I am six years sober and counting."

When the discussion wrapped up and Brother Jim had dismissed us, Sally followed us out to Jake's truck. Unsure of how to act or what to say, I stood beside Jake, feeling completely uncomfortable.

"How've you been?" Jake finally asked.

"Good," Sally said, "really good. This is my last visit here. I've decided to attend services with Dan at his church on Wednesday nights. I came to tell Brother Jim how much I appreciate all he's done for me. And I also wanted to say goodbye to the two of you. And Jake, words could never begin to express how much you've helped me. I just needed to say that and tell you thanks."

She wrapped her arms around his neck. Jake hugged back, and when she pulled away, tears were flowing freely down her face. She shook my hand and headed back into the church.

"You okay?" I asked.

"Yeah," Jake's voice broke a little. I looked down at my boots and waited. After a moment, he asked, "How's that proposal coming?"

So, I told him about the ring.

WEEK 48—DEFINING SEXUAL ABUSE

Dottie and I spent Thanksgiving with Granny. We had the traditional turkey dinner and visited. In the middle of the afternoon, Pops dropped Luke at the house. Somehow, just having him there made our whole family seem infinitely bigger. As we sat around a fire in the backyard, I thought about all the years I'd missed being with family. It made me sick to think of it, and I knew I never wanted to lose another minute.

Luke stayed through the weekend, and I took him back Sunday evening. I had been asking around about various contractors in the area, and Monday morning, I called what I figured to be the best choice and set up an appointment to have them come out and discuss building the house. When I told Granny, she was giddy as a schoolgirl and made me drive her out to the building site.

"So, how many bedrooms will there be?" she wanted to know.

"I'm thinking three," I told her, "a master and two kid's rooms."

"That's good," she said with a grin. "I was sure hoping for some more great-grandkids."

She had a hundred more questions, some I could answer, others I hadn't even considered myself. By the time, I took her back home, I realized there was going to be a lot more to building this house than I'd originally thought.

* * * * *

"How many of you are married or have ever been married to a Victoria's Secret model?" Miz Nancy stood in the doorway one hand on a hip, the other arm loaded with copies of the night's lesson.

No one spoke. No one raised their hand. We all just sat staring at her.

"That's what I figured," she said as she began to hand out the lessons, "but every one of the women you are with wants to be looked at, respected, and adored just as if she was one of those models."

As she spoke, she circled the table, laying packets in front of each member she passed, "How many of you feel like you treat your wife or girlfriend like she is the most beautiful woman on the earth?"

Bo and Jake raised their hands. Miz Nancy paused and looked Jake in the eye, "So blacking her eye was treating her like the most beautiful woman in the world."

"No, I suppose not." Jake met her gaze. "I reckon, up to a point, I did treat her well, but towards the end, not so much."

When she turned to Bo, he was busy studying his packet. Miz Nancy finished handing out the packets and stepped to her usual spot near the door.

"Tonight, we're going to discuss what makes a healthy sexual relationship." As she spoke, I snuck a peek around the table. Every one of the guys had their eyes fixed on their packets, "We will discuss how using sex to control someone can ruin a relationship and the negative effects pornography can have on a relationship."

"Man, this is really uncomfortable stuff," James spoke from the far end of the table.

"Yes, it can be," Miz Nancy agreed, "but how many of you would have no problem laughing and discussing it if you were with just a bunch of your guy friends."

"That's different," Tex interjected.

"How so?" Miz Nancy wanted to know.

"Well," Tex replied, "what guys and gals say when they're not in mixed company is one thing, but when they're together, it should be different."

"So, you think girls talk about sex when they get together?" Miz Nancy asked.

"Sure, they do," Catfish chimed in. "I once had a girlfriend who told me some of the things she and her friends discussed. It made me blush like… well, like a schoolgirl."

Catfish has a way of saying just the right thing to break up the tension. Several of the members chuckled aloud, and even Miz Nancy grinned.

"You're right, Catfish," she grew serious. "Women do talk about sex when men folks aren't around, but for purposes of this class, the state requires that we discuss these topics. So, you might as well get comfortable because tonight is just the first night of three nights on the topic."

After the introductory material and Miz Nancy's customary smoke break, we discussed how our present attitudes about sex in a relationship had been molded by people and events in our lives. Most of us had been introduced to sex in our teenage years by someone slightly older than us. Many of us had also been introduced to pornography, in one form or another, about the same time.

"How many of you have used sex to control someone?" Miz Nancy asked.

Garret was the only one to raise a hand. As he looked around the table and the rest of us looked at him, Miz Nancy said, "This is not unusual."

"Really?" Garrett seemed astonished.

"Yes," Miz Nancy nodded. "How many of you have ever had someone try to control you using sex?"

Every hand in the room went up.

"And once again," Miz Nancy said, "this is not uncommon. Sex should never be used as a tool of control."

After several minutes of discussion about using sex as

control in a relationship, Miz Nancy shifted to pornography. "How many of you would say you use pornography on a regular basis?"

The room fell silent.

After a moment, Miz Nancy asked, "How many of you have ever looked at a pornographic magazine?"

Several hands raised as Catfish asked, "You mean like Hustler?" then blushed.

"Yes, Catfish," Miz Nancy said, "like Hustler."

"I have," he said, reddening even more.

"So, is pornography okay when you're in a relationship?" Miz Nancy asked.

"No," Jake answered.

"Why not?" Miz Nancy asked.

"Because it hurts the relationship," Jake answered.

"And you know this how?" Miz Nancy pushed.

"My first wife was into it pretty hard. I was young and had been sheltered, so I thought it was a normal part of a marriage. It ruined our relationship," Jake explained. "With my last wife, she was very paranoid about pornography. I was so in love with her and so into her, I never had any desire to look at the stuff, but it was still a big problem in our relationship."

"Jake is right," Miz Nancy said. "Pornography in a relationship causes problems, and often the problems ruin the relationship."

At the end of the discussion, on my exit paper I wrote: Tonight, I learned that pornography can and does ruin relationships and should be avoided. I also learned that using sex to control another person is wrong.

* * * * *

Walking into the Neon Church and knowing Sally would not be there hurt for some reason. Jake and I slid into our usual seats, and I left an empty chair between us. I wondered how he was feeling about Sally not being there but figured it best not to ask. When the service was over and Brother Jim released us with a prayer, we wandered out to Jake's truck.

"How'd Thanksgiving go for you?" I asked him.

"Good, really good," he said. "We all gathered at my sister's home. I guess there must have been about forty of us all together. Had a big spread and ate too much. How about you?"

I told him how me and Dottie and Granny had lunch together, and how Luke coming over seemed to make it so much better. Somehow, the conversation shifted, and soon, we were discussing the new house. I filled him in on the contractor I'd called and the meeting I had coming up on Friday. He knew the contractor and had used him to build the house his ex-wife had gotten in the divorce.

"You won't find a better group of guys anywhere around here," Jake said.

"So, how's it going with your house plans?" I asked.

"It's done," he said. "I signed the papers last Monday. I am now the proud owner of eighty acres, and I've leased another three hundred."

"Dang!" I grinned. "Well, congratulations. Now all you need are some cows."

"In time," he grinned back, "in time."

WEEK 49—USE OF SEXUAL ABUSE

The contractor showed up Friday morning bright and early. By ten-thirty I'd shown him the blueprints I'd had drawn up and walked him through the building site. He told me his crew was finishing up a house out east of town, and I would be next on his list. If the weather held, he'd start sometime in January. What a way to start the new year. I could only think of one thing that would make it better.

Monday morning, after a wonderful weekend with Dottie and Granny, I jumped on the four-wheeler and headed out to check fences. Twenty minutes out snow began to fall, and before I could get my slicker on, big fluffy flakes filled the sky. The fences looked fine, and the cattle bunched against the blowing snow left me with nothing to do, so by noon, I was back at Granny's with a cup of coffee cradled in my hands and my sock feet inches from the wood burning stove.

"How many more meetings have you got left?" Granny asked.

"Four," I answered, "but there won't be a meeting the week of Christmas, so it'll still be five weeks before I'm through with the classes."

"Getting close." She eased into her favorite rocker and set her coffee cup on the side table beside it. "Do you think the classes helped at all?"

"Yes, Granny, I do." I smiled, blowing across the top of my cup.

"I do, too," she agreed. "I've seen a change in you that I never believed was possible."

"Thanks, Granny," my smile widened. "You'll never know how much I appreciate you saying that."

"You're welcome, Runt." She grinned back with a wink.

* * * * *

By Wednesday night, the snow had melted, and the daily high temperature was back to a tolerable sixty degrees. When I parked in front of the counseling center and got out, I realized there was absolutely no wind, uncommon for December. I shed the light camouflage jacket I was wearing and tossed it into the truck before walking across the parking lot and into the building.

After the normal Wednesday night routine of greetings, packet distribution, and signing in, Miz Nancy stepped into the room. She stood just inside the door as usual and looked around the room.

"Tonight, we will attempt to dispel some common myths about sex," she announced. "Someone, please, begin reading the first page of the introduction."

Jake read half of the first page. James took the second half. I started the second page and Catfish finished it.

"I think tonight, we'll do the questions together as a group," Miz Nancy said, drawing more than one questioning look from the guys.

She ignored us and read, "Men shouldn't discuss their feelings. Why?"

"It makes them look weak," James answered.

"That is the number one reason given in every one of the classes I've ever taught on this subject," Miz Nancy agreed, "but is hiding how you feel really healthy in a relationship?"

"No." This from Jake. "Keeping it all bottled up only causes serious problems when it reaches the boiling point."

"You're right, Jake," Miz Nancy nodded her head. "Discussing your feelings is an important part of a healthy relationship."

"My old lady don't want me getting all mushy and shit with her," James scoffed.

"You're also right, James," Miz Nancy said. "Women don't want a mushy or sappy or a blubbering man, but they will respect you if you have the courage to talk about your feelings with them. It doesn't have to come across as a weakness if it's done correctly."

The next myth was that sex equals intercourse. It took a bit before anyone was willing to open the ball for the discussion around this one. Miz Nancy asked for a show of hands to see how many of the guys believed this myth, and it was unanimous. Even after explaining that there was more to sex than the actual act itself, many of the guys just weren't buying it.

"Ma'am," Catfish finally spoke up, "sex is sex."

As I looked around the table, I noticed several of the guys were nodding in agreement, but a few, myself included, were seeing sex in a whole new way. Walking into the meeting tonight, I would have bet a crisp new hundred-dollar bill that there was no way I was going to learn something new about the birds and the bees. I would have lost that Benjamin.

By the end of the session, I felt like my head might explode. I had instruction on sex from a woman's point of view. To say it was somewhat different than what I knew, or thought I knew, would be an understatement. I'm not planning on running out and buying any 'how to' books, but I definitely plan on having some open, honest conversations with Dottie on the subject.

At the end of the night, on my exit paper I wrote: Tonight, I learned that men and women have some very different thoughts about sex. I also learned that it would be good for me to share my thoughts and feelings, not only about sex but about everything I'm feeling.

By the time we got out to the parking lot, the congregation from the church was already filing out. I was surprised that our class had run so long but seemed so short. I said as much to Jake.

"It was a good class tonight," he said, "a very interesting class. Some of what we discussed, I was aware of, but as they say, you're never too old to learn, and I learned plenty tonight. I just wish I'd known some of what I learned when I was your age."

After a moment's thought, I said, "You know, I think these classes should be taught in high school. If not these, something like them. And I'm not just talking about the sex sessions, I'm talking about all the sessions. I know they sure would have helped me if I'd had them earlier in life."

"Maybe," Jake said with a grin. "Maybe they would help a few, but mostly, youngsters hear what they want to hear and do what they want to do."

"Yeah," I grinned myself, "you're probably right. Speaking of youngsters, how's your son doing? The one in college, the younger one?"

"He's doing good. About to finish his first semester," Jake answered, adding, "He's not sure how well he likes living on campus, so he's thinking about moving out to the house with me and commuting back and forth. It's just thirty minutes to the college. He's still got a few weeks to decide."

"You okay with him commuting?" I asked.

"Sure," Jake nodded. "I'm fine with him staying at the college, but I'm also fine with him commuting. I'll support whatever he decides to do. I've decided to retire at the end of December and do a little traveling, so if he does decide to move in, it will be nice to have someone there while I'm away."

"Retire?" I was shocked.

"Yeah," Jake chuckled, "I've been considering it for a while. Got places I want to photograph, and then in a year or two, I want to stock the ranch, set back, watch the cattle graze, and maybe write a book or two."

As I drove through town, I thought about the future, first Jake's and then mine. It seemed like things were falling into place for both of us, and I realized I was okay with it. I wasn't scared. I wasn't looking back over my shoulder, waiting for something bad to catch me off guard. I was looking forward, seeing the future and all it's wonderful possibilities.

As I left the city limits, I called Dottie. We talked about our plans, and I couldn't stop smiling.

WEEK 50—CONCLUSION OF SEXUAL ABUSE

"What is your definition of rape?" Miz Nancy asked. She stood just inside the doorway holding the evenings packets. As she waited for a response, her eyes scanned the room. The air seemed to grow thick, and I found it hard to breathe.

Finally, Jake said, "Having sex with someone against their will."

"Anyone else have another definition?" Miz Nancy continued to scan the room.

Heads began to shake. Everyone was in agreement with Jake. Without another word, Miz Nancy began to hand out the packets. When she had finished, she began to read the introductory material herself. It contained two full pages of statistics and one page of law.

"This is material that is required for this class. I realize it is not a comfortable subject," Miz Nancy said, "but it is one we must cover. Instead of answering a lot of questions for this topic, we will have an open discussion. Let's begin by a show of hands. Who knows someone who has been raped?"

A few of the guys raised their hands and the discussion began. I had never known anyone who'd been raped, so for the most part, I just listened. Miz Nancy gently guided the conversation and several of the members joined in. By the end of the session, we had covered every possible aspect of rape and sexual assault. When Miz Nancy called an end to the class, I wrote on my exit paper: Tonight, I learned that if someone says no and a person continues to have sex with them, it is rape.

Sitting in the Neon church fifteen minutes later, I felt like I needed a shower. I was glad we only had one class in which we were required to discuss rape. The thought of something like that happening to someone I knew turned my stomach. As the congregation discussed the chapter for the night, I found myself praying earnestly to God that I would never be put in a position like some of those discussed in our session.

The service ended with prayer. Brother Jim said it himself and then dismissed the congregation. Jake and I shook hands with Catfish at the door and headed for our pickups.

"You okay?" Jake asked as we walked across the parking lot.

"I feel like I need a shower," I answered.

"Yeah, that was a hard one," he agreed. "I don't even like to think about it."

"Me either," I nodded.

"Well, then," he smiled weakly, "how're things going at the ranch?"

Our conversation turned to ranching and family. Jake's son had decided to move back in with him and commute to college. We chatted for a while, but it was evident that we both wanted to be away.

On my way out of the parking lot, I called Dottie. I told her I need to talk about something other than class, so we talked about what type of furniture we each liked. By the time I pulled into the driveway, I felt some better but still wanted that shower.

WEEK 51—DEVELOPING HEALTHY RELATIONSHIPS

"What do you want for Christmas?" I asked my son as we pulled out of his mother's drive.

He shrugged, "I don't know, Dad. Hadn't really thought about it much."

As we made the trip to Granny's, he filled me in on his week. He was excited about being out of school for two and a half weeks. I listened and he chattered on. I was hoping to find an idea for a Christmas present but was still no closer to one when we pulled into the gravel lane that led to Granny's.

Because I wasn't allowed to have guns in my possession, I'd missed deer season for the most part. If I got lucky, I'd have about two weeks after I finished my class to get one with my bow. I spent the weekend showing my son the ins and outs of hunting white tail. He was a good student, eager to learn, and seemed to be picking it up quickly. I'm not sure how good a teacher I was, but it felt good to be passing my knowledge on to him.

The weekend rolled by and Wednesday was upon me before I knew it. On the drive to the counseling center, I began to think about what I would say at my last meeting. I was sure we wouldn't meet next week since Christmas day fell on that Wednesday, but I still felt the need to start planning. It takes me a while to mull things over in my mind.

There were several new guys seated around the table when I arrived. Jake was in his usual chair, but someone had claimed my customary place. The only chairs left at the table were beside

Jake and at the far end between Bo and James. Tex had not arrived, and he usually sat next to Bo, so I took the chair next to Jake.

"How was your week?" he said softly without taking his eyes from his packet.

"Good," I said, "and yours?"

"Real Good." He gave me a sideways look, smiled, and returned to his reading.

I picked up the top page from the pile in front of me and stared at it blankly. After tonight, I had only one meeting left. I had grown used to the routine of coming to class, the weekly greeting from Jake, the lessons themselves. The Neon Church crossed my mind and for the first time it dawned on me that I wouldn't be here for the services. Sure, I could make the forty-minute drive over, but I knew I wouldn't. I made a mental note to talk to Dottie about what church she thought we should attend. Man, for such a long year, it sure had gone by fast.

"How many of you have ever been in a healthy relationship?" Miz Nancy asked as she stepped into the room.

Caught off guard, everyone sat silently staring at her until finally Jake asked, "Are you talking about any relationship, or with a woman?"

Miz Nancy grinned, "Good question, Jake. Tonight, we're going to discuss what makes a good relationship. Most of you have family or close friends with whom you have good, healthy relationships. All of you are here because, for some reason, you haven't been able to take the elements from your healthy relationships and apply them to the relationships you have with women."

Fifteen minutes later, the initial material read, the question answered, and Miz Nancy's cigarette break over, we began our discussion. The first thing she asked us to do was to think of someone, anyone, we felt like we had a good relationship with and ask ourselves if it was a healthy relationship.

"Hank, who is yours?" Miz Nancy called on me.

"My Granny," I said. "There's no one else who has been there for me as long as she has and no one who has stood with me no matter what was going on in my life."

"So, there's respect and trust?" she asked.

"Yes," I answered.

"Does the respect and trust go both ways?" I wasn't ready for her question, and I took me a minute to think before answering.

"Now," I finally spoke, "I'd have to say yes, but there have been times in my life where I was really doing some stupid things, and I can't say Granny had a lot of respect or trust for me then."

"What's changed?" Miz Nancy was just full of questions tonight.

"Well," I shrugged, thought a moment, and said, "I reckon, I've changed."

"How?"

I was beginning to feel like I was the only one in the room. I kind of wished someone else would chime in.

"I guess I've matured," I answered. "I don't know. Maybe at some point, I started to respect myself a little. All I know is I feel different now."

"Good," Miz Nancy smiled. "Now we have a place to begin. Respect and trust, those are two of the most important things in a healthy relationship. Bo you're next?"

As we began to compare the dynamics of a healthy relationship with an unhealthy relationship, I began to examine the relationships in my life. It occurred to me that my life had begun to change for the better when I walked away from the people in my life who were toxic, not only to me, but to themselves. As I listened to each of the guys talk, I realized that most of them were saying the same thing, just in different ways. Life gets better when you surround yourself with people whom you trust and respect, and who trust and respect you.

Of course, there is the matter of being worthy of trust and respect, and looking back, I realized I had not always been worthy. I promised myself that this would never again be a problem in my life. When the class ended, on my exit paper I wrote: Tonight, I learned that a healthy relationship is based on trust and respect. I learned that to maintain healthy relationships, I must be worthy of another's trust and respect, and I must trust and respect them.

Before she dismissed us, Miz Nancy announced that there would be no class the week of Christmas, and since New Year's Day fell on the next Wednesday, she was moving class that week to Monday. I hadn't thought about New Year's being on a class night and was sure glad she had decided to move it. Now, I would be finished before the new year started. Of course, there would be final paperwork that I'd have to attend to at the district attorney's office, but I'd be finished with the classes.

* * * * *

It seemed strange walking into the Neon Church knowing it would most likely be the last time I would ever attend. The discussion for the night was over the prodigal son. Brother Jim answered a question here and there, but mostly, various members of the congregation spoke about what they had gotten out of the reading. Nearly every testimony was a story of how badly the teller had messed up and how they had found their way back to the Lord.

As I listened to one after another, my eyes began to fill, and my chest began to ache. Finally, I stood and spoke.

"My name is Hank. I don't know most of you. I've been attending Brother Jim's services here for nearly a year. Tonight is the last night I'll be attending. Next week, I finish my court ordered Batterer's Intervention Program that's held next door. As I listened to you all speaking tonight, I realized that I, too, have been like the prodigal son. It has been a long trip back from the darkness I was in, and I want to thank God for His help and His patience. I also want to thank Brother Jim for these services. They have been a great help and very instrumental in my journey."

At the end of the service, Brother Jim came by and shook

my hand. I thanked him again for what he'd done for me and wished him well.

"That was a nice thing you did in there," Jake said as we walked to our trucks. "I'm proud of you."

Besides Granny, I can't remember another person in my life telling me they were proud of me. It felt good to hear; actually, because it came from Jake, it felt great.

"Thanks," I said then asked him if he had plans for Christmas.

"Yeah," he grinned, "I'm gonna make the rounds of my kid's houses, dropping off presents, then have dinner with my mom and dad. And you?"

"I reckon it'll be like Thanksgiving," I told him. "Me, Dottie, and Granny until the afternoon, and then they'll drop Luke off. Which reminds me, I haven't figured out what to get him for Christmas."

"Well," Jake chuckled, "seems like you had the same problem last month with his birthday."

"Yeah," I laughed. "I guess I got a long way to go, huh?"

"You're gonna do fine," Jake assured me. "Have you got anything at all in mind?"

"I'd still like to get him a rifle," I confessed, "a little .22 and teach him how to use it, but I won't be able to before Christmas."

"Well, he'll be getting lots of presents on Christmas," Jake pushed his Stetson back on his forehead. "Here's an idea. Why not give him a box of .22 shells and a card with a coupon for a trip to the gun shop after New Year's?"

"That's not a bad idea," I said.

"He'll get his rifle, he'll get to spend time with you picking it out, and it won't get lost in the jumble of other gifts," Jake nodded thoughtfully.

"I like it, thanks," I told him.

Jake shook my hand and climbed into his pickup. I walked across to my truck and got in. I hoped someday I would be able to help someone the way Jake had helped me this past year.

As I pulled away from the center, I called Dottie. By the time I reached the house, I felt like I was about to burst with excitement. I couldn't remember the last time I'd looked forward to Christmas. It felt great.

WEEK 52—DEFINING PARTNERSHIPS

"This is Hank's last meeting," Miz Nancy announced at the end of our discussion.

Amid congratulations and wise cracks, I stood to my feet. I couldn't tell you a thing about the packet we'd just gone through except that it had something to do with partnerships. During the entire session, my mind had been focused on what I would say, and as I looked around the table, I felt completely unprepared.

"A little over a year ago, I walked into this room, a bitter broken mess," I began. "The second week I attended; I was asked to define love. I had no idea if I knew what love really was and had no way to define it. I discovered that I couldn't stand to look at myself in the mirror because I couldn't stand the man who stared back at me. Then little by little with the help of these classes, some new friends, and the Neon Church next door, I realized I could change. I realized I didn't have to be the man I used to be, and more importantly, I figured out that I wanted to change. Miz Nancy, I still don't have a definition for love, but I do know what it is, of that I have no doubt, and I want to thank you for all the help you have given me. Thank you."

I borrowed a line from a Tim McGraw song and wrote it on my last exit paper. It read: I've learned that I have a ways to go, but the path ahead doesn't scare me anymore. I've learned who you've been ain't who you've got to be, and the future is in front of me, not in my past.

I took a last, long look at the Neon Church as Jake and I stood beside his truck visiting. The neon palm trees made me smile. A young couple pulled to a stop in front of Suzy Q's, got out giggling, and disappeared inside. It was the first time in weeks, I'd even thought about or remembered that the adult toy store was there. It's funny how once you start down a path, you're kind of blind to other paths. I'm sure glad I'm on the path I'm on now.

"So, I guess, this is goodbye," Jake said.

"I sure hope not," I grinned. "I've been thinkin', and I'd like to run an idea by you."

"Okay, shoot." He said.

"Well, I know you've got plans to ranch," I told him. "How would you feel about us working out something where we help each other out. I checked and we're about twenty minutes from each other. I know you want to travel some, and I might want to take my family on a vacation now and again."

"What were you thinkin'?"" Jake asked.

"To be honest," I answered, "I haven't worked all the details out, but you're part of the reason I'm where I'm at today, and I'd sure like to be able to come to you for advice now and then. I know a little about cattle, so in return, if you need help with getting a herd started, I could be there for you."

"Okay," he said, "but I think you're giving me too much credit and yourself not enough. You are the biggest reason you are where you are today, and don't let anyone tell you different."

"Thanks." I stuck my hand out.

"Now, what's this about a family vacation," he chuckled as he stuck his hand out, "Don't you need a family first?"

"I sure do," I said, "and I wanted your opinion on something, now that you mention it."

"What's that?" he said as we shook.

"I picked up the ring from the jeweler's last Thursday," I explained, "and I was thinking I would take Dottie out to the building site just before midnight on New Year's Eve. I've already staked out the whole house, and what I plan to do is walk her through it, show her where all the rooms are going to be and then take her out to where the front porch will be and propose just as the New Year comes in."

"Okay." Jake was smiling.

"So, is it too cliché?" I asked. "Should I wait and do it another day?"

"No, it's not," Jake shook his head, "and I think you'd be foolish to do it any other way or any other day."

We made plans to meet for coffee on the first Friday of the new year, he climbed into his truck, and drove away. The young couple came out of Suzie Q's laughing harder than when they had gone in. As they drove past me, headed out of the parking lot, the guy raised a hand, and I waved back. With them gone, mine was the only vehicle left. I got behind the wheel and I took one last long look at the building that had been the biggest part of my Wednesday nights for more than a year. So much had changed in my life in the last year, and a lot of those changes had happened right here.

I looked at my reflection in the rearview mirror and said aloud, "It's gonna be okay."

SIX MONTHS LATER—MID-JUNE

It's been nearly six months since I wrote in this journal. When my B.I.P. classes ended, I had no reason to write in it anymore; plus, I didn't know if or how I should end it. I was looking for something to write a note on today and ran across it, and realized that if someone were to read it in the future, they might want to know a few things, so here goes.

Dottie said yes and tomorrow is our wedding day. Jake has become a big part of our lives. Over the months we've gotten to know most of his family, and he's gotten to know our little clan as well. My son has taken to calling him Uncle Jake, which seems strange to me because he's so much older than me, but Jake doesn't seem to mind. Since neither I nor Dottie have living parents, we asked Jake to give Dottie away, and he agreed.

The house is finished. The ranches, both mine and Jake's, are doing great. Jake's youngest son has turned into quite a hand. Every minute he's not busy with schoolwork, he's working on one of the ranches. He's really taken my son under his wing, and it's great to see the two of them working together.

Jake just got back from a trip last week. He's taken several since he finished his last B.I.P. class and retired. Usually, he's gone a week or two, taking pictures. He seems to be enjoying life. I asked him when he got back from this last trip, if he was ever gonna fine a good woman, settle down, and stay home.

"No, maybe, and some day," was his answer.

"Still don't think you could love someone like you loved her?" I asked.

"If something happened to Dottie, could you ever love someone else the way you love her?" he asked in return.

Without hesitation, I answered, "No," and that's where we left it.

273

DEAR READERS,

First and foremost, I want to say *Thank You* to all of you. Without you, the reader, this book is simply pages of words glued together. It took you reading it to make it what it was meant to be—a story I wanted to share in hopes that it would help those of you who are currently, or have at some point in your life been, caught up in the cycle portrayed within this book.

While this story is a work of fiction, the subject matter is not. Domestic abuse and domestic violence are very real. Thankfully there are many people, counselors, social workers, and many others, who dedicate their lives to help those who find themselves part of these circles of abuse and violence. For those of you who have stepped up to help, I would like to thank you for all you do. And while I do not know each and every one of you, I am compelled to give a special thanks to one I do know: Theresa Barton, *Thank You.*

As with any story, taking this one from an idea to the reality of a book, took a number of special people. With that in mind, I would like to thank my mom and dad, who are the major driving forces behind my writing. A big shout out to my dad for all the commas, editing, and encouragement he provided along the journey. A huge *Thank You*, to my developmental editors, Joani Hartin and Denise Sanders, and my formatter, Judi Fennell. And a special thanks to my agent, Erin Niumata, and her beta readers.

Until next time,
Charles Lemar Brown

THE SEVENTH DATE

Dub Taylor has traveled the world and now he is back, if only for the amount of time it will take to settle his family's estate. Two hundred acres of prime pastureland in south central Oklahoma. Katherine wants the land, but the only purchase price Dub will agree to is seven dates. Will she agree to his terms? And if she does, will she be able to complete the seven dates without killing him?

ABOUT THE AUTHOR

Charles Lemar Brown is a retired high school science teacher, who now spends much of his time writing and traveling. In addition to this work, he has also published The Road to Nowhere and a book of short stories entitled Raised Redneck, Vol. 1. He is also an avid photographer whose photographs have been sold around the world. He lives in rural Love County, Oklahoma, where he enjoys spending time with his seven children and nineteen grandchildren. Left alone too long, he is likely to be found making TikTok's, working out in his home gym, or kicked back with his cat, Tilee, watching whatever football game he can find on the television. His favorite quote is—what doesn't kill you makes you stronger and I ain't dead yet.